With a shrug, the dress fell to the floor. Dee's panties were skimpy, no more than a g-string in fact, with a thin black cord that ran between the cheeks of her bottom, accentuating their firm pertness. Still swaying to the beat, she turned to show Jon her breasts.

They were lovely, not too large and perfectly shaped. The nipples were pink in colour and hard with desire.

Then she began to slip her panties down her thighs . . .

Indecent Display

Samantha Austen

HEADLINE
DELTA

First published in 1996
by HEADLINE BOOK PUBLISHING

A HEADLINE DELTA paperback

10 9 8 7 6 5 4 3 2 1

ISBN 0 7472 5325 0

Typeset by Palimpsest Book Production Limited,
Polmont, Stirlingshire
Printed and bound in Great Britain by
Cox & Wyman Ltd, Reading, Berkshire

HEADLINE BOOK PUBLISHING
A division of Hodder Headline PLC
338 Euston Road
London NW1 3BH

Indecent Display

Chapter 1

With a clash of cymbals and a throbbing chord, the song came to an end, though the sound of the band continued to echo about the small room long after the girls had lowered their instruments and taken a bow and the man watching had ceased to clap.

Dee, the singer, propped her instrument against one of the amplifiers and stepped down off the stage. It felt odd to be facing an audience of one. Under normal circumstances it would have been a roomful of enthusiastic youngsters dancing the night away and impatient for another number. But auditions weren't like that. Here there was only one person who they had to please.

Dee wasn't really the band's leader. Officially speaking there wasn't a leader, all four members of the group having an equal say in what they did. But it always seemed to be Dee who set up the gigs and made sure they got there on time, and the tendency of the others was to seek her opinion on all matters concerning the band. Now, as usual, she took the initiative, approaching the man sitting in the single chair that faced the stage.

As she came closer she eyed him critically. He wasn't bad looking, actually. He was in his early thirties, his slightly greying hair worn almost to the shoulder, but swept back and carefully coiffeured. He was broad in the chest, his waist slim and he smiled at her as she approached.

Dee walked with a slight swagger. She had the air of a woman who looked good and knew damned well that she did. She was twenty-three, the oldest member of the band and by far the most experienced. She was tall and slim, with long naturally blonde hair that hung down to below her shoulders. Her breasts were firm and full, pressing hard against the fabric of the short one-piece dress she wore, putting the buttons that ran down the front under considerable tension. The dress hugged her figure tightly, accentuating the curve of her slim waist and round, pert backside. Beneath the hem of the dress a large expanse of leg was visible, long and shapely, tapering to neat ankles. She knew the man was watching her, and she knew he liked what he saw.

'So, Mister Howland, what did you think?'

'Call me Jon. You're not bad at all. How long have you been together?'

'Just over a year.'

'Get many jobs?'

'It's not bad, but getting this one would improve things.'

He eyed her up and down. 'Can we go somewhere and talk business?' he asked.

Dee studied his face. His eyes betrayed nothing, yet there had seemed to be a tone in his voice that conveyed a hidden agenda. She turned to the other band members.

'Hey, girls,' she said. 'Why not take five? There's a café across the street. Go and grab a coffee and I'll meet you there as soon as I'm done.'

The three others had been watching from the stage. Now they took their cue perfectly, abandoning their instruments where they were and trooping out through the door. Dee watched them go, chatting and giggling together. There was no doubt that if sexiness was a criterion for getting this commission, the band would win it hands down.

The door closed and she turned back to Howland.

'Pull up a chair,' he said. 'And let's talk.'

Dee dragged a chair across to where he was sitting, putting it down immediately opposite him. She sat down and crossed her legs, revealing a lot of creamy thigh.

'Okay,' he said. 'Let's talk about the job.'

'How many other bands are in the frame?' she asked.

'There's one other. A bunch of guys calling themselves the Purple Shades. Have you heard of them?'

'Yeah. They're pretty good. But we're better.'

He smiled. 'That's what I like, positive thinking.'

'So tell me about the contract.'

'It's for four months. On board the cruise ship the *SS Diana*. She runs down from Southampton and all around the Med, stopping in European and North African ports.'

'What are the hours like?'

'You'd be expected to play six nights a week. You'd get full accommodation and food. Basically it's a working holiday.'

For the next fifteen minutes the pair of them discussed the details of the contract, arguing over various issues of pay and conditions. At last Dee sat back.

'Well, Jon,' she said, 'it all sounds okay to me. When will you make your decision?'

'I don't know,' he said. 'Those guys in Purple Shades

are pretty good. And they're asking for slightly less money.'

'Yeah, but an all-girl band is quite an attraction.'

He leaned forward and placed a hand on her knee.

'Yes,' he said, staring into her eyes. 'There are some things you could do much better than any of those guys could.'

He began to slide his hand up her leg, inching it ever closer to the hem of her skirt.

She took hold of his hand and removed it.

'Listen, Jon,' she said. 'I never mix business with pleasure. I've never fucked my way into a job, and I don't intend to start now. You take my band on its merits, or not at all.'

He leaned back, smiling slightly. 'Yeah,' he said. 'Sorry about that. It's just that you're a very sexy lady.'

She smiled. 'You're not so bad yourself. But we're negotiating right now. So when can we have an answer?'

He glanced down at the paper on his lap, on which he had been taking notes. He studied the figures carefully, then looked up at her.

'Aw, what the hell,' he said. 'I'm still within budget. And you're right. You girls are a damned sight prettier than the Purple Shades. You get the job.'

Dee gave a little squeal of delight.

'Great,' she said. 'When do we start?'

'The *SS Diana* sails in ten days' time. Come into my office tomorrow and I'll have a contract for you.'

'Fantastic. Thanks, Jon, we really wanted this job.'

He grinned. 'Don't thank me. You negotiated that pretty professionally. Besides, you're a great band to hear and to look at. I'm looking forward to seeing more.'

A faint smile played about Dee's lips as she rose to her feet. She turned her back to him and strode up to the stage, her backside wiggling provocatively. She went up to the keyboard and flicked a switch, and at once a beat started up. It was a slow, insistent rhythm, reminiscent of jungle drums, and it echoed about the empty room.

Dee turned round, striking a pose, her hands on her hips, her body turned slightly sideways so that she looked at him askance. Then she began to dance, a sensuous dance, her body keeping perfect time to the music as she slunk about the stage. Howland watched in fascination, marvelling at the way she moved, his throat dry as his cock slowly stiffened in his pants.

Dee danced on like this for two or three minutes, fully aware of the effect she was having on him, and enjoying herself immensely. She loved to show off like this. It was one of the reasons why she had joined a band in the first place. But Howland was about to get a show that few of her customers ever saw.

Without breaking the rhythm of the dance she reached up and flicked the top button of her dress undone. It was such a swift and subtle moment that for a second he wasn't sure if he had seen correctly. But when he looked again, the button was certainly undone.

Dee gave a little swirl, spinning around on one foot, and when she faced him once again he realised that the bottom button on the dress was undone also. He licked his lips.

Dee continued to bump and grind her way about the stage, her hips swaying back and forth, and the buttons came undone one by one, first from the top, then from the bottom. Soon only two buttons remained at her waist, her plump young breasts, unfettered by a bra, forcing their way out of the top whilst the skirt parted with every step, revealing an acreage of thigh.

She slipped the penultimate button undone, then the last one.

She clutched the dress to her body, still dancing, moving back and forth across the stage, her head cocked on one side as she eyed him. Then she stopped in the centre and turned her back on him.

With a single shrug, the dress fell to the floor. Dee's panties were skimpy, no more than a g-string in fact, with a thin black cord that ran up her backside, accentuating the firm pertness of her buttocks. She stayed where she was, her body still moving to the rhythm of the beat whilst Howland watched in wide-eyed disbelief. Then she turned to face him.

Her breasts were lovely. Not too large, but perfectly shaped with barely a hint of crease beneath them. The nipples were pink in colour, hard and long, the tips pointing upwards. As she danced they moved up and down with a mesmerising elasticity. She smiled and blew him a kiss. She could see he badly wanted to come up onto the stage with her, but this was her game and she would play it in her own time.

Her hands dropped to her crotch and she began to rub herself over the thin panties, her finger tracing out the valley of her sex. As she did so she knew the material was darkening with the liquids that flowed from inside her.

If the dance was having an effect on Jon, it was having no less of one on Dee. The girl was feeling very turned on indeed now, and she knew she wouldn't be able to resist his cock for much longer. She slid her hand underneath the small black triangle that covered her crotch and gasped as her fingers sought out her clitoris. She began to masturbate herself, her eyes still fixed on Howland's as she did so. She was trying her best to stay cool under his gaze, but the pleasure was becoming too much for her.

Suddenly her hands went to the waistband of her panties and she simply tore them off, snapping the thin cords so that the garment came away in a single movement. Howland's eyes opened wider still as he feasted them on her crotch.

Her pubic hair was blonde and wispy, barely covering her mound. The lips of her sex were thick, with a prominent slit between them. From this protruded her love bud, glistening with wetness.

She had stopped dancing now, and as he watched she widened her stance and forced two fingers into her pussy. Then she began to masturbate in earnest. She had abandoned all traces of modesty now, such was her arousal, and she slid her fingers in and out vigorously, her body shaking as she frigged herself.

Then, suddenly, she could resist it no longer. The bulge in Howland's pants was so large now that she could clearly make out the shape of his cock through his denims. She abandoned her slit and leapt down from the stage, making straight for him. She pushed his legs apart then dropped to her knees between them, reaching for his zipper at once, the wetness of her fingers making dark stains on the denim.

She delved into his underpants and freed his cock. It sprang up at once, stiff and hard, the vein throbbing under her fingertips. Wasting no time, she opened her mouth and took him inside. He gasped as her lips closed about his swollen glans and she began to suck hard, her tongue working back and forth over his thick helmet as she did so.

'Oh shit, Dee,' he muttered. 'I've just got to screw you.'

She looked up, a mischievous grin on her face.

'I guess the business is over, then,' she said. 'Time for the pleasure.'

She took his hand and pulled him to his feet, dragging him across to the stage, his cock still rampant. The stage was about three feet off the ground, and Dee turned as she reached it, hoisting herself into a sitting position. Then she spread her legs and leaned back, shuffling forward slightly so that her backside protruded over the edge.

Howland's eyes drifted over her lovely young body, his cock twitching as he took in her breasts, flattened slightly, but with the hard little teats still pointing straight up, and her pink, wet slit, open for the taking. Dee glanced down between her twin mounds and blew him a kiss.

'Come on, Jon,' she said. 'Stick that lovely fat cock of yours into my cunt. Fuck me, Jon.'

He needed no second bidding. Moving forward between the white, open portals of her thighs he took his erection in his hand and ran the tip of his cock up and down her glistening hole, teasing her clitoris with it and making her writhe about with the ecstasy of the stimulation. Then he moved it lower, to the entrance to her vagina.

He began to press, his swollen glans gently easing apart the pink flesh and making her groan aloud. Then, suddenly, he was inside her, his cock sliding deep within her, forcing apart the walls of her sex and sinking in to the hilt. He paused for a moment once he was all the way in, and she knew he was enjoying the feel of her sex as the muscles convulsed about his weapon, massaging it with their undulating movement. It was an automatic reaction, one over which she had no control, but she knew it drove her lovers wild, and she smiled slightly as she watched the intense expression on his face.

He began to move, taking her thighs in his hands and pumping his backside back and forth so that his cock slid in and out. She groaned and arched her back, pressing her sex against his rod with a new urgency, an urgency that seemed to transmit itself to him as the movement of his hips increased.

Dee gasped and panted under his ministrations. This was sex as she enjoyed it most, with no ties, no responsibilities or recriminations. Just two consenting adults taking pleasure in one another's bodies. She began to moan aloud, her entire being alive with the intensity of the sensation.

Howland's cock was working like a piston now, thrusting into her with an energy that told her his orgasm was close. Dee's whole body was being shaken by his onslaught, her breasts bouncing back and forth with every stroke. She gazed up at him. His eyes were closed, his teeth clenched, the veins in his forehead prominent.

'Aaah.'

He came with a cry, his cock suddenly seeming to inflate inside her as the spunk began to pump from him. With an equally loud cry she came too, the sensation of the hot semen spurting against the very entrance to her womb sending wave after wave of sensuous pleasure through her.

To Dee, the pleasure seemed unending, hoarse shouts coming from her throat as she thrust her hips against his, milking every drop of spunk she could from him until he was spent, his body collapsed over hers, both of them gasping for breath.

So overcome were they that they didn't hear the door open. But Dee did hear the gasps of surprise as the three other members of her band stood, their eyes wide, staring at the naked girl, her legs spread open, her face flushed with pleasure.

'What on earth—'

She grinned. 'Hi, guys. Guess what? We're going on a cruise.'

Chapter 2

It had been Dee's intention to form an all-girl band ever since she had begun performing on stage. Once the decision had been made, it was simply a case of finding the right talent, and she had set out with determination to do so. It had taken some time to find the girls she wanted, and the ones she had finally chosen all had an abundance of the talent she had been seeking. But it was about the only thing they had in common. Otherwise they were completely unalike.

Lisa Smythe was an aristocrat, tall and auburn-haried, with a slim, willowy figure and an English rose complexion that attracted prospective suitors like bees to a honeypot. Her father was an earl with a vast country estate and she had had all the advantages of a privileged upbringing. Expensive public school had been followed by attendance at one of the country's finest music colleges. It had been her parents' intention that she train as a concert pianist, and indeed she had shown a good deal of talent in that direction, pleasing her music teachers greatly with her performances. But whilst she loved the classics, Lisa also had a penchant for more modern music, and she liked nothing better than to sit at the piano bashing out popular

11

tunes. Then, unknown to her parents, she had diversified, taking up the guitar, then the saxophone, and in both cases she learnt quickly and was soon playing with confidence.

She had met Dee quite by chance. It was at a party thrown by one of her friends, a grand affair at a country house. Dee had been filling in as vocalist and bass guitarist for a member of the band, who was off sick that day. They weren't a particularly good oufit and, despite her best efforts, she had found it difficult to find the harmony required to play really good music together.

They had been on a break, and she had taken her drink out onto the terrace for a breath of fresh air when a young man had joined her. He was a hulking, rugby-playing type, not really her sort at all, and he was more than slightly drunk. Still, he was company and she needed something to help her relax after the session with the band.

They had made small talk for a while, then he had suggested a walk round the grounds. Dee had complied, having no better plan, and they had set off.

He walked with his arm about her. He said his name was Bob, and he'd just graduated from Cambridge, though he seemed a little hazy about precisely what subject his degree was in. As they strolled along he moved his hand down to her behind, squeezing it clumsily.

It was when they reached a secluded corner of the garden that he made his move, pulling her up short and pushing her back against a tree, his palm flattening the front of her dress. He placed his mouth over hers and forced his tongue between her lips, his hands fumbling for the buttons of her blouse. Dee let him have his way for a while, allowing him to slip his hand into her top and under her bra, his fingers groping for the soft flesh of her breasts. It was when he reached under her skirt that she stopped him. It wasn't that she was being prudish, or that she didn't fancy the idea of a cock penetrating her cunt at that moment, it was just that it wasn't the place, and she didn't want to get grass stains all over her costume before the second act.

He grumbled when she pushed his hand away, trying to force it back underneath, but Dee was having none of it.

'Stop it,' she said. 'Not here.'

'But I want you, dammit,' he slurred. 'My John Thomas is like a fuckin' ramrod. You're so fuckin' sexy.'

She reached down to his crotch. Sure enough she could feel his stiffness through the material of his trousers.

'All right,' she said. 'Turn round and lean back against the tree.'

She dragged him round and pressed him back against the trunk, then reached for his flies.

He was right, his prick was like a ramrod. No sign of brewer's droop there, thought Dee. She closed her hand about it and he gave a gasp of surprise as she began to masturbate him.

She wanked him hard, her hand flashing up and down his shaft whilst the other caressed his balls. He began to make moaning noises, his body slumped back against the tree as she worked him. In fact so loud were his moans that neither of them heard the footsteps approaching.

'Bob! What the hell do think you're playing at?'

Even as the girl spoke a spurt of semen erupted from his cock, describing a wide arc through the air before splashing onto the grass. A second one followed, then a third. And all the time he was staring wide-eyed at the figure who had just emerged from the bushes.

'Lisa . . .'

He tried to place his hands over his twitching cock, but this simply served to deflect the thick white liquid onto his trouser leg, where it trickled down, leaving a long pale streak.

Dee, apparently unworried by the appearance of the girl, continued to work his foreskin until the flow of semen stopped. Then she licked the droplets from her fingers and pecked him on the cheek.

'Better get those pants cleaned, Bob,' she said, and turned to go.

'Wait a minute,' said Lisa indignantly. 'What do you think you're up to?'

'Sorry, Lisa,' mumbled Bob. He was frantically trying to brush the spunk from his trousers, but merely succeeding in spreading the stain.

'Not you, you drunken bugger,' she said. 'This little slut you've picked up.'

'Who are you calling a slut?' said Dee indignantly.

'You. Who else but a slut would wank off a bloke she scarcely knows?'

'If I was a slut, I'd have let him fuck me,' spat back Dee. 'Anyhow, if he's your fella, how come you're not tending to his needs?'

'I threw him out because he's so pissed.'

Dee giggled. 'He is rather, isn't he? Look at the mess he's making of those trousers.'

By now the stains were even bigger as Bob tried frantically to remove them.

'Fuckin' suit's hired too,' he mumbled. 'Dunno what they're going to say.'

Lisa glared at him for a moment, then burst out laughing.

'I guess you'd better find yourself a dry cleaners that opens on Sundays,' she said. 'Come on, let's leave him to it.'

She turned and set off toward the house. Dee hesitated for a moment, then started after her.

'Sorry about that,' she said. 'I didn't know he was your boyfriend.'

'Oh, he's not my boyfriend,' laughed Lisa. 'He's just a boy my parents approve of. Though I'm not sure what they'd make of him at the moment. He's supposed to be my escort for the evening, but all he's done so far is get pissed out of his brains and try and grope me.'

'He tried that on me too. That's why I thought I'd try and calm his ardour.'

'Maybe that's what I should have done. What's your name?'

'Dee.'

'How long have you known Fiona, Dee?'

'Fiona?'

'The girl whose party this is.'

'Oh.' This time it was Dee's turn to laugh. 'No, I'm not a guest. I'm with the band.'

Lisa turned to her with interest. 'You're in the band?'

'Not exactly. I'm filling in for their bass guitarist and vocalist, who's sick.'

'So you don't normally sing with them?'

'No.'

15

'Thank goodness. I thought I was going to have to be polite about their playing. I mean, you sound great, but that keyboard player's not up to much, is he?'

Dee sighed. 'No, I'm afraid not. There's so few decent ones about nowadays.'

'Why, are you looking for one?'

'Kind of. You see I'd really like to form a band of my own. An all-girl band.'

Lisa stopped and faced her. 'You're really planning to start a band?' she said, her eyes shining.

'If I could just find the talent.'

'I can play keyboards. And guitar. And sax.'

Now it was Dee's turn to look surprised. 'Really?'

'Really. You want to hear me?'

'Yeah. Yeah, why not? Can we get together?'

'I'm free tomorrow.'

'Great. Why not come round to my place and we'll give it a whirl?'

'I'd love to.'

'Right, it's a date. I'll give you my address. Meanwhile, I'd better get back. I think that awful noise is the band warming up.'

Chapter 3

The session between the two girls on the day after the party had been a great success. Lisa had proved a positive virtuoso on all three instruments and she and Dee had enjoyed a great afternoon harmonising with one another. By evening they had agreed that they wanted to play together on a more permanent basis. The trouble was, where was the rest of the band to come from?

'The first thing we need is a drummer,' said Dee.

'But where the hell do we find one? Girl drummers are pretty few and far between.'

'I've got a couple of friends in the business,' said Dee. 'I called them this morning to see if they could suggest someone.'

'And could they?'

'Oddly enough, they both came up with the name of the same club. Some girl plays there every night.'

'Maybe we could go along and hear her play.'

'That's what I had in mind.'

Thus it was that the following night they found themselves at the Pink Gin, a so-called cocktail lounge in South London.

On first inspection, the Pink Gin didn't look too promising.

It was in a rather shady alley off the main street, and the neon sign that flashed outside was clearly in need of repair, with half the letters of the club's name extinguished. The pair of them stepped rather nervously through the doorway and into the entrance hall, where a bored-looking girl in a sequinned leotard sat behind a desk.

'You members?' she asked.

'No. We're just here to see the show,' replied Dee.

'You wanna see the show? You dykes or something?'

'What do you mean?'

'I mean most of our customers are guys. It's that kind of club.'

'Listen,' said Dee impatiently. 'Can we go in, or not?'

'Fiver each.'

Dee passed over a ten pound note, and the girl gestured towards a door.

'In there.'

The noise, heat and smoke were almost overpowering as the pair pushed open the door and entered the club. They found themselves in a large, dimly lit room, with tables set all around. At the far end was a stage, the only part of the place that was brightly lit. A girl stood on the stage, wearing an identical leotard to that worn by the one in the entrance hall. She was swaying gently to the music that blasted from the speakers on either side.

'Where's the band then, Dee?' shouted Lisa. 'You sure this is the right place?'

'The Pink Gin, that's what they told me,' replied Dee.

'It's not exactly the Café Royal, is it?'

Dee laughed. 'Don't be such a snob, Lisa. Come on, let's get a drink.'

Beside the stage was a small bar, and the two friends made their way across to it. Dee ordered the drinks, then she turned and the two of them surveyed the club.

The clientele was almost exclusively male, sitting down at the tables or crowded about the stage. Most of them were young men in suits, obviously arrived straight from the office. Almost to a man they clutched lager bottles in their hands as they laughed and joked noisily together.

The only women in the room sat quietly in the corners. All were flamboyantly dressed in tight, brightly coloured outfits, some in pairs or threes, others with solitary men, much older than those about the stage.

'What the hell kind of club is this?' asked Lisa. 'Are those women what I think they are?'

'Whores? I think so.'

At that moment a man in his early forties sidled up to them.

'Can I buy either of you ladies a drink?' he asked.

Dee smiled. 'No thanks. We're just here to meet someone.'

He moved closer. 'I'd pay well,' he said.

'How much?' asked Lisa

Dee turned to her in amazement. What was she saying?

'Two hundred,' said the man.

'Nah,' said Lisa. 'That would hardly buy you a hand job. Try the girls in the corner.'

The man's face fell, and he turned and shuffled back to his table. Dee collapsed into hysterics.

'Lisa! What on earth do you think you're doing?' she gasped.

'Just telling the truth.'

'But what if he'd offered more?'

'I should hope he would. Two hundred indeed. Why, my female ancestors never sold their cunts for less than a baronesship and a share of a stately home.'

Dee shook her head. 'You're priceless, Lisa,' she said.

Just at that moment the music died away, and there was a roll of drums. Both girls turned toward the stage. As they watched a curtain was drawn back at the side, revealing a glittering drum set, behind which sat a young woman.

She was about twenty years old, with flaming red hair that flew in all directions as she attacked the drumskins. She wore a spangled bikini top that strained to contain one of the biggest pairs of breasts Dee had ever seen. They fairly wobbled as she moved, drawing every eye in her direction. Apart from the top, all she wore was a pair of similarly decorated briefs, her slim torso and long legs left bare.

But it was her drumming that caught the attention of the two girls at the bar. The drumsticks simply seemed to fly over the drums, beating out an extraordinarily exciting rhythm. So engrossed were they in the girl's playing they barely noticed the slim young dancer who had appeared centre stage and begun to strip.

'Christ, she's good,' said Lisa. 'Just look at her go.'

'A real virtuoso,' replied Dee. 'She's carrying the whole show on her own.'

'I wouldn't quite say that,' said Lisa. 'Most of the guys have got their eyes on the stripper.'

The girls sat back to watch the show. The stripper was slim and dark, of Oriental appearance, and she knew exactly how to hold the attention of her audience. She slid across the dance floor, her body shaking to the beat of the drummer, who slowed and increased her tempo as the girl went through her routine.

Suddenly Lisa nudged Dee.

'Look,' she said, pointing to the drummer.

'Wow!'

With a shock Dee realised that the girl had removed her top, baring her breasts. And what breasts! They were not only large, they were firm, standing proudly from her chest, the areolae big and brown, the nipples hard. As she beat a tattoo on the drums they bounced up and down in a way that was drawing attention from the stripper and towards her.

The act went on for another five minutes, the naked stripper teasing the young men who hung about the edge of the stage with her lovely young body before a final crescendo sounded and the lights went down. When they came back up again, the stage was deserted.

'Phew, some drummer,' said Dee.

'Yeah. We've got to talk to her. You reckon we can get backstage?'

'We can try. Come on.'

Dee took Lisa's hand and the two of them set off for the stage. Now that the act was over the young men were crowding about the bar ordering more drinks, and nobody noticed as they stepped onto the platform and, pulling aside the curtain, slipped through the opening behind.

In the back the club seemed even more dingy than it had from outside. The hallway they were in was grubby, with peeling wallpaper, the only light a naked thirty-watt bulb that hung from the ceiling. The two friends crept down the passage, peering into the rooms that led out to right and left.

Suddenly there was a moaning sound, and the pair of them stopped and listened hard.

'Where's it coming from?' whispered Lisa.

'That room at the end, I think,' Dee replied. 'Come on.'

The two of them crept forward toward the open doorway. When they reached it, Dee peered round. Then she froze, her eyes fixed on the tableau in front of her.

The drummer was bent forward, her hands placed flat on a chair, her backside raised. She was totally naked apart from a pair of high-heeled shoes. Behind her stood a man, about twenty-five years old. He was wearing a suit, and Dee recognised him as one of those who had been standing by the stage in the club. His flies were undone, a long pink cock protruding from them and disappearing into the girl's vagina.

'My god, they're fucking,' gasped Dee.

'Let me see.' Lisa craned round, and her jaw dropped as she saw the sight, the young man pumping his hips back and forth as the girl gasped and moaned with passion, her breasts hanging pendulous beneath her and swinging to and fro. As Lisa watched, a hoarse cry escaped from the man's lips and he came, triggering an orgasm in the girl at the same time, their bodies locked together in mutual passion.

No sooner had he finished than the man pulled his cock from her. He turned and, seeing Lisa and Dee, blushed red, trying desperately to stuff his still-erect cock into his trousers. He pushed past them, obviously flustered and almost ran down the corridor. The cheer that greeted him as he pushed through the curtain confirmed that he still hadn't been able to contain himself.

'Who are you two? A pair of voyeurs?'

The drummer had straightened up, her hands on her hips, apparently unworried by her nudity, or by the semen which was already leaking from her sex onto her thigh.

'Sorry,' said Dee. 'Didn't mean to interrupt.'

'That's okay. He's just a punter. It's his birthday and his mates had a whip-round. It all helps to pay the bills.'

'This place doesn't pay well, then?'

'You're joking. My talent's wasted amongst this lot. I can't even do a gig without having to flash my tits.'

'Ever thought of joining a band?'

'They'd have to be good.'

'We are.'

'What, you two? You're the band?'

'At the moment, yes. I play bass guitar and do the vocals, Lisa here is the best all-round piano, sax and guitar player you've ever heard. I'm Dee, by the way.'

'Hi. I'm Trixie. Trixie Ballantine. You serious about the band?'

'We certainly are. Why not come along to a rehearsal? If you don't like what you hear you don't have to stay.'

'I might just do that,' said Trixie. 'When do you rehearse?'

'Saturday afternoon,' said Dee. 'Here's the address.'

Trixie took the card from her and read it. 'You got a drum kit I can use?'

'Sure. Just turn up.'

At that moment a man in jeans and a T-shirt glanced round the door.

'Come on, Trixie,' he said. 'You're on in five minutes. Get your costume on and get out there. And clean that spunk off. You'll get the place a bad name.'

Trixie turned to the others.

'Nothing like being appreciated for your art, is there?' she laughed.

Chapter 4

The discovery of the fourth and final member of the group was a fortuitous one, and happened almost by chance. It was about a week after Trixie had agreed to join the band, and the three girls had met in a pub in Soho to discuss how they would go about finding a lead guitarist for the group.

'Maybe we should just do the rounds of the clubs and see what talent's available,' suggested Lisa.

'That'd just take too long,' replied Dee. 'And there's no guarantee of success.'

'I know a couple of guys who play pretty well,' put in Trixie.

'Yeah, that's the trouble,' replied Dee. 'If it was a guy we wanted we could get one tomorrow. But I want this to be an all-girl band.'

'Is that really so important?' asked Trixie. 'After all, there's things you can do with a guy that you can't with a girl.' She winked at them.

'Trixie!' exclaimed Lisa. 'Don't you ever think of anything else?'

'Sometimes,' she replied. 'But my thoughts have a habit of always coming back to sex.'

'There's nothing else for it,' said Dee. 'We'll have to advertise.'

'Where?'

'In a trade publication.'

'Isn't that a bit risky?' asked Lisa. 'How will we know if they're any good?'

'We'll just have to hold auditions.'

'But there could be dozens of them. It might take ages.'

'It's still the only way. We're not going to stumble over a good guitarist in the street.'

'Funny you should say that,' said Trixie. 'I've got a feeling I did. This very evening.'

'What do you mean?' asked Dee.

'Well it's only just occurred to me. It was whilst I was walking through the tube station tonight. There was a girl, a busker. She was playing a guitar. Real bluesy stuff. It was damned good.'

'Where was this?'

'Just down the road. Didn't you come that way too?'

'Wait a minute, I did hear something,' said Lisa. 'Trouble is I come from the other direction, so I never saw the player. It was a girl, was it?'

'That's right. Pretty little thing. Long brown hair. She looked a bit down and out though.'

'Do you think she's still there?' asked Dee.

'Might be. It wasn't that long ago.'

Dee rose to her feet. 'Only one thing for it,' she said. 'Let's go and find out.'

In the tube station tunnel, Jenny Lovejoy put down her

guitar and examined the open case on the ground in front of her, sifting through the coins. Twelve pounds fifty. Not much for a evening's work. She sighed. That certainly wasn't going to buy her a room for the night. It looked like another cardboard box for her. More seriously it meant no opportunity to buy new batteries for her amplifier, and the ones she had were running pretty low. Lose her amp and she'd lost her sole source of income. Then where would she be?

She began packing her instrument back into its case. So intent was she on doing so that she scarcely heard the footsteps of the man as he stepped up behind her.

'Bad night, Jenny?'

She turned. 'Oh, it's you, Danny,' she said quietly.

'That's right. How are things?'

'Oh, so-so.'

'Doesn't look like it to me. Looks like times are hard.'

'I'll get by.'

'Bet you could use a few more quid, though.'

'I'm okay, I said.'

'How does twenty-five sound?'

'Danny, please. I said I'd stopped that. No more.'

'But you could use the money. Come on, Jenny. I've got a punter.'

'No.'

She bent down to pick up her amplifier, but he placed a hand on it. He flicked the switch and watched as the power light glowed dimly.

'Nearly out of juice, Jenny,' he said. 'What are you going to do then?'

'I'll get by.'

'Another twenty-five would help though, wouldn't it?'

Jenny looked at him. He was right, the money would come in handy. She hadn't eaten properly for a couple of days, and she was beginning to feel it.

'Where?' she asked.

'Just up above. He's in the pub opposite.'

'Twenty-five?'

'That's what I said.'

She sighed. 'All right then, Danny. Show me.'

She picked up her equipment and followed him up the long empty corridor that led to the surface.

It was a warm evening, and it felt good to be out in the open air again, even if it was just the busy streets of London. She followed Danny out of the entrance to the station and into the pub next door. Inside it was noisy and smoky as they pushed their way to the bar.

The man was about forty, rather paunchy and balding on top. He was clutching a whisky glass and looking rather nervous.

'Jenny, I want you to meet Mister Smith,' said Danny.

'Hello.' Jenny did her best to sound enthusiastic. There was a mirror on the wall and she eyed her reflection. She wasn't exactly dressed for seduction, she thought, though it could have been worse. She had on a pair of tatty jeans that clung tightly to her, showing off the slimness of her legs and the roundness of her pert backside to good effect. On top she wore a shirt, in a man's style, that hung outside her waistband. She was no more than five foot two, but her body was perfectly proportioned, her neat little breasts pressing out the front of the shirt.

The man nodded to her. 'Want a drink?'

'Scotch, please.' She might as well milk the situation for all it was worth.

The man ordered the drinks and Jenny took hers, downing it in a single gulp.

'You want another?' he asked.

She shook her head. What she wanted was her money, and a chance to get some sleep.

'Where can we go?' the man asked Danny.

'There's a little alley out the back. It's perfectly safe.'

Jenny looked at him. An alley? Some women got a suite at the Ritz. Others at least had the comfort of a bedroom. It seemed all she rated was an alley.

'Shall we go then?'

Danny led them outside. Jenny felt her heart pounding as she followed, still carrying her stuff. She contemplated what was to happen. She hated the idea of prostituting herself. She had done it only once before, the first time she had met Danny. Then it had been a foreign businessman on the back seat of his car, a swift and loveless coupling that had left her unsatisfied. Yet somehow, the idea that she was about to be fucked was igniting an unexpected fire inside her. It had been ages since she had felt a cock inside her. In fact, apart from the businessman her only sexual experience had been with a boy at college, who had got her drunk and had come too soon, leaving her to finish herself off with her own fingers. Now, suddenly, she felt desire stirring within her, and with it a warm wetness that permeated her sex.

Danny led them out of the pub and up a narrow, dark alley that ran alongside. It opened into a small yard at the back, where empty beer crates were stacked. A light on the side of the building illuminated the area. Jenny stared about her. It wasn't exactly what she would have chosen, but it would have to do. She looked questioningly to Mr Smith.

'Take the shirt off,' he said. 'Show me your tits.'

She turned to Danny, but he showed no sign of leaving. Slowly she reached for the buttons on the shirt.

She undid them one by one. When she had reached the bottom she let her hands hang by her sides. The shirt opened an inch, revealing that she wore no bra underneath. The man moved close to her, taking hold of the garment and pulling it aside. Her breasts were perfect, the size and shape of ripe oranges, the nipples erect. He pushed the shirt back and slid it off her shoulders. Jenny made no move to stop him, letting it fall to the ground behind her.

He reached down and cupped her breast, squeezing it. His touch was firm, but gentle, and it sent a thrill through her body. He grasped her other breast and began working his hands in circles, making the nipples harden still further and eliciting a sigh of pleasure from the girl. He lowered his head and planted his lips on hers, his tongue forcing itself between her lips. Despite herself, Jenny found herself responding eagerly to him, intertwining her tongue with his as the wetness inside her sex continued to increase.

They kissed long and hard, his hands all the time fondling her breasts. When at last he pulled away she was breathing heavily, her chest rising and falling.

'Take off the jeans,' he said.

Jenny didn't need asking a second time. She was feeling hot now, and the only thing that would give her relief was a stiff cock. She undid the jeans as quickly as she was able, peeling them off her legs and tossing them aside. Now all she wore was a pair of scanty briefs. She looked into his face, her eyebrows raised. He nodded.

As she hooked her thumbs into the waistband of the panties she suddenly remembered Danny. He was still watching, a faint smile on his face. Jenny reddened as she considered the wantonness of her behaviour. For a second she hesitated. Then she pulled down the briefs and kicked them aside.

She stood, her hands at her side once again as the man took in her lovely young body.

Beneath her breasts her stomach was flat, with a neat little pit of a navel. Her pubic hair was short and dark, forming an almost perfect triangle. Her thighs were creamy white in the light of the bulb.

The man reached for her crotch, and she gasped as his fingers sought out her clitoris. He teased her lips apart, allowing it to show though, pink and moist. He worked his finger round in a little circle, making her moan aloud. Then he ran it down her slit.

'Open your legs.'

Jenny obeyed at once, placing her feet apart and thrusting her pubis forward to allow him better access. He slid a finger into her and a shudder ran through her diminutive frame.

Jenny glanced down at his trousers. They were bulging at the crotch. All at once she wanted to feel him. She reached eagerly for his fly, fumbling with the zipper before dragging it down and freeing his cock. She grasped it. It was thick, and as hard as iron. She ran her fingers along its length, tracing the thick vein that ran up it.

Now it was his turn to gasp.

On impulse, Jenny dropped to her knees. She took him in both hands, marvelling at the hot, throbbing weapon she held. She licked her lips, then took him into her mouth. He tasted salty, and she licked a bead of moisture from his glans. She sucked him further inside whilst her hands gently caressed his balls. He let out a low moan, clutching at her hair and holding her whilst his hips pumped back and forth.

She went on fellating him for some time, her hair flying as she bobbed her head up and down. He was emitting whimpering sounds now, his stiff weapon pressing to the back of her throat. Jenny sensed that his climax might be close, and she drew back from him and looked up, her hand still working his foreskin.

'Do you want to come in my cunt?' she asked.

He nodded.

Jenny rose to her feet and, taking his hand, pulled him across to where the beer crates were stacked.

'How do you want me?' she asked.

'Face down over those beer crates,' he croaked.

Eagerly she prostrated herself over the crates. The plastic was hard against her bare skin and the bottles felt cold as she squashed her breasts against them, but she didn't care. Jenny's body was tingling with anticipation now. Gone were her inhibitions, in their place only desire. It shocked her slightly that she could act in so wanton a manner. Even the twenty-five pounds seemed trivial now compared to the pleasure his cock would give her.

'Ah!'

She gave a cry of pleasure as she felt him press his stiff

member against her slit. She pushed her backside back at him, unambiguously urging him to enter. He needed no urging however and, with a thrust of his hips, he was inside her, pressing his thick cock deep into her sex.

He wasted no time, beginning to fuck her at once with massive thrusts, squeezing the breath from her lungs as he forced himself down on her prostrate body. She responded enthusiastically, moving her hips back and forth in rhythm with him. Her pubis was resting against the edge of one of the crates and her clitoris was in contact with its rough surface, so that each stroke sent an extra thrill of pleasure through her.

Jenny was in seventh heaven. There was something about giving herself like this, naked in a sordid back alley with a total stranger, that appealed to her most base desires. The presence of a watcher only served to increase her wanton lust. Here she was, Jenny Lovejoy the slut, whoring for a mere twenty-five pounds, and loving every moment of it, her cunt fairly pulsing with gratification. She pressed her bottom back at him all the harder, matching his rhythm, her body alive with pleasure.

His movements were becoming frenzied now, his stomach slapping noisily against her backside, and she guessed that he was approaching his climax. With a moan of delight she braced herself to accept his sperm.

He came with a hoarse shout, his cock twitching violently as spurt after spurt of hot semen squirted into her hot and willing hole. The sensation of his orgasm triggered her own, and she screamed with passion as she came, the bottles rattling in their crates as her body rocked back and forth.

Her orgasm seemed to go on and on, wave after wave

of sensuous pleasure washing over her as he continued to squirt his seed deep inside her. It was not until she had milked the last drop from his balls that she relaxed, her body slumped over the pile of crates.

He withdrew, and she heard the sound of his zip being pulled up, then a mumbled thanks and retreating footsteps. She rose to her feet and turned to face Danny, who was still standing where he had been all along. Now that the passion of the moment had departed she found herself blushing as he eyed her nakedness.

'You really enjoy a bit of roughhouse shagging, don't you?' he asked.

Jenny did not reply, suddenly ashamed of her wantonness. He moved closer, his hand cupping her breast.

'You and I could make a fortune together if you'd just do this more often,' he said.

She shook her head. 'Give me the twenty-five, Danny,' she said.

'Don't I get some fun?' He squeezed her nipple.

'No, Danny. Some other time, maybe.'

'Come on, babe.' He slid his other hand down to her backside.

'No, Danny. Now give me my money.'

He stepped back and reached into his pocket, pulling out two ten pounds and a five pound note.

'Here it is,' he said. 'Come and get it.'

'Danny, stop buggering about. Give me my money.'

She snatched at it, but he withdrew his hand.

'Come on, Jenny,' he urged. 'Take the money.'

She lunged at it again, but in vain.

'Danny!'

He held the money aloft, then turned and ran off. Jenny dashed after him, shouting angrily. He made for the exit to the alley, and she followed him, momentarily forgetting her state of undress. Danny laughed aloud as he ran, emerging from the shelter of the narrow lane and running across the street with Jenny not far behind. Then, just as she reached the road, someone stepped out in front of her. There were three of them, all girls, and she ran headlong into them, causing all four to sprawl into the road.

'What the—'

'What on earth—'

Dee, Lisa and Trixie sat up and stared at the naked girl who had just bowled them over. Jenny stared back at them, then down at herself, suddenly realising where she was and what she was doing.

'Oh, shit!' she cried, hugging her arms about her body and springing to her feet. Then she was running back down the alley, her pert, white behind the last sight they had of her as she disappeared into the gloom.

'Who the hell was that?' said Trixie as she hauled herself to her feet.

'I think that was our guitarist,' replied Lisa.

'What, her?' said Dee.

'I'm afraid so.'

'Do you think she does that sort of thing often?'

'What, run around the streets naked? I don't think so.'

'Pity,' said Trixie. 'It'd be great for the act.'

'Come on, girls,' said Dee. 'I guess we'd better follow her.'

And the three of them set off down the alley in pursuit of the naked girl.

Chapter 5

And so the Kool Kittens were born. Dee hated the name, but when she finally found them an agent he was enthusiastic.

'After all,' he said. 'We've got to emphasise the fact that you're all chicks. It's a real gimmick.'

'If we're chicks, how come you want to call us kittens?' she asked, but he simply waved aside her protestations.

And in truth he turned out to be an asset to them, finding them gigs all over London and ensuring that people knew who they were. It was him that had got them the audition for the cruise and now, as they packed their bags, they had reason to thank him for what he had done, despite the dreadful name.

'After all,' as Trixie had said, 'what's in a name? We're working, aren't we?'

In another part of London, Les Cargill's mind was also preoccupied by work, but work of a very different kind. He was sitting up in bed studying the blueprint of a building, making notes with a pencil as he did so. He wrote carefully, referring to the diagram frequently, occasionally picking up a small calculator into which he intermittently tapped some figures. It was some time before he put the pencil down. Then he gazed closely at his notes, and nodded his satisfaction, tossing the notebook aside. If he wasn't prepared now, he never would be.

Forgetting the job in hand for a moment, he lay back, lifted the sheet and stared down at his body. There was no doubt that his figure was athletic, his body bronzed all over, barring only a very thin white stripe across his groin, where his large cock nested amid a tangle of thick, dark pubic hair. The colour of his nether bush belied the streaked blond of his carefully manicured hair. Les would have passed for a Bondi beach bum any time, and he knew he was attractive to women.

The room in which he was lying was shabby, with peeling wallpaper and a threadbare carpet. He snorted to himself. He wasn't born to live in squalor. He should be leading a better life. And after tomorrow he would be. All this was going to change and he would be a rich man.

The door opened and a woman came in. She was tall and leggy, with a large bust and slim hips. She wore a short negligee which hid very little of her curvaceous figure and in her hands she held two glasses of wine. To the casual observer she might have appeared sophisticated, though the moment she spoke her broad Cockney accent betrayed her origins.

'You still lookin' at that plan thing, Les?' she asked, placing the glasses on the bedside table and sliding into bed beside him.

He grunted noncommittally.

'What's it all about, Les? You've bin staring at it for ages.'

'It's work. I told you, I've got an important job on tomorrow, before I go away.'

'Why've you gotta go away, Les?' She snuggled up to him. 'Why not stay here with little Doll?'

'You know why. It's business.'

'Then why not take me with you?' Her hand moved to his chest and she began toying with the dark hairs there.

'I can't take you, Doll. Now stop asking, would you?'

She pouted. 'You haven't got someone else, have you, Les?' Her hand began to slide down his body, the palm flat against his skin.

'Don't be daft, Doll. Why would I want someone else?' Why wouldn't I, he thought privately. When he was rich there would be no more slags like Doll. He'd have proper, sophisticated women who knew how to behave in society.

'Mmm. Show me you still want me then, lover.' Her hand ran over the wiry curls of his pubic hair and grasped the thick shaft of his cock.

'Not just now, Doll,' he said. 'I'm trying to concentrate.'

'Why not concentrate on me?' She squeezed his member gently and was rewarded by a slight swelling as she did so.

'Later, Doll.'

'But who knows when you'll be back? I've got my needs, you know, Les.'

'I told you. I don't know myself yet. Now let me concentrate.'

'Mmm?' She scarcely seemed to be listening to him as she slid her head down under the bedclothes. He shuddered slightly as he felt her hot little tongue on his belly.

He lifted the plan again, determined to concentrate upon it, but at that moment he felt her lips close about his cock and the gentle sucking began. Despite himself he felt his penis begin to stiffen.

One thing he had to concede about Doll. She was bloody good in bed. And enthusiastic, too. She was the best fuck he'd come across for a long time and he'd be sorry to leave her behind. But greater things beckoned for Les Cargill, and there was no place for Doll in them.

'Mmm.'

He groaned as she began to work her head up and down on his now erect penis. He stared hard at the plans, but his mind was filled with the sensation in his groin as Doll sucked and licked at him, her fingers massaging his balls. He flung back the bedclothes and stared down at her. Her nightdress had ridden up to her waist now, revealing the pink rosebud that was her sex, the wetness already showing on the outer lips. He ran a hand up her inner thigh, fascinated by the smoothness of her flesh. His fingers found her sex and he slid a digit inside, making her start. She removed his cock from her mouth and stared back at him.

'Mmm, that's nice, Les,' she said. 'Put two in.'

He did as she requested, smiling slightly at the instant effect this had on her, her hips writhing back and forth as he frigged her. She turned her attention back to his penis, and it was his turn to writhe as she sucked greedily at it, a trail of saliva running down the shaft and into his pubic hairs.

There was no doubt, Doll was an expert at giving head. He had never known a woman with such a sensuous touch, her tongue worming its way under his glans whilst her teeth just scraped gently along the flesh, their sharpness somehow adding to the sensation. He was thoroughly aroused now, his cock as hard as iron, his balls feeling almost uncomfortable, such was his desire to come. He frigged her hard, his fingers soaking with her juices, the wetness leaking out onto her thighs as she writhed about above him.

She seemed to sense the imminence of his orgasm and allowed him to slide from her lips, kneeling up on the bed so that his fingers came out of her. She turned to face him, licking her lips sensuously, then took hold of the hem of her nightie and pulled it over her head.

He stared at her. He never tired of the sight of her breasts, full and rounded, sagging slightly with their own weight. The nipples were brown and hard, set high on her twin mounds so that they pointed proudly upwards.

'Would you like to suck my tits?' she asked, once again sensing his desires almost before he was aware of them himself. He nodded.

She moved closer and leaned over him, letting her luscious mammaries dangle above his face. He reached up and placed his palm flat over the left one, feeling for the stiff, rubbery teat. She pressed lower and he opened his mouth, taking the hard brown knob inside.

He loved to suck her tits. They seemed to have been designed for his mouth alone and he devoured them greedily, his hands squeezing the soft, pliable flesh whilst he ran his teeth back and forth over the protruding nipple. As he did so, Doll's hands found his penis again and she began gently working the foreskin back and forth.

'Shit, Doll, I need you,' he muttered, pushing her backwards. 'I just gotta fuck you.'

Doll flopped onto her back, spreading her legs wide and smiling up at him. 'I'm all yours, lover,' she said. 'Fuck me, Les.'

He sprang up onto his knees and crawled forward until he was above her, gazing down at her nakedness. She reached between his legs and took hold of his stiff erection, pulling him forwards and guiding him to her honeypot.

He sank his cock into her, his long pink spear of flesh piercing her vagina and sliding deep within her until their pubic hair was intermingled. There he paused, savouring the closeness, his face gazing into hers, her stiff nipples brushing against the dark hair on his chest. Then his hips began to move.

He fucked her slowly, savouring the sensation. Her cunt was tight, as it always was, giving him the most incredible sensation as he slid in and out, his pace increasing with every stroke as he felt his orgasm build once more. Beneath him Doll writhed and moaned, her body bucking with every stroke, her breasts lolling to one side then the other as she gave voice to her lust.

He wanted to make it last as long as he could, but the foreplay had already raised him to a state of high arousal and once again he felt the pressure building in his balls.

'Oh, Christ, I'm coming,' he gasped, and as he did so he felt her tighten the muscles of her vagina about his member.

'Ah! Ah! Ah!'

She screamed aloud as he began to pump his spunk into her, great floods of semen springing from his throbbing organ, filling her hungry cunt as she too allowed her orgasm to overtake her. The two of them rolled about on the bed, their bodies locked together, their fluids mingling in the most intimate manner possible.

When, at last, he was spent, he rolled off her, leaving her gasping, her breasts rising and falling as she regained her breath. He reached for the packet of cigarettes on the bedside table and lit two, passing one to her.

'Bloody hell, that was good,' she said.

He grinned. 'Yeah. You're the best, Doll. I'm gonna miss you.'

'Don't say it like that,' she said. 'It sounds as if you're not coming back.'

He made no reply, sitting up and picking up the blueprint that had fallen to the floor. He folded it carefully and slipped it into a document case that lay beside the bed. As he did so something fell out. It was some kind of travel agent's document, and written on the front was the name *SS Diana*. He picked it up and replaced it in the case. Then he put his wine glass to his lips and took a long drink.

Chapter 6

Detective Inspector Kathy Prender closed the file in front of her and sat back. There was no point in reading it again. There was nothing new in there and she was in danger of confusing herself by constantly re-reading it. She picked up her coffee cup. It was cold. She put it back down with a gesture of annoyance and checked her watch. It was one in the morning. Any sensible person would have been in bed, yet here she sat waiting for something to happen. She had been so sure it would be tonight. So what was holding things up?

Kathy Prender was one of a new breed of police officers. Recruited from university, she had been thoroughly trained in the science of forensics and detective work, then deployed to a branch of the Metropolitan Police that specialised in the solving of major crimes. She had been with them more than a year now, and had acquitted herself well, with a number of convictions to her credit. So why couldn't she solve this one?

If truth were told, this case was slightly unusual. In fact she couldn't even be certain that there was a case. Normally her squad would have been called in after the crime had taken place. This time they were anticipating the offence.

It had all started when a constable on the beat had, quite by chance, apprehended a car thief. He had rounded a corner to be confronted by a young man opening the door of a powerful BMW coupé, a man who he knew to be too short of money to afford even a bicycle. A short chase had ensued, and he had eventually trapped the young man down an alleyway.

As it transpired, the thief had previous convictions, and was, in fact, on probation at the time of committing the theft. But what really aroused the arresting constable's suspicions was the type of car being stolen. All the man's prior offences had been for taking small hot hatchbacks for joyriding. The expensive BMW seemed a long way out of his class, particularly considering the specialist equipment needed to lift such a vehicle. It was for this reason that he had had the suspect closely questioned, and the story that had emerged was one that he had felt important enough to pass on to Kathy's department.

It seemed that the thief had been approached in a pub. Nothing unusual about that, of course, except that the man who had approached him was a complete stranger, and what was more, had a very clear idea of the type of car he wanted. He had handed over a list of vehicles, none of which was particularly conspicuous, but all of which were capable of a very swift getaway should the need arise. It soon occurred to Kathy that the intention was to use the vehicle to escape from the scene of a crime.

The car thief had had little else to offer apart from a vague description of the instigator of the crime. So Kathy had been forced to search elsewhere to obtain more details.

After a period of trawling the various local officers'

informants, with little success, she finally found a clue. Someone had heard about a man who was seeking a good diamond fence. The rumour was that a receiver was being sought for a large quantity of finest quality stones that would be on the market in the near future. Kathy spent some time visiting likely dealers and, whilst she received little firm information, it quickly became clear to her that the amounts of money involved were beyond the means of the East End dealers.

A check had been made around London's jewellers and gem merchants for any large shipments of jewels. The trouble with that, Kathy reflected, was that many of these dealers' clients were not particularly honest themselves, and it was not always in their interests to let the police know precisely what their plans were.

The police had done the best they could, staking out officers at the most likely targets for the last three nights. And nothing had happened. Now, with yet another night apparently passing quietly, Kathy was worried. What if she'd been wrong all along? What if the whole thing was just a wild goose chase? She couldn't keep the watch up for much longer, it was using up too much resource.

The telephone on the desk suddenly rang, making her start. She snatched up the receiver.

'Prender.'

'Control here, ma'am. Just had a call. There's an alarm going off at one of the south London dealers.'

'Anyone seen breaking in?'

'No. The owner's on his way down there now with the keys. Lavers is on the spot already. Should he break in?'

Kathy thought for a second. 'No,' she said at last. 'We've

got no proof that a crime's taking place. Better hold off until the owner gets there. Call my car.'

Five minutes later she was speeding through the streets of London in an unmarked police car.

The gem merchant's premises were in a narrow road flanked by tall Victorian buildings. As the car slowed to turn into the road, another car suddenly shot out of the turning. The police driver had to brake hard to avoid hitting it. As it sped past, Kathy swung round and recognised it as a BMW coupé. She swiftly made a note of the number.

'Put out a call on that car,' she said. 'Find out if it's stolen.'

They pulled up outside a building, above the entrance to which an alarm bell was ringing. On a plaque outside the door were the words *JJ Arons. Gem Merchant*. As they climbed from their vehicle, an elderly gent was stooping down to unlock the door. With him was a younger man whom Kathy recognised as the detective who had been on watch. Kathy joined them.

'Anything to report, Lavers?'

'Didn't see a thing, ma'am. The place has been quiet.'

'Did you see that car just now?'

'Just glimpsed it. It pulled out from about two streets down.'

She turned to the older man. 'Mr Arons?'

'Yes.'

'Is there a back way in?'

'No. The building backs onto an old factory. There's a high fence and the door's been bricked up.'

'Let's go inside then.'

The man led them through the entrance. He went to a panel on the wall and turned a key in it. At once the alarm stopped ringing. He unlocked the door to the office and glanced around.

'Nothing's been touched here,' he said.

'Where do you keep the gems?'

'In the strong room behind. I'll show you.'

He led them through a door at the back of the office and down a short passageway to another. This one was made of metal, with two heavy locks. He undid them both and pushed the door open.

'Oh, shit.'

Opposite the door was a brick wall. In the middle of it was a hole about two foot square. The bricks had been simply smashed by some kind of heavy instrument. Kathy cursed quietly as she surveyed the damage. They were too late.

Chapter 7

'She's beautiful, isn't she?'

The four girls stood, gazing up at the sleek lines of the *SS Diana*. The ship was a modern one, long and sleek, with steep sides, the funnels raked back to give an impression of speed. The Kool Kittens were standing on the quayside watching as the passengers trooped aboard.

'Wow,' said Jenny. 'This is really going to be some kind of adventure.'

'It certainly is,' said Dee. 'Listen. I want to go aboard and get our on-board passes. Trixie, why don't you come with me and we'll leave these two to get the equipment and baggage through Customs.'

'Okay,' said Trixie. 'That all right with you guys?'

'Sure,' said Lisa. 'Come on, Jenny, let's go.'

Jenny followed Lisa into the Customs shed. It was a long, narrow building that sat on the quayside alongside where the ship was moored. As they entered they found it almost empty, most of the passengers having checked in earlier in the day. The band's instruments and baggage were piled onto trolleys and the two girls pushed them down the long passageway flanked on either side by low counters behind which the Customs men stood. They had nearly reached the end when they were stopped.

'Hang on, ladies.'

They turned to see a man dressed in the uniform of a Customs official. Beside him was another man, similarly dressed.

'Yes?' said Lisa.

'Can you tell me what you're carrying?'

'Our luggage. And our instruments.'

'Instruments?'

'Yes. We're the Kool Kittens.'

'The cool what?'

'The Kool Kittens. We're the ship's band. Or half of it, anyhow.'

'I see. Would you mind bringing your luggage over here with you please? Just a routine check.'

'Of course.' Lisa smiled, though inwardly she was cursing their ill luck.

The two men led them through a gap in the counter and into a back room. There were one or two other passengers in the room, all with their bags open and Customs officers rummaging inside. The girls were led to a table onto which they unloaded the luggage.

The men began opening the bags, checking carefully through the contents of each, even removing the instruments from their cases and examining them.

'Are you looking for anything in particular?' asked Lisa.

'Just routine,' came the reply.

The search went on for about fifteen minutes, with no bag left unchecked. By the time the men had finished the girls felt as if every item of clothing they possessed had been scrutinised. At last, though, the officials seemed satisfied and closed the cases.

'Right,' said the first man. 'Now we just need to see your tickets.'

'But we haven't got any,' said Jenny. 'We told you, we're the band.'

'In that case I'll need to see your on-board passes.'

'We don't have them yet. Our friends went ahead to pick them up.'

'Where are your friends?'

'I'm not sure. I guess they're on the ship.'

'We can't let you through without them, I'm afraid.'

'But you've got to,' protested Lisa. 'We'll miss the boat at this rate.'

'You say your friends are already on board?'

'Yes. The idea was that they would get the passes whilst we took the baggage through.'

The man turned to his companion. 'Maybe we should give Svetna a call. She deals with passes.'

'You're right.' He turned to the girls. 'Wait here and I'll see what can be done.'

The man crossed the room to where a telephone hung from the wall. He picked it up and began to speak. The conversation lasted no more than two minutes, then he was back.

'There's a bit of a hold-up with the issuing of the passes, apparently. The purser's had to go ashore and he won't be back for half an hour.'

'What does that mean?'

'It means, I'm afraid, that you'll have to wait.'

'We're not going to miss the boat, are we?' asked Jenny.

He smiled. 'No chance of that. Apart from anything else they won't sail without the purser.'

'What do we do meanwhile?' asked Lisa.

'You'll have to stay here. There's a waiting room over there.'

He indicated an area at one end of the room, where a number of chairs was set out.

'Is it safe to leave the luggage here?' asked Lisa.

'Certainly. It'll be fine.'

The two girls looked at each other. Clearly there was nothing else for it. They had to wait. Reluctantly they made their way across to the waiting area.

'Just our luck,' grumbled Lisa. 'I could have done without this.'

'Where do you suppose Dee and Trixie are?' asked her friend.

'Search me. I guess they're in a waiting room somewhere too. What a place. There's not even a coffee machine.'

The two girls sat down side by side and stared at the blank wall.

Behind them another figure was being led into the searching area. It was a man in his early twenties, and he looked decidedly disgruntled.

Les Cargill was worried. This was just what he hadn't wanted to happen. The gems were carefully hidden inside the cassette recorder in his bag. But if the Customs were at all vigilant, he was in trouble. And from what he had seen so far they certainly were just that. It was clear they had had some kind of tip-off that the thief was sailing aboard the *SS Diana*.

Les's mind raced as he tried to decide what to do for the best. If only he could get rid of the diamonds until after the search was completed. But where? Then he spotted the pile of baggage and musical instruments on the trolley beside him, and an idea began to form in his head.

'Excuse me, ladies.'

Lisa and Jenny looked up. In front of them were two men, somewhat younger than those who had intercepted them earlier. They were dressed differently too, in brown overalls, though there was no mistaking the badges on their hats, which bore the seal of HM Customs.

'Yes?'

'Would you mind coming with us?'

'Have our passes arrived?'

'Not yet. Just another formality.'

Lisa and Jenny exchanged a glance. What now? This whole thing seemed to be getting out of hand. Reluctantly they rose to their feet and followed the two men.

They were led through a door on the far side of the waiting area. Beyond was a long passageway, then another door. The room in which they found themselves was barely furnished, with a wooden bench running down the middle and rows of lockers on either side. The men took them to the centre of the room, then turned to face them.

One of the two men began to speak. He was the taller of the pair, with short fair hair and blue eyes. His lapel bore a badge with the name 'Eddie' on it.

'Right, ladies,' he said. 'I'd like to look in your handbags, please.'

'Is that really necessary?' asked Lisa.

'It's our job,' said the second man. He was slightly shorter with dark curly hair and a droopy moustache. His badge revealed his name to be Jake.

Reluctantly the two girls handed over their bags and stood back whilst the two men emptied them onto a bench. They went through the contents for a few seconds, then Jake turned to Jenny.

'This is your handbag?' he asked.

'You know it is.'

'Then can you explain what this is?'

He held up a small plastic sack. Inside was a quantity of white powder.

'That didn't come from my bag,' protested Jenny.

'I'm afraid I have a witness,' said Jake. 'You saw her hand the bag over, didn't you, Eddie?'

'I certainly did. This is a serious matter.'

'But I tell you that wasn't in my bag,' said Jenny despairingly. 'You believe me, Lisa, don't you?'

'Of course.' Lisa turned to the two men. 'You can't possibly think she's a drug smuggler.'

'We see all kinds here, miss,' said Eddie. 'Now I'd be grateful if you'd both cooperate. Then maybe we can get to the bottom of this. We're going to have to search you.'

'Search us?'

'I'm afraid so. Now would you please remove your clothes.'

'What?'

'Strip please, so that we can search you properly.'

'But that's outrageous,' said Lisa.

'It's the law,' said Jake. 'Now, come on, ladies, please do as I ask.'

'What, now?' asked Jenny, her voice shaking slightly.

'Wait a minute,' said Lisa. 'If we're to be strip-searched, shouldn't there be a lady officer present?'

'Normally, yes,' said Eddie. 'Unfortunately there's none on duty at the moment.'

'Well, can't we wait until one's available?'

'Certainly, if that's what you'd prefer. The next shift comes on in about three hours.'

'Three hours? But the ship sails in less than two.'

'That can't be helped, I'm afraid. You could always fly down and join it at one of the stops.'

'But that's no good. We've got work to do. We're supposed to be playing tonight.'

The men shook their heads. 'Well, we can't let you board until you've been searched,' said Jake.

'Wait a second.' Lisa turned to Jenny and lowered her voice. 'You sure that powder wasn't in your bag?'

'Of course not, Lisa. I don't use that stuff,' whispered Jenny.

'Then it was planted.'

'Planted? But who would have done that?'

Lisa glanced at the two men. 'I have my suspicions.'

'What do you mean?'

'I mean that once we've got our clothes off, these two are going to want to do more than just search us.'

Jenny's eyes widened. 'You mean . . .'

Lisa nodded. 'You fancy being fucked by one of them?'

'But they can't.'

'Not officially, maybe. But they can certainly make sure we miss the ship if we don't co-operate.'

'So there's not much choice, really.'

'Not really.'

For a second Jenny hesitated, then she shrugged. 'I suppose we'd better go along with it, then.'

Lisa turned back to the men. 'It seems we have no choice,' she said. 'Where do we go?'

'Right there will do,' said Eddie, a slight grin on his face.

Lisa had worn jeans and a shirt for the journey, whilst Jenny was dressed in a short summer frock. As the two men watched they both began to undress.

Lisa undid the buttons on her shirt, pulling it from her waistband and shrugging it off. Her bra was underwired, so that it pressed her breasts together and upward, enhancing her cleavage. She began to undo the fly of her jeans. Jenny, meanwhile, released the catch at the back of her dress and slid down the zipper. Soon both girls were clad only in their underwear.

Lisa's panties were white, matching her bra, with a high tanga waist. Jenny wore a black lacy set, the pants small and wispy. In addition she had on a suspender belt which supported her sheer stockings. She blushed as the two men eyed her appreciatively.

The two girls hesitated, unwilling to go any further.

'Come on now, ladies,' coaxed Eddie. 'The underwear as well, please.'

Reluctantly both reached behind their backs for their bra catches, snapping them undone and allowing the garments to fall away from their breasts. Then each hooked their fingers into the waistband of their panties and slid them off. Jenny went to undo her suspender belt.

'No, you can leave that on,' said Jake.

The two naked girls stood side by side whilst the men admired their bodies. It was difficult to choose which was the lovelier; Jenny, with her petite frame and neat round breasts or the taller Lisa, with her lissom shape and large, firm breasts that jutted forward as if inviting a lover's caress.

'Right, ladies,' said Eddie, an edge of excitement in his voice. 'Please go to the wall and face it, your palms flat against the surface.'

'Here we go,' muttered Lisa.

The two girls crossed to the wall and did as they were asked.

'Hands lower down the wall, please,' said Eddie. 'And spread your legs apart.'

Jenny felt extremely vulnerable, standing as she was. She knew that the position showed off her backside perfectly to the watching men and she knew too that they could clearly see the pink lips of her sex.

She stared at the wall as she heard the men cross the room, her palms sweating slightly.

'Oh!'

The touch of Jake's hands made her jump. He had placed them on her back, and was rubbing them over her soft flesh. From the corner of her eye she saw that Eddie was doing the same to Lisa.

'Is this really necessary?' asked Lisa.

'We have to check for concealed goods,' replied Eddie.

Jenny's body trembled slightly as she felt Jake's strong hands rove over her back. She thought about what was about to happen. It was outrageous really, but in another sense it was quite exciting. Besides, Lisa was receiving the same treatment, and that made Jenny feel much better.

In fact, when she came to think of it, having a man's hands on her naked body was rather nice. It was a relaxing feeling, almost like a massage and, despite her unusual stance, she felt her body begin to relax, the closeness of his body somehow rather arousing.

He placed his arms about her waist, his fingers seeking out her navel. Then his hands began to slide upwards and she closed her eyes.

'Mmm.'

She couldn't suppress the groan as his hands found her breasts. He cupped them from underneath, squeezing them gently, then his fingers sought out her nipples, which puckered to hardness at once as he rolled them between finger and thumb. Jenny stole a glance at Lisa, who was receiving similar treatment, her breathing sounding loud as Eddie fondled her breasts.

Jake's hands left her soft mammaries, causing Jenny to give a little sigh of disappointment. They didn't leave her body, though, creeping round behind her once more and sliding down to the rounded flesh of her behind. He took hold of a buttock in each hand and pulled them apart. Then she felt a finger slide down the crack and pause over the starred hole of her anus.

'Ah!'

He slid a finger into her nether hole, once more making her start as he rotated it.

The sensation was delicious, and Jenny found herself pressing back at him. There was something unexpectedly arousing about her situation, standing naked in this bare room with her friend whilst the two men fondled their bodies. Something that was making her flesh tingle with anticipation.

Jake slipped his finger out of her rear and Jenny's breath quickened as his hand began to creep down between her legs, towards the place where she now longed to be touched. He ran his palm over her inner thigh, making her shudder with pleasure. Then he moved his hand higher toward her slit. She braced herself for his touch, knowing that she was very wet, and that he would feel that wetness and see how turned on she was.

His fingers sought out her clitoris and she felt it harden under his fingers. Then she gasped as two fingers penetrated her with a slight squelching sound.

She wondered for a second whether Lisa was feeling the same. Certainly the heavy breathing of her friend seemed to indicate as much. She stole a glance to her left, and her eyes widened as she saw that Lisa's hand was reaching behind her, her fingers wrapped round the long, thick cock that protruded from the man's trousers. Lisa was wanking him gently whilst he frigged her with one hand, the other still caressing her breast.

'I want you.'

The words were murmured into Jenny's ear by Jake as he worked his fingers in and out of her vagina. It was all Jenny needed to hear. She straightened and turned, opening her legs and pressing her pubis forward as he reinserted his fingers from the front. She began to unbutton his overall, her fingers moving quickly down until the garment hung open. She slipped it from his shoulders and let it drop to the ground. Underneath he wore only a pair of briefs that bulged impossibly, looking as if they could be torn apart at any moment. She pulled them down and his cock sprang to attention at once, projecting from his groin like a thick, veined cannon, the end of his glans shiny with lubrication. She took him in her hands at once, thrilled by the hardness of his weapon under her fingers.

Jenny looked across to see that Eddie too was now naked. He had taken Lisa across to the bench in the centre of the room and she was lying back along its length, her legs spread on either side, her sex wide open. Even as Jenny watched, Eddie lowered his body over hers and Lisa gave a cry as his cock slipped into her.

It was all too much for Jenny and she pulled Jake's erection closer to her.

'Fuck me,' she whispered.

'Turn back to the wall,' he said. 'And spread your legs.'

Jenny complied at once, taking up her stance facing the wall once more and bending forward, thrusting her backside back at him. He moved closer, and she felt the hard tip of his penis press against her behind. She reached back and took him in her hand, guiding him to the centre of her desires.

'Ahhh.'

The cry that escaped her lips was one of pure lust as he rammed his weapon into her, filling her with the most delicious sensation. Its length and girth seemed almost too much for her and she spread her legs still further in order to fully accommodate him. He pressed on and on until she felt his skin come into contact with her own, his breath rasping in her ear. Then he began to move his hips.

There was no finesse in his technique, he just fucked her hard, his belly slapping against her backside as he thrust at her with vigour. She was reminded of her encounter with the john in the alley behind the pub. This, like on that occasion, was raw sex. Simple copulation for the sheer pleasure of it, and despite the men's trickery she found herself loving every moment.

He slipped his arms about her waist, one of them grasping for her breasts whilst the other dropped to her sex, teasing her clitoris out and rubbing it vigorously, making her scream aloud with the delicious sensation this gave her. Jenny was in ecstasy, her body shaken by Jake's violent thrusts, her sex on fire with pleasure as she struggled to keep her balance. She glanced behind her at Lisa, who was stretched out along the bench moaning aloud whilst Eddie rammed his cock into her, making her breasts shake back and forth with the force of the onslaught.

Suddenly Jenny felt Jake's rhythm change, and at the same time heard him draw in his breath, signalling the imminence of his orgasm. He thrust into her two more times, then gave a hoarse cry and began pumping his seed into her. With a shout Jenny was coming too, her sex convulsing about his cock as she felt spurt after spurt of hot semen splash against the entrance to her uterus. From the bench behind them similar lustful sounds were ringing in the air and she knew that Lisa was climaxing at the same time.

Jenny knew of no more exquisite sensation than that of having her cunt filled with sperm, and her small frame swayed and shuddered with sheer pleasure as Jake's tool went on pumping the contents of his balls into her. He stayed deep inside her until his cock stopped twitching and every last drop of his seed was inside her. Then he eased himself out and she turned, leaning against the wall, panting for breath, an expression of pure satisfaction on her face.

For a while she remained where she was, leaning back, her breasts rising and falling as she fought for breath. Jake reached out and stroked her hair, then turned. He crossed and sat down on the bench beside the still panting Lisa. Jenny eased herself off the wall and went to join them. As she did her foot struck something and she bent down to see what it was.

It was an identity card, with Jake's photo on it. But it wasn't the photo that held her attention. It was the job description beneath it.

'Domestic Cleaner.'

Chapter 8

Jenny stared at the card, unable to believe her eyes. A domestic cleaner! And she and Lisa had stripped off in front of him and his friend without complaint. The seduction was something else, of course. They had both gone into that with their eyes open. But the whole thing had been based on trickery, and she felt a sudden anger as she realised how they had been fooled.

She looked across at him. He hadn't noticed her pick up the card. His eyes were fixed on Lisa, and he was toying with her breasts as she lay beside him. Jenny's mind worked fast. She had to tell Lisa what she had discovered. She knew her friend would know what to do next. Lisa's hand was trailing on the floor beside where she lay, and that gave Jenny an idea. She palmed the card and made her way across to them. Jake looked up to her and smiled.

She knelt down at his feet and reached for his cock, which had already softened. He turned to her, his hand still squeezing her friend's breasts, and Jenny took the chance to slip her hand over Lisa's, dropping the card into her palm as she did so. Then she knelt up and put Jake's cock in her mouth, tasting herself on him. He looked down, and as he did so she saw Lisa sneak a glance at what was in her hand.

65

Jake stroked Jenny's hair. 'Why not sit with Eddie?' he said, grinning. 'Your friend and I were just getting acquainted.' Clearly the two of them were not finished yet.

Then Lisa spoke. 'Not just at the moment, guys,' she said, reaching for Jenny's hand. 'Right now, I fancy Jenny more.'

Eddie's eyes widened. 'You mean you're lesbians?'

'Not specifically,' said Lisa. 'We swing both ways.'

Jenny had no idea what Lisa was playing at, but she allowed herself to be pulled to her feet so that she was looking down at her prostrate friend.

'Come here,' urged Lisa, pulling her down on top of her.

Jenny straddled Lisa's body, the spunk that oozed from her sex forming a shiny streak across Lisa's stomach as she lowered herself. Then, at Lisa's urging, she leaned forward until their breasts were touching. Lisa lifted her head and planted a kiss on her friend's mouth. Jenny was staring at her in amazement as Lisa began to fondle her breasts, kissing the smaller girl's neck, then working her mouth round to her ear.

'So they're not Customs men after all,' she breathed. 'The bastards fooled us. They're just a pair of cleaners.'

Jenny nodded almost imperceptibly. Her head was spinning slightly as she felt her friend's hands on her body. She had never been caressed in such a way by another woman, and she was finding it hard to concentrate on what Lisa was saying.

'Mmm, you feel nice,' said Lisa. 'Here, let me kiss you.'

She placed an arm round Jenny's neck and pulled her closer, nuzzling against her ear once more.

'Will you do as I say?' she whispered.

Jenny gave her a squeeze of affirmation.

'I need to get close to the door. We're going to have to make this convincing, though. Just do whatever I tell you.'

'Mmmm,' replied Jenny.

Lisa didn't move for a few seconds, then she suddenly pushed up at Jenny.

'Come on, lover,' she said. 'I want to feel your tongue in my cunt. You can lick out the spunk that's in there. You'd like that, wouldn't you?'

Jenny tried to hide the shock in her voice. 'Y-yeah,' she stuttered.

Lisa rose to her feet as the men looked on. She knew she looked good in the buff, and she swaggered across the room, her neat backside swaying back and forth. She made for the door through which they had entered the room. It was a single door that opened inwards, with a small window at about head height. She turned and leaned against the door, her hips pushed forward, her legs wide.

'Lick me, Jenny,' she said. 'Lick me clean.'

Jenny was still uncertain what her friend was playing at, but she had agreed to go along, so go along she must. The petite girl dropped obediently to her knees between Lisa's legs. She studied the pink flower of pleasure that was presented so beautifully to her. The lips were spread apart and she could see the spunk that trickled from inside and onto Lisa's thigh. She licked tentatively at the white fluid, swallowing it down.

She had never been so close to another woman's sex before, and the scent of female arousal mingled with the distinctly male smell of fresh semen made for a heady cocktail. She protruded her tongue, then licked again at her friend's sex.

Lisa gave a little gasp as her friend's tongue came into contact with her love bud. The sensation of turning on another woman was, to Jenny, extraordinary. She felt Lisa's muscles contract as her own little pink muscle delved into her friend's vagina. Jenny sucked and slurped at the juices that flowed from the girl's love hole, suddenly incredibly turned on by the intimacy of their contact. She could sense Lisa's arousal as she worked her, and somehow that arousal was transmitting itself to her, so that once again her own juices were flowing.

On the other side of the room the two men were watching, amazed. Both had recovered their erections, their cocks standing out like flagpoles as they witnessed the scene. It was clear that they would be ready for more once Jenny had finished.

When the orgasm came it almost took Jenny by surprise. Lisa had been standing against the door, her body stiff, her breaths coming in short gasps. Then, suddenly, she cried aloud and her body gave a violent shudder beneath the onslaught of licking. She grasped hold of Jenny's hair and pressed her sex hard against her friend's mouth, small, staccato grunts escaping from her lips as she rode out her pleasure. Across the room the two men had started to masturbate, their hands working their foreskins back and forth as they fixed their eyes on the two naked girls.

Jenny withdrew her tongue and stared up at her panting

friend. Lisa was leaning against the door, her head back, her breathing heavy. She smiled down at her companion.

'Thanks, Jenny.'

She turned her head and looked through the window.

'Oh shit, it looks like one of your colleagues is coming,' she said to the men.

'Does that mean he'll want to fuck us too?'

'What did you say?' said Jake.

'One of the other Customs guys. The ones who searched our bags. He's just come through the door at the end and he's heading this way.'

'Oh hell!' exclaimed Eddie. 'We're in for it now. Quick, girls, follow me.'

He snatched up the girls' clothes from the floor and tossed them across. Then he and Jake rushed through a door at the back of the room, with Jenny and Lisa following swiftly. By the time the girls reached the next room the two men had already pushed open a pair of doors marked 'Fire Escape'. Through them the quayside could be seen, and the *SS Diana*, with crowds of people lining the decks.

'Quick, out,' panted Eddie. 'Before he gets here.'

'But there's another Customs man just outside on the quay,' said Lisa.

'Where?' Both men turned and stared out the doorway.

Lisa nudged her friend and nodded. As one the pair ran at the two men, striking them in the centre of their backs. They staggered forward a couple of paces, and that was all the girls needed. They grabbed a door each and slammed them shut, snapping the bolt into place.

'Quick,' said Lisa. 'To the window.'

Both girls ran to the window and gazed out. There were

the two men, both stark naked, their cocks as hard as ever, banging against the doors. Behind them someone on the ship had spotted them, and already hoots of laughter were ringing out. The pair swung round and suddenly realised their predicament, naked and rampant in front of hundreds of laughing people. They tried to cover themselves with their hands, but in vain. At last they simply made a dash for it, running alongside the ship, their cocks bouncing up and down as they desperately sought refuge.

Lisa and Jenny collapsed into one another's arms, both helpless with laughter.

'Where do you think they'll end up?' gasped Jenny.

'In a police station at that rate,' her friend replied.

'That'll teach them to take advantage of a pair of innocent young girls.'

Lisa looked her in the eyes. 'Hardly innocent,' she said. 'That was quite a show you put on there by the door. I hadn't intended to come, but I couldn't help myself. You must have done that kind of thing before.'

Jenny blushed. 'No, that was the first time with a woman,' she said.

'You're a natural, then,' said Lisa. 'Let's hope it won't be the last.'

Chapter 9

Trixie Ballantine dumped her suitcase on the floor of the cabin and looked about her. It wasn't exactly the Ritz, she decided, but it was comfortable. And it was all hers. She sat down on the bunk and bounced up and down a couple of times. Quite firm, with no squeak, she mused. That should serve her purpose.

She stood up and began to strip, watching herself in the full-length mirror on the door as she did so. She undressed slowly, imagining herself doing it in front of a lover. Trixie loved her body, and she loved to give it to men. Next to playing in the band, her greatest pleasure was fucking, and she intended to do a great deal of both during this trip.

She stripped to her underwear and stood sideways to the mirror, her eyes roving up and down her tall frame. She undid her bra strap and noted with satisfaction that her large, full breasts barely dropped at all when the support was removed. All those exercises in the gym certainly paid off. She slid down her panties and eyed her pubic bush critically. It was ginger, as was her hair, the curls cut short into a neat triangle. It needed a trim, she decided. She liked her mound prominent, but wanted her sex to be visible when she was naked.

Trixie stepped into the shower and turned it on, allowing the water to cascade over her shapely frame. She soaped herself slowly, enjoying her own caresses. When she was through she ran the water cold, the thin spray making her flesh tingle with excitement and causing her nipples to stand out stiffly.

When at last she was done, she towelled herself, lovingly dabbing at every cranny of her body. Then she stepped back into the cabin. A shower always made her feel extremely sexy, and today was no exception. On an impulse she reached into her handbag and withdrew a thick vibrator. She switched it on and ran her hand up and down its length, caressing it as she would a real penis. She lay back on the bunk, spreading her legs wide and pressing it against her sex. It slid in easily and she lay back, her eyes closed, her body thrilling to the vibrations from the humming phallus.

She was just deciding whether to simply relax and enjoy the sensation or to bring herself to orgasm when the telephone shrilled beside her ear.

'Damn,' she exclaimed, reaching for the instrument.

'Trixie?' It was Dee's voice on the other end.

'Yeah?'

'You free?'

Trixie gazed down at the thick object that hummed between her legs. 'Kind of.'

'We need to do a sound check in the entertainments lounge. Can you be there in half an hour?'

'I guess so.'

'Well, don't put yourself out.' Dee sounded slightly irritated.

Trixie laughed. 'Don't worry, Dee,' she said. 'I wouldn't miss it for the world.'

Dee laughed back. 'Great, Trixie,' she said, all traces of impatience gone from her voice. 'See you in half an hour.'

Trixie slid the vibrator out of her vagina and placed it on the table by her bed. Then she reached down and pulled back the zip on her travelling bag.

'That's funny.'

She reached inside and took out the cassette recorder. She studied it carefully. Where on earth had that come from? It certainly wasn't hers, and it hadn't been there when she was packing. So what was it doing in her bag?

Then she remembered. The bags had all been searched by Customs. Lisa and Jenny had told them how all the luggage had been unpacked by the men. Obviously the tape recorder belonged to one of the others and had been put in her bag by mistake. She dropped it into the bottom drawer of her dresser, and piled a load of clothes in on top. She would ask the girls when she saw them.

She suddenly giggled as she thought of the tale Lisa had told them about the bogus Customs men. She herself had been there when the two men had run the gauntlet of the ship, and she thought of the men's stiff cocks as they had run by, cocks that a short time earlier had been stimulating her two friends. The thought of it brought back the familiar feeling of arousal. She looked again at the vibrator. After all, she had half an hour.

Trixie lay back on the bunk once more and reached for the device, smiling as it hummed into life.

* * *

Dee gazed at the telephone headset after Trixie had rung off, still grinning. The trouble with Trixie was that it was impossible to be cross with her. Anger rolled off Trixie like water from a duck's back. It was as if she didn't have time to be angry with you. She was a real asset to the band, Dee thought. Not just because of her virtuoso drumming, but because of the way she always had of cheering the rest of them up, even during the blackest moments.

Then there were her stories. If Trixie was to be believed she had had more men than the rest of them put together, and each one had possessed the most extraordinary prowess. Trixie would talk endlessly about where, when and with whom she had had it to anyone who would listen. But she didn't talk in a boastful way. On the contrary, her stories tended to be rather self-deprecating, and she had a knack of having everyone in stitches as she described the most unlikely of escapades.

Dee's thoughts drifted to the other two band members. She had a special affection for Lisa, being her first 'recruit' and the one who had helped her set up the band. There was something very steadying about having Lisa along. She was especially pleased with the way she had taken Jenny under her wing. The youngster was still a little naive compared to the rest of them, and needed Lisa's more mature influence.

She wondered about that for a moment. The two were extremely close. She thought of the story they had related about their escapade in the Customs shed. Something about it seemed to embarrass Jenny, though it evidently wasn't the fucking she had received from the man called Jake. Lisa sensed that something else had occurred, and that the two of them were not telling the full story.

She shrugged. If they didn't want to tell her, then it really was none of her business. The important thing was that the band was a unit, and that they were all firm friends.

She shook her head. This was no time for idle speculation. She had to meet Jon Howland in the entertainments lounge to discuss the setting up of the equipment before the rest of the girls arrived.

Jon Howland. He was another piece in the odd jigsaw that made up this cruise. Since that first day they had not screwed again, but she knew that if he needed her, she would not say no. That was the kind of relationship she preferred. She was not exactly promiscuous in the way that Trixie was, but she liked a man who could satisfy her carnal desires without bringing too much emotional baggage with him. There was no doubt in her mind that if Jon wanted her again she would be there for him.

Speaking of which, she thought, glancing at her watch, she was supposed to be there for him right now.

In his cabin at the opposite end of the ship, Les Cargill was also thinking about the members of the band. But his thoughts were a good deal less sanguine than Dee's. He sat, staring at the porthole, trying to plan his next move. At the time, in the Customs shed, it had seemed a good idea to drop the tape recorder, and with it the diamonds, into the open case. In fact it had saved his skin, since his bags had been subject to just as rigorous a search as had the girls'. Now, though, he had the problem of getting the machine back, and he wasn't certain yet how he'd go about it.

He considered his position. At least he had some idea who the bag belonged to. There was no doubt that the pile of musical instruments belonged to a band, so it shouldn't be too hard to trace the owners during the trip. Then it was simply a case of breaking into their cabins and finding his loot. Assuming it was still there, of course. What if they had found it before boarding and handed it in somewhere? Or they had thought it a bomb and turned it over it to the authorities? But that was absurd, surely. Nobody bombed cruise liners, did they? Once again he cursed his luck in being picked out for a random search. One thing was for sure. He'd have to find the diamonds before they arrived in Panavia, the small North African state where the man to whom he intended to sell the gems lived.

Suddenly an idea struck him. Lying on the table beside his bed was a folder marked 'Welcome to the *SS Diana*', and underneath 'Your Entertainment Guide'. He picked it up and opened it. It contained a number of pamphlets advertising the various diversions on offer to passengers during the cruise. His eyes lighted on one entitled 'Night Life'.

He opened it and read it carefully.

'Nightly in the Entertainment Lounge, dancing to the Kool Kittens, the classiest act on board.'

Les studied the photograph that accompanied the words. There were four of the most gorgeous girls he had seen in a long time. He stared at the faces carefully, then a slow grin of recognition spread across his features. He had seen two of them before. The one with the auburn hair and the small dark one. They had been in the Customs shed when he had been stopped. So it was their luggage he had seen.

His eyes roved over them and their two companions. An all-girl band, eh? And he had to befriend them and win their confidence. He felt something begin to stiffen in his pants as he studied their lovely bodies.

Perhaps retrieving the diamonds wasn't going to be such a chore after all.

There was one other person aboard the *SS Diana* whose mind was concentrated on the stolen diamonds. Detective Inspector Kathy Prender stared out from the rail of the ship as below her the mooring ropes were untied. She still hadn't quite got over the shock of finding herself here, aboard the cruise liner and sailing for the Mediterranean. It had been no more than a matter of hours ago that she had received her orders to join the ship.

Since visiting the scene of the jewel robbery, Kathy had had a pretty busy time. They had ascertained that the cache of jewels stolen was a particularly fine collection of unmounted gems that the dealer had been holding for no more than a few days. There was no doubt that the hoard had been specifically targeted by the thief, since nothing else in the strong room had been touched. It was clear that whoever had committed the crime had known exactly what they wanted, and had made sure that the robbery was over very quickly, with a fast car in which to make their escape from the scene.

And the car had been their first clue. They had found it abandoned a few miles away and had subjected it to the usual forensic tests. It was then they had found the ticket envelope, with the name of the travel agent on it and the words *SS Diana* scribbled on the cover.

The travel agent's premises was a small one in East London where the sale of a cruise ticket was not a particularly common occurrence. Unfortunately, though, the man behind the counter had a poor memory, particularly where helping the police was concerned. He apparently had no recollection of when the ticket had been sold. He couldn't even recall whether the purchaser had been a man or a woman.

There was one other clue, though. In the boot of the car they had found a screwdriver, and a box that had once contained a cassette recorder. Putting two and two together, Kathy had decided that this was probably where the gems had been hidden and at once had visited a local retailer and bought a similar model. On dismantling it she had soon confirmed that there was ample space inside the case to conceal the gems and reassemble the machine without impairing its operation. Their quarry had been careless, though. On the floor of the boot the police had found a corner of plastic about an inch across that had evidently snapped off whilst he had been taking the machine apart.

So now they knew they had to find a passenger aboard the *SS Diana*, who posessed a tape recorder of precisely that make and model with a corner chipped off.

There had followed a flurry of activity during which it was ascertained that the *SS Diana* was sailing that very afternoon. In no time the decision was made. Kathy Prender would sail with her, and would continue her investigations on board whilst her colleagues followed up whatever clues they could back home.

So here she was, off to the Mediterranean on a luxury

cruise. She sighed. In a way it seemed like a dream, but it wasn't exactly going to be a holiday. Any other girl might be thinking of a shipboard romance, or at least a fling, but she knew she had work to do.

Kathy turned away from the ship's rail and surveyed the other passengers. There were hundreds of them lining the decks, waving and shouting to friends and relatives on the dock below. Amongst them was a number of very attractive men, and for a moment she allowed herself to consider some of the more obvious attractions of a Mediterranean cruise. It had been some time since she had last had a man. Indeed her sex life had been decidedly arid during recent months. Maybe she should at least have a look around. After all, she thought, she might be a policewoman, but above all she was a woman, and she had her desires like any other. Perhaps she would allow herself to let her hair down occasionally during the trip . . .

Chapter 10

The atmosphere in the Entertainment Lounge was thick with smoke, and the sound of the band was almost deafening. Trixie looked up from her drum kit over the crowd of dancers as they celebrated their first night on board. She couldn't remember when they had played to a more receptive audience. A silly grin stretched across her face as she pounded away at her skins.

It was all going better than they could have hoped. Jon Howland had proved an excellent Master of Ceremonies and everyone seemed to be having a good time, applauding loudly every time the band completed a number. She watched as Dee pranced about the stage in her star-spangled costume, the dress cut extraordinarily short so that with every swing of her hips her briefs were displayed to an enthusiastic crowd.

Trixie glanced sideways at the other two members of the band. As always Jenny was completely absorbed in her playing, the notes booming from the speaker as she plucked out a fast and complex riff, her playing precisely in time with Trixie's own drumbeat. Lisa too was clearly enjoying herself, catching Trixie's eye and grinning broadly at her as she laid down the backing to the number.

This was what Trixie enjoyed most about playing with the Kool Kittens. There was a real togetherness in the way they played. It was as if they had never performed with anyone else. There was no doubt about it, this trip was going to be bloody good fun.

Speaking of good fun . . .

Trixie eyed the audience. Most of those on the dance floor were couples or young women, but beyond she could see the men, leaning against the bar, their drinks in their hands, eyeing up the dancers. Trixie licked her lips. There was certainly plenty of scope, and she intended to play the field.

The number came to a crashing crescendo and the applause echoed round the room. Jon stepped briefly on stage to announce that the girls were taking a break, and at once the disco speakers roared into life.

The four girls stepped down from the platform, Dee joining Jon at the bar, whilst Lisa and Jenny headed for the ladies. Trixie, with nothing better to do, wandered out onto the deck.

It was a lovely evening, the reflection of the moon making a sliver of silver across the gentle swell of the sea. In the distance she could just discern the flashing of a lighthouse, but otherwise the ship seemed completely alone.

'Enjoying the air?'

Trixie turned. She hadn't heard the man approach. He was tall and well built, with his hair streaked blond. He was smiling as he addressed her and she found herself smiling back.

'It's a lovely night,' she said.

'You're the drummer, aren't you?'

'That's right.'

'I was listening. You're very good.'

'Thanks. I aim to please.' As she spoke the words she was looking directly into his eyes and she sensed that he had caught the barely hidden ambiguity in her words.

'How long's your break?'

'About forty minutes. Long enough.'

'Long enough for what?'

'What did you have in mind?'

'A drink? A walk round the deck? Maybe something else?'

'Maybe something else.'

He moved closer, and she could smell his aftershave. It was an expensive brand and she found the scent alluring.

He reached out and took her hand, pulling her close to him. She made no attempt to resist as he wrapped his arms about her and pressed her body to his, crushing her breasts against his broad chest.

He placed his mouth over hers, and his tongue darted between her lips. She opened up to him, and their tongues met. He kissed her long and hard, crushing his body against hers, the hardness at his crotch pressed against her in a way that fired her passion almost at once.

He broke the kiss and stared down at her.

'You're a fast mover,' she said. 'What's your name?'

'Les. What's yours?'

'Trixie.'

'You're a gorgeous woman, Trixie. I'd like to see more of you.'

Once again she could hardly suppress a smile. 'How much more?'

'Couldn't we continue this conversation somewhere more private?'

'What about my cabin?' she suggested.

'Sounds good to me.'

Trixie took his hand and pulled him along the deck. 'Come on,' she said. 'That forty minutes is wasting.'

They reached Trixie's cabin in no time at all. She pushed open the door and they almost fell inside, Les grabbing her at once and pressing his body to hers.

She giggled. 'Let's get naked,' she said. 'I want to see if that cock of yours is as big as it feels.'

She began unbuttoning his shirt, revealing his dark, hairy chest as she did so. As soon as it was undone she opened it and began kissing his flesh, her teeth nibbling gently at his nipples. Her hands dropped to his pants and she fumbled with his belt, undoing it then setting about his fly. His trousers dropped to his ankles, followed swiftly by his underpants, and at last Trixie had his erection in her hands.

His cock was massive, standing stiff and proud, and she ran her fingers up and down its length, its hardness sending a frisson of excitement through her. She reached underneath and felt for his balls. They were large and heavy, his scrotum stiffening as his erection grew even harder.

'My, what a big boy,' she whispered. 'I bet he tastes nice too, doesn't he?'

'Why not suck it and see?' he said with a grin.

Trixie needed no further encouragement. With a little squeal of laughter she dropped to her knees. His cock seemed even bigger from that position, rearing up just in front of her face, and she stared at it as her fingers closed around its shaft. It had swelled so much that the glans had forced his foreskin apart and she could see the slit in the end and the sheen of moisture on it. She opened her mouth and pulled him toward her.

Trixie closed her lips about his thick shaft, sucking hard at him as her nostrils took in the scent of his manhood. His cock fairly throbbed as she sucked at it, little pulses running down its length. She pursed her lips and began moving her head back and forth, her tongue flashing to and fro over his glans as she worked him. He was moaning softly now, his hips jabbing against her face as she fellated him.

Trixie was an enthusiastic cocksucker, and she slurped greedily at his erection, sensing his arousal increase as she did so. She loved to turn a man on like this, knowing how much pleasure her mouth could give. Her sex fairly ran with wetness at the sensation of his member pressing against the back of her throat.

But the wanton young beauty wanted more, and suddenly she sat back and slid his weapon from her. 'You're not coming in my mouth,' she said, grinning slyly. 'I want to feel this feller in my cunt.'

She stood up and unzipped her dress, pulling it over her head and tossing it onto the bed. She paused for a second, striking a pose in front of him. She wore a pair of scanty briefs and a matching bra that lifted her breasts beautifully, enhancing her cleavage so that he gaped at the twin mounds of flesh.

She reached behind her and undid the catch, and his jaw dropped still further as he feasted his eyes on the expanse of her breasts. They were the most magnificent pair he had ever seen, standing firm and proud from her chest, the nipples pink and hard. She smiled at him.

'Your turn to suck, I think.'

Les stood mesmerised as she lifted her breasts with her hands and offered them up to him. For a second she thought he was in a trance. Then he brought his head forward and his lips closed over her left nipple. At once he began to suck at it, whilst his hands closed over her other breast, almost mauling it, such was his excitement.

'Now, now,' she said, stroking his hair. 'Take it gently. There's plenty for you. Let's get on the bed.'

She took him by the hand and led him to the bunk, laying back and pulling her down on top of her. As she prostrated herself her breasts fell apart slightly and he buried his face between them, his stiff cock pressing against her leg as he sucked and licked her.

Trixie lay back, her eyes closed, savouring the moment. She loved men who paid attention to her breasts, and she knew it was difficult for them not to, such was their size and prominence. And Les certainly knew how to treat them, his actions gentle yet positive as he slurped and kneaded the soft flesh.

He lifted his head, like a diver coming up for air, and gazed into her eyes. 'Oh Christ, Trixie,' he gasped. 'They're gorgeous.'

'I know,' she giggled. 'But it's my cunt that needs attention now. Come on, Les, I'm dying to be fucked.'

She reached down and slid her panties down her legs, kicking them onto the floor. Then she spread her thighs, allowing him his first view of her love hole, the pink leaves of flesh glistening with wetness as she pressed her hips up at him.

'Come on, Les,' she said. 'Don't hang about. Stick your cock in me.'

He manoeuvred himself over her, his face close to hers, and she reached down for his member, positioning the head at the entrance to her vagina, she gave a little tug and he pressed down. There was no resistance, his cock slipping easily into her well-lubricated hole. Even the experienced Trixie was surprised at the way it filled her, plunging ever deeper until she thought she could take no more.

He began to fuck her, his movements gentle at first as he found his rhythm. She moaned and gasped beneath him as he pumped his hips back and forth, each stroke sending a wave of undiluted pleasure through her body. She wrapped her arms about him, pulling him closer to her, enjoying the feel of his warm skin against her own.

His cock felt gorgeous, sliding back and forth over the sensitive walls of her sex, each stroke bringing a sigh of gratification from the wanton girl. She arched her body up at him, loving the way the hairs on his chest rubbed against her long, stiff nipples. He slid a hand up over her quivering mammaries, his fingers teasing the teats in a way that sent a tingle through her excited body.

'Oh shit, that feels good,' she murmured.

'Good for me too,' he replied. 'I don't think I'm going to last much longer.'

'Come then,' she replied, ramming her hips up against his. 'Do it, Les. Come inside me. Fill me with spunk, Les.'

The coarseness of her words seemed to spur him on, and his movements quickened, making Trixie moan aloud as he rammed his cock deep into her. He too was starting to breathe harder now, and she could sense a tension in him that had not been there before. She looked up into his face. He was a picture of concentration, his brow furrowed, his lips drawn back, sweat pouring from his forehead.

Then he was coming, his cock twitching violently as spurt after spurt of hot semen forced itself into her cunt. One spurt, two, and then she too felt her orgasm overwhelm her as, screaming with pleasure, she writhed about beneath him, pressing her sex upward against his groin, her lovely breasts shaking back and forth with every stroke.

The two of them rode out their passion together with mutual abandon, bucking and bouncing on the bunk until Trixie felt sure that the springs must break.

At last, though, she sensed his body relaxing as his passion finally began to ebb. She tightened the muscles of her sex about him, wanting to hold him in her as long as possible, extracting every last ounce of pleasure from him until he finally collapsed over her, his breath coming in rasping gasps.

He rolled over, his penis slipping from her sex as he

flopped onto the bunk beside her. She reached down for him, feeling his wet cock soften in her hands.

'Wow, that was great,' she sighed. 'Any chance of getting him hard again before my break ends?'

Chapter 11

Les Cargill leant against the ship's rail and gazed down at the dockside below. He was watching the men unloading the ship, though his brain barely registered what he was seeing. His mind was elsewhere, concentrating on his problem. How to find that damned cassette recorder.

He had thought his job would be a simple one after the first night. After all, Trixie had been a pushover. The trouble was, it was all very well getting into her cabin, but searching it for the machine was another thing altogether. The woman was sex mad, not leaving him alone for a second, then throwing him out the moment her break was over. Since then he had tried in vain to approach her again, but it had proved harder than he had thought, and he soon realised that she had an extremely catholic taste in men. It seemed that hardly had the band finished playing than some stud had his arm about her and was leading her away. And the more the other men realised her appetite for sex, the harder it was to get near her.

It had been a week now since that first delicious fuck, but nothing since. Trixie, it seemed, was determined to work her way through every man on the ship before giving anyone seconds. In despair, he had tried changing his tack and making approaches to the other three members of the band, but without success. The lead singer seemed more preoccupied with the entertainments officer, whilst the other two spent all their spare time together. This whole thing was proving to be much more difficult than he had anticipated.

The sound of female voices just above him shook him from his reverie, and he glanced up at the deck above. There, right above him, were three-quarters of the Kool Kittens, the singer, the lead guitarist and Trixie herself. Quick as a flash he sank back so as to render himself invisible from where they stood, then listened intently. It was the petite guitarist that was talking.

'A whole day off. Isn't it great? What are you going to do, Dee?'

'I thought I'd find a beach. There's supposed to be a really great one about five miles down the coast. It's close to a town, but very secluded.'

'Where did you hear about it?'

'From Jon, of course. He knows this area really well.'

'I suppose he's going with you?'

'No. He can't get away. Too much work, I guess. Why don't you come?'

'No thanks. Lisa wants to stay on board, so I said I'd stay with her.'

'You always seem to do what Lisa wants.'

'Why shouldn't I?' The girl's voice sounded defensive.

'No reason. Hey, Jenny, you're free to do as you please. Anyhow, I've got to get moving. There's a bus in fifteen minutes and I don't want to miss it.'

Les listened as the footsteps above receded. He was

thinking fast. With the girl off the ship it was an ideal opportunity to search her cabin. But how? How on earth could he get inside? After all she was bound to take her key with her, and breaking in was out of the question. It would simply draw attention to what he was up to.

Then a glimmer of an idea dawned in his mind. Of course she'd take her key with her, but if she was sunbathing on the beach she'd hardly have it on her person. If he could find an opportunity to steal her bag, he could be back at the ship and have searched her cabin before she'd have a chance to suspect what he was up to. All he had to do was dash down to the little garage by the docks and hire a scooter, then follow the bus to wherever she was going.

He paused for a second. It wasn't a great plan. It wasn't even that likely to work. But at least it was a plan, and it was all he had just at the moment. Anyhow it meant he'd be doing something, rather than standing around all day. He gave a shrug. He'd do it. There seemed nothing to lose. He turned and hurried off down the deck.

Above him, Jenny lingered at the rail with Trixie, watching the figure of Dee retreat toward her cabin.

'How're you spending your day, Trixie?' she asked.

'Oh, I'm sure I'll find someone,' replied her friend with a grin.

Jenny giggled. 'You're incorrigible, Trixie,' she said.

'But great fun to know. What are you and Lisa going to get up to?'

'We were just going to spend the day sunbathing. There's a quiet little spot we found up by the funnel. The passengers aren't allowed up there.'

'What, just lie in the sun all day? You lazy things.'

'It's okay. It's a pity we haven't got a cassette player or something, though. I brought some tapes but nothing to play them on.'

'You didn't lose the player, did you?'

'No, I just forgot to bring it. Why?'

'Well,' said Trixie. 'It's a funny thing. When I unpacked my bags on the first day there was a tape machine in with my stuff, and it wasn't mine. I put it in the drawer meaning to ask whose it was, then forgot about it.'

'How odd. And you've still got it?'

'Yes. It's in my cabin. You can borrow it if you like.'

'That'd be great. Let's go and get it, shall we?'

The two girls turned away from the ship's rail and headed off toward Trixie's cabin. Down below neither of them saw Les Cargill head down the gangway onto the dockside, blissfully ignorant of the fact that, had he remained where he was for a few more minutes, all his troubles would have been over.

Chapter 12

Dee Masters stepped down from the bus, glad to be in the open air again. It had been hot and crowded inside, the passengers all chattering loudly to one another in the way that Latins so often did. She had been exposed to another typically Latin trait as well, with more than one hand having to be brushed away from her thigh as the bus lurched along. Now, however, she was out of it, and she breathed the fresh air deeply. There was a definite tang of the sea in the air, and she had the whole day to herself. She was really looking forward to the rest.

The town itself was surprisingly busy, with cars buzzing up and down the main street and people laughing and gossiping outside the gaily painted shops. There was little or no sign of tourists though, a fact that pleased her. Jon had been quite right about the town being off the trail of most tour itineraries. It was precisely what she needed after a week on board ship.

She pulled a piece of paper from her pocket and read Jon's directions. She looked about her and checked the street names. Soon she was setting off down a narrow road which opened into a track running down toward the coast.

Dee felt good in the sunshine. She was wearing a very short frock over her bikini, and once away from the houses she unbuttoned it and let it fall open, enjoying the cool air against her skin. There was almost nobody about, just as Jon had promised.

After walking for about ten minutes, Dee spotted a fork in the path by a tall rock. The fork was barely visible. Without Jon's instructions she doubted she would have found it. She turned down it, dodging under the low branches as she headed into the undergrowth. She walked for a further minute, then the path suddenly opened out and she found herself gazing down into a secluded little cove.

She gave a little squeal of joy. It was perfect. Just what she wanted.

A steep path ran down to the golden sands of the beach and she picked her way carefully over the rocks. When she reached the bottom she slipped off her shoes and stepped out onto the sand. It felt pleasantly warm as it ran between her toes and she ran down to the water's edge. The sea was an ideal temperature, the waves lapping about her feet. Dee looked about her. The spot was just perfect.

She made her way back up the beach to a shady spot at the foot of the cliff, where she dropped her small beach bag. She slipped off her dress, folding it carefully and placing it in the bag. Her bikini top followed, her firm young breasts a creamy white in contrast with the rest of her skin.

Dee hesitated for a moment, gazing about herself. Dare she strip completely? Well, why not? There was nobody about, and anyhow, who could possibly be offended by the sight of a lovely girl like herself worshipping the sun? With a decisive movement she hooked her fingers in the waistband of her bikini bottoms and slipped them off, dropping them into her bag along with the top.

Dee stretched in the sun, her lovely body taut as a bow, her breasts pulled slightly oval as she leant backwards, her face turned up toward the sky. She felt wonderfully free. Just at that moment she didn't care if someone did come along. She felt good, and she looked good, that was all that mattered.

On the other side of the cove was a stretch of flat rock, and the naked girl wandered across to it. The rock was smooth and warm to the touch, leaning at an acute angle to the horizontal. Dee stretched herself out on it, lying back and luxuriating in the sun's rays. She gazed down at her body, revelling in her nakedness. If only Jon were here with her. They could have fucked to their hearts' content in this secluded spot.

The thought sent a sudden thrill through her. It always turned Dee on to be naked, and she loved to show her body off. She let her mind wander. Imagine if someone were watching her now, and could see her stretched across this rock. She felt her nipples harden at the thought and a warmth creep into her groin. Almost unconsciously her right hand strayed down between her legs, sliding over her pubic hair and seeking out the little bud there that was already hardening.

Dee began to play with herself, her finger teasing her clitoris out from between her sex lips and running over its surface, gasping slightly at the delicious sensation this gave her. She spread her legs, opening up her sex and allowing her fingers to explore it more fully. She ran a digit down her slit, feeling the wetness that had already begun to seep from her.

With a groan she slipped a finger into her vagina. Then another. Then she began to frig herself, raising her backside from the rock and pressing her sex hard against her fingers.

At the top of the small cliff that overlooked the cove, Les Cargill was enjoying what he saw. He had been feeling more than a little hot and bothered a few minutes before when he thought he had lost track of Dee. He had been very careful not to be spotted whilst following her from the town. Almost too careful. At first he had missed completely the fork in the path that led to the cove. He had backtracked four times before he had finally found it and made his way stealthily down to the sea.

What he saw now, though, made it all worth it. There, stretched out on the rock below, the stark naked girl was frigging herself for all she was worth. And he had a grandstand view. More to the point, she was absolutely gorgeous. Until now he had only had eyes for Trixie, but now that he saw Dee in all her glory, and clearly as horny as hell, he found his cock stiffening uncomfortably in his pants.

For a moment he thought of revealing himself. Of descending to the beach and offering her what she clearly wanted. But only for a moment. He was here for a purpose. He had to get hold of that tape recorder. His future livelihood depended on it. Still, there was no harm in watching . . .

He slid down the zipper on his fly and pulled out his

rampant cock, running his hand up and down it as he watched. He knew of few more arousing sights than that of a naked woman pleasuring herself, and he began to wank as he watched. The girl was clearly very turned on indeed, her low cries of pleasure easily reaching his ears as she thrust her pubis forward, her wet fingers glistening in the sunlight. As he watched her firm breasts bounce with the rhythm of her masturbation, Les began to wank in earnest, his rod grasped in his fist, his knees bent, his hand working back and forth with vigour.

Suddenly the girl's cries became loud and shrill, and a shock of pleasure ran through his body as he realised she was coming. A few seconds later it was he who had to suppress a shout as gobs of his semen began to shoot from the end of his cock, describing a long arc through the air and splashing onto the rocks in front of him.

He continued to watch the girl as he emptied the contents of his balls onto the ground, until just a dribble hung from the end of his tool. He stared down at the wet marks. It seemed a waste in a way. Much better to have pumped his spunk into the cunt he had been watching, but at least the relief of his passion allowed him to concentrate on the job in hand.

Dee lay panting on the rock, her body relaxed now that she had achieved orgasm. She raised her head and looked guiltily about her. She hadn't known what had come over her. Masturbation wasn't something she usually did, especially in so exposed a spot. Suppose someone had seen her? Yet that thought gave her a kind of perverse thrill. You're turning into a bloody exhibitionist,

Dee Masters, she told herself, and allowed herself a quiet grin.

She sat up and gazed out at the ocean. Perhaps a swim would help. After all, she had heard that men took cold showers to calm their ardour. Maybe it would work for her. Besides, she was feeling very warm, and a dip in the ocean was just what she needed.

She rose to her feet and padded across the sand, making a striking picture in the bright sunlight, her pale, slim body with her firm breasts and neat pubic bush contrasting starkly with the bare rocks behind her.

She strode into the sea. It was clear and cool, making her shiver slightly as it covered her ankles and began to immerse her legs. As soon as the water was deep enough she plunged in, her body scything gracefully through the water as the green shroud closed about her, momentarily cutting her off from the world.

She surfaced a few yards further on, then struck out toward the open sea, swimming with the agility of a born athlete. It wasn't until she was some way out that she turned and gazed back toward the shore.

Then she saw him.

He was scrambling down the rocks towards the beach. She was too far away to be able to make out his features, particularly since the shadow from the peak of the baseball cap he was wearing obscured half his face. She froze where she was. Perhaps he was just passing. Or maybe he too had heard of the secluded beach and wished to share it. Either way it left her in a somewhat compromising position, naked and separated from her clothes by the stretch of beach.

At that moment he picked up her bag, and she knew things were more serious than she had thought.

'Hey!'

He had begun to rummage in the bag, and he looked up as she shouted. She was swimming hard now, heading for the shore as fast as she could. He seemed to hesitate for a moment, then he slung the bag over his shoulder and began to climb the rocks.

He was nearly halfway up by the time Dee reached the beach. She raced across the sand toward him, still shouting, and began to scramble up the rocks. Encumbered by the bag he was slightly slower than her, and she began to gain ground. He had too good a start though, and she watched with frustration as he disappeared over the brow.

Dee pulled herself up the last few feet and headed off in pursuit, dodging the bushes that threatened to scratch her bare skin. By the time she reached the main track he was a good hundred yards ahead and running hard. Dee ran too, pursuing him with all the vigour she could muster from her athletic young body. He had reached the houses that straggled out at the end of the town now, though she seemed to be closing on him. She ran into the little street, unaware of the astonishment on the faces of the few people who sat in the shade by the houses, suddenly disturbed from their siestas. She saw the man disappear down an alley up ahead and she headed for it.

As she turned the corner she heard the rasp of the scooter's engine. The man was astride the machine, her bag flung across his shoulder. She made a final effort, just failing to grab it as the scooter lurched forward. Then it was speeding away, the engine screaming as the man gunned the throttle.

Why she continued to chase, Dee couldn't say. It was just pure instinct, she supposed. Whatever the reason she stopped short when she suddenly burst into the centre of the main street, still bustling with people.

It took a second for the enormity of her situation to sink in, then she glanced down at her naked body, and around at the astonished shoppers, who were stock still, staring wide-eyed at her.

'Oh shit,' she muttered.

Chapter 13

Kathy Prender made her way along the narrow corridor that led through the crew's quarters aboard the *SS Diana*, peering right and left into every nook and cranny. She knew that her plan was flawed, stupid even, but after nearly a week on board, anything seemed better than just sitting and waiting for the thief to show him or herself. At this, their first port of call, she had hoped for more news from London, perhaps some identification of whoever had been driving the getaway car. Instead there had been nothing. Simply a short note asking how her own investigation was going.

Investigation, she mused. Some investigation. Just day after day of watching a crowd of people enjoying themselves, and being quite unable to join in. Standing on the periphery, aware of the fun and fucking that was going on all around her whilst she kept to her solitary existence, simply watching and listening.

The plan to check the crew's quarters had been more out of desperation than anything. She had approached one of the ship's officers and shown her identity card to him, and he had agreed to allow her into this part of the ship, normally off limits to passengers. Now she was making her way down through the corridors, searching vainly for some kind of clue to the whereabouts of the stolen diamonds.

She pushed open a door and found herself back on deck. The crew accommodation was rather dark and stuffy compared to that of the passengers, and she was grateful to be out in the open air again. She leant on the rail, breathing deeply and staring out across the harbour. She was getting tired of this fruitless search. One more deck, then she would call it a day.

It was then that the sound of music reached her ears. It was a beaty pop melody, and it seemed to be coming from above her. Suddenly curious, she looked about for a way to get aloft.

At the end of the deck on which she stood was a stairway that led up to the next level. She made her way along to it and climbed up. As she emerged she found herself alongside the funnel. It towered above her, emitting a steady hum. There was still no sign of the source of the music, though.

Kathy cocked her head, trying to ascertain the direction from which the sound was coming. Puzzlingly it still seemed to be above her, though as far as she could tell she was on the highest deck on the ship.

She spotted a ladder that ran up the side of the funnel. From where she stood it appeared to lead to the very centre of the funnel itself. Surely the music couldn't be coming from there?

In a sudden moment of decision, Kathy took hold of the sides of the ladder and began to climb. The rungs were spaced quite wide apart and it was not the easiest of ascents, but she persevered, taking one step at a time.

At last she reached what appeared to be the top. She hauled herself up another rung, then realised that she was not, in fact at the rim of the funnel, but that it was stepped at the back, with a small deck about twenty feet across on the lower part. Then she froze. She was not alone.

There, stretched out on the deck were two young women. Both were totally naked. One, a petite dark-haired girl lay on her back Above her was a rather taller auburn-haired woman, who was leaning over her, their breasts pressed hard together. The pair were kissing passionately. The smaller girl had her legs spread wide apart and her companion's hand was at her sex, two fingers sliding in and out of her as they embraced. The small girl was emitting muffled cries of pleasure, and her hips were gyrating wildly as the other woman frigged her.

Kathy stared at the scene, unable to take her eyes off the beautiful, naked pair as they enjoyed one another's bodies so intimately. There was something unmistakably erotic about the scene, and she felt an unexpected pang of jealousy as she watched.

So captivated was Kathy by the sight of lesbian passion before her that it was a good thirty seconds before her eye alighted on the tape recorder. But when it did she almost gasped aloud with surprise.

That was it! That was the machine she had been seeking! The make was right, the model was right. She could even discern the piece of plastic that had been snapped off when the thief had been taking it apart. She could hardly believe her eyes. The machine held more than five million pounds' worth of diamonds, and here it was, lying on the deck.

The noises from the prostrate girl were becoming louder,

and it was clear that her excitement was increasing. Suddenly Kathy realised that she must not let herself be seen. That she needed time to think.

She ducked down beneath the parapet and began to descend the steps. As she did so, the cries from the girl indicated that she had, indeed, achieved orgasm, and once again that strange sensation of jealousy filled Kathy as she lowered herself silently to the deck.

Once down she leant back against the funnel, her heart racing. Somehow she had expected the thief to be a male. To see the two women with the machine had been quite unexpected. There was something else, too. She felt as if she knew the girls from somewhere, but she couldn't quite place where. The problem was, what to do? She could hardly approach them as they were. The whole thing would be far too embarrassing. Besides, she couldn't be sure that the diamonds were still in the tape recorder. Perhaps the best thing would be to contact London and seek advice. After all, the ship was due to sail in a few hours, and the girls were showing no sign of leaving. Even now she could still hear the sound of the music.

Yes, that was it. She would call London first. Then she would find out who the voluptuous young pair were who disported themselves so shamelessly above.

With a determined look on her face, Kathy headed for the radio room.

Chapter 14

Dee stood, rooted to the spot, as more and more eyes turned toward her. It was like a bad dream. In fact it was precisely like a dream she had had time and again at night, in which she was standing stark naked in a busy street full of normally-clad people. But this was real, not a dream, and the colour shot to her cheeks as she realised what the people could see.

And there was no shortage of people. More and more were stopping short and staring at the naked lovely standing in the middle of the main street. Some stood and gawped, their mouths open. Others, mostly young men, grinned broadly and made lewd gestures to one another. Some of the older women shouted in outraged voices as the crowd grew.

Dee glanced behind her. There were crowds in that direction too, their eyes fixed on her nakedness. They were beginning to close in, and she knew that if she was to escape it was now or never.

She spotted a small gap in the crowd and ran for it. They tried to close in on her, grabbing at her body from all sides and for a second she was trapped, her breasts and sex mauled by numerous hands. Then, with a final desperate twist of her body, she was free and running down the street. From behind her came shouts, and she knew she was being pursued. The shouts alerted those in front as well, and others tried to intercept her as she raced past. She could see still more people ahead of her and she knew she had to get out of the main street.

In front of her was a narrow alley, and she darted into it, the sound of her pursuers still ringing in her ears. To her right was a second alley, and once again she raced down it. She was beginning to tire now, the run up from the beach starting to take its toll, and she wasn't certain how long she could maintain the pace.

She continued to take the twists and turns in the dark streets, occasionally encountering an astonished passer-by as she raced along. Those following her were beginning to drop back now, and for a moment she felt she might be safe. Then she rounded a corner and found herself in a blind alley.

Dee looked to right and left, but there seemed no escape apart from back the way she had come, and even now the sound of her pursuers was dangerously close.

Then she spotted the shop. It was quite small, the windows almost covered by blinds. The entrance too was hung with a screen of thin plastic strips of the sort used to keep insects out. She stared at it for a second, then made up her mind. It didn't look promising, but there was nowhere else to go. She raced across and threw herself through the door almost as the first of those chasing her rounded the corner behind her.

Once inside the shop she paused, blinking. It seemed dark after the brightness of the Mediterranean sun. To her relief she saw that the place was empty, with even the counter deserted. She looked about her. It was a very unusual shop indeed. On one side the wall was covered with magazines and videos. When she looked closer she discovered their covers to be festooned with photographs of naked men and women in various sexual positions. Glancing across to the other side, where the shop's counter was, she saw lingerie in bright colours and various leather goods, with gleaming studs and buckles. At the back were racks of whips, gags, handcuffs and other similar items. Dee didn't need a translator to tell her this was a sex shop.

All of a sudden she heard voices outside and was brought back to reality with a start. She looked down at herself. She was far from being out of the woods yet, still stark naked, with no money and a long way from the ship. And it was only a matter of time before those outside followed her into the shop. Even as the thought struck her, she heard a voice call from a door behind the counter and the sound of a chair scraping back.

At the far end of the shop was a door. There was a neon sign above it, written in a language she did not understand, with an arrow pointing through. Dee did not hesitate. There was nowhere else to go. Even as she heard her pursuers outside approach the door of the shop she dashed across and through into the room behind.

It was more of a corridor, really, lit by a single bulb. Along its length were six doors, each sequentially numbered. Dee grasped the handle of the first one and turned it. The door opened and she slipped inside, closing it behind her. The room was very small, no more than ten feet long and six wide. Inside it was even darker than had been the corridor, the only source of light a screen flickering on the far wall. Dee blinked in amazement. On the screen was a couple, both totally naked. The man's penis was erect, and the woman was masturbating him with her hand, to the sound of a rather whining music track.

Then, with a start, Dee realised she was not alone.

The man was sprawled on a kind of low couch that ran along the left-hand wall of the cubicle. It was difficult to see in the gloom, but Dee estimated he was in his early forties, with dark hair and a drooping moustache. One thing she could see though, was the erect cock he was still holding in his hand. It was clear he had been wanking when she had entered.

It was difficult to tell who was the most embarrassed at that point. Dee clutched her hands to her breasts and sex at the same moment as he tried to cover his penis. He opened his mouth to speak, but she put a finger to her lips, shaking her head urgently. This meant uncovering her breasts and his eyes dropped to them at once.

Dee's mind raced. It was clear to her now what this room, and the others like it was. It was a place for watching blue movies in private, evidently one of the sex shop's services. It was also a dead end. There was nowhere else to run.

Suddenly there was the sound of people talking outside, and Dee's heart sank. They must surely catch her now. She gazed down at the man in front of her. He seemed to have got over his initial shock, and was now admiring her body with undisguised interest.

There was a rap on the door, and a shouted question.

Once again Dee shook her head violently. The man hesitated for a second, then he let his eyes drop to her crotch, still covered by her hand. He raised an eyebrow.

Dee didn't need a translation. She glanced at the door then, with a shrug of resignation, let her arm drop to her side. Her bare sex was just two feet in front of his face now, and he licked his lips.

The man shouted something toward the door. There was a brief exchange, then she heard those outside move on to the next cubicle. She leant back against the wall and gave a sigh of relief.

Then a hand touched her on the inner thigh, sliding slowly up toward her crotch.

She gave a little start as the fingers brushed against her sex lips, but made no move to stop him as he slid a finger into her vagina. This was the price of his silence, and it seemed a cheap one under the circumstances.

She glanced down at his groin. His penis was thick and bulbous, standing proud from his flies. He was still wanking himself slowly, and she turned her eyes to the image on the screen, where a dusky young woman was going down on a well-endowed stud with some relish.

Dee dropped to her knees, brushing aside his hand from his erection and reaching for it herself. She closed her hand about his shaft, enjoying the feel of his hardness. He lay back, his finger still exploring her sex, watching her face with expectation.

She leaned forward, her face close to his penis, studying its shape and size. Then she opened her mouth and took him inside. He grunted with pleasure as her lips closed about his glans and she began to suck. From the corner of her eye she noted that her counterpart on screen was already sucking her partner eagerly and this spurred her into renewed activity.

Dee loved to suck cock. The feel of a truly hard erection filling her mouth was something that aroused her totally, and she began to work her head up and down with enthusiasm, her breasts shaking with the rhythm as she pleasured him. Her hands reached into his fly and sought out his balls, fondling them gently and eliciting a gasp from him as she did so. He continued to finger her, his motions gentle, keeping her passion alive without threatening to bring her to orgasm. Dee enjoyed his touch, aware that this was his show, and that his orgasm was the important one. She wondered at her own lasciviousness, kneeling totally naked before a complete stranger and fellating him with enthusiasm. It wasn't quite how she had planned to spend her day, but right now she couldn't think of anything she'd rather be doing.

The sounds from the movie made her glance once again in that direction. As she watched, the man snatched his cock from the woman's mouth and pumped white creamy sperm into her face. At the same time she felt the penis in her mouth twitch and she sensed the man's orgasm was near.

Unlike her counterpart on the screen, Dee wasn't about to miss the opportunity of swallowing her partner's spunk, so that when he came she kept her lips clamped about his prick, happily gulping the hot liquid down with relish, her hand working up and down the shaft in time with his ejaculations. His cries of passion were almost as loud as those of the girl on the screen, his hips pumping back and forth against her face as she sucked him dry. When at last there was no more to come she raised her head, licking away the dribbles of white fluid that still trickled down the length of his cock, then gazing triumphantly into his eyes.

He smiled back at her, his face a picture of contentment. On the screen, the credits were running and Dee knew her timing had been perfect. She rose to her feet, staring down at him. As she watched he reached into his pocket, extracting a banknote from it. He folded it carefully into a long strip, then, to her surprise, slid it into her vagina, causing it to twitch as a spasm passed through her body. Then he nodded toward the door.

Dee was dismissed. She had performed as required, and now was no longer needed. Never before had she been quite so blatantly used by a man for his pleasure. Yet there was a strange sense of satisfaction as she reached for the doorhandle. She had read once that the only way for a man to fully possess a woman for his pleasure was to pay for the privilege, and that was what had happened here. She had prostituted herself, yet she felt no regrets whatsoever. She opened the door and slipped into the corridor, closing it behind her.

Once outside, Dee recalled her predicament. She was still stranded and naked, although the immediate danger of the pursuit was now past. Still she had to form a plan as to how she was to get back to the ship. Leaning back against the wall she spread her legs and slipped the banknote out from where he had placed it. She examined it. It was quite a lot. More than enough to pay her bus fare, but still insufficient to solve her immediate problems.

The sound of music suddenly caught her attention and she turned. It was coming from behind one of the doors further down the corridor. She glanced down at the note in her hand, then across at the door again. An odd feeling of warmth began to fill her as the idea formed in her mind. On the wall at the end of the corridor was a mirror, and she gazed at her reflection, taking in her jutting breasts, slim waist and prominent sex. She knew she would be irresistible to any man who saw her like this.

She moved across to the mirror. There was a narrow gap between it and the wall, and she slipped the precious banknote into it. Then she went across to the cubicle from which the sound was emanating and opened the door.

The room was identical to the one she had been in earlier. Once again the only illumination was from the screen at the end, where a naked pair were locked in a passionate embrace. The man on the couch looked up in surprise. Surprise that turned to amazement when he saw that she was naked. He was much younger than her previous partner, almost boyish. He wasn't wanking, but the bulge in his trousers testified to the effect the film was having on him.

'Mind if I join you?'

Dee didn't know whether he would understand English, but all the same she slipped onto the couch beside him, pressing her body against his. His face was a picture, a mixture of surprise, nervousness and lust as his eyes took in her body. She smiled at him, planting a light kiss on his lips. At the same time she slid her hand down to the front of his trousers and squeezed his erection, making him give a strangled squeak of surprise.

Slowly, deliberately, she began to unfasten his jeans, unbuckling his belt and undoing the button at the waistband. She slid down his zip, then reached into his pants, her fingers seeking out the stiff rod that seemed to be about to tear them apart. She freed it from its confines, and found herself holding her second cock in the space of less than five minutes.

The young man whimpered slightly and his stiff weapon twitched under her fingers as she ran her hand down its length. Dee guessed he was inexperienced, possibly even a virgin. The idea thrilled her, and she felt a warm sensation in her groin as she contemplated his seduction.

On the screen the woman was down on all fours whilst the man rammed his penis into her from behind. Dee indicated the action with a wave of her head, then raised her eyebrows.

'You wanna try that?' she asked.

He nodded dumbly.

She smiled and got up from the bed. She made him move aside, then climbed up onto her hands and knees. She pressed her breasts downwards and raised her behind as high as she was able, spreading her legs and presenting him with what she knew was a perfect view of her sex. He climbed onto the couch behind her, pressing his cock against her flesh as he tried to force himself into her.

'Steady,' she remonstrated. 'There's plenty of time. Here, let me.'

She reached behind and took his erection in her hand, squeezing it gently. Then she pulled him forward, placing the tip against the entrance to her vagina.

'Now push,' she urged.

He did so, and in a second his thick penis was sliding into her, penetrating her deliciously and making her gasp with pleasure.

He began to fuck her at once, ramming his prick into her with an urgency that confirmed to her that this was his first time. There was no craft to his fucking, simply the urgency of youth as his belly slapped noisily against her backside. To Dee the sensation was fabulous. Normally she preferred a man with some finesse, but somehow, in her current situation, the fact that she was being taken with so little consideration seemed to her perfectly apt, and she found her own orgasm building fast as he rogered her with enthusiasm.

She looked up at the screen, where the woman was receiving precisely the treatment she was, her large pendulous breasts swinging back and forth with every stroke from the stud behind her. She felt her own breasts bounce in rhythm to the young man's efforts and found herself wanting to laugh aloud with the pleasure he was giving her.

He came suddenly, almost taking her by surprise. One second he was pounding into her, the next his body was stiff as his hot spunk filled her love hole. With a cry of joy, Dee came too, her backside thrusting back at him as the waves of pleasure flowed over her. And still he was coming, spurt after spurt of his semen blasting into her until she could feel it begin to leak out and trickle down her thigh.

At last, though, even his energy began to sap and, with a sigh, he fell forward onto her, his arms about her, his hands fondling her breasts gently.

She allowed him to rest on her like that for about a minute, then eased herself forward so that he slid from within her. She slipped from the bed and stood beside it, gazing down at him, a smile on her face.

'You're going to be quite a stud one day, young man,' she said. 'But right now, I've gotta go. How about a little gratitude, meanwhile?'

She held out her hand, rubbing her thumb and forefinger together. For a second he stared blankly, then an expression of recognition crossed his features. He reached into his pocket and pulled out a banknote, which she took with a nod. Then, with no further ado, she turned to the door.

'So long, lover,' she called over her shoulder, then she was back in the corridor again.

She slid the note behind the mirror next to the other, then paused to examine herself in the mirror. Her hair was a bit of a mess, and there was a streak of sperm running down her leg, but otherwise she was okay. The sound of music reached her ears again and she turned. Then, a smile on her face, she made her way to yet another of the closed doors.

Chapter 15

Detective Inspector Kathy Prender leant against the ship's rail, her eyes fixed on the gangway. She had been there for more than two hours now, and she was getting more than a little bored with the vigil. But she knew she had to stay where she was. It was the only way to ensure that neither of the girls she had encountered up by the funnel attempted to leave.

She shuffled impatiently. This was a side of police work she had never enjoyed, the waiting. It was surprising how much of the job involved just that. Sitting in a van or a deserted flat waiting for something to happen.

She had called headquarters immediately after her encounter with the two girls. She had explained what she had seen, though omitting the details of the girls' demeanour. She had expected to be ordered to retrieve the tape recorder at once, but instead was surprised to be told to await further orders. Meanwhile she was to ensure that the machine did not leave the ship, but without drawing attention to herself. Thus she had positioned herself here, watching the gangplank.

'Miss Prender?' The voice by her ear made her start, and she turned to face the new arrival. It was a young ship's officer. She recognised him from her trip to the radio room earlier. In his hand was an envelope, and he held it out to her.

'This has just arrived for you,' he explained. 'It's confidential.'

She took the envelope and thanked him. He replied with a kind of salute, then turned and walked away. Kathy tore open the envelope and examined its contents. It was a single sheet, torn from a teleprinter. She read it carefully.

'Confidential. For the attention of Detective Inspector Prender.

'Essential you keep tabs on tape machine. On no account is it to leave the *SS Diana*. Investigations show that intention is to sell goods in Kulfra as part of drug money laundering operation. Agent from Kulfra due to join ship in Naples, where deal will be struck before your arrival Kulfra. Essential you keep a close watch and identify this agent. Interpol think he's a big fish. You must try and infiltrate the perpetrators to gain more information, meanwhile. Will contact you as information becomes available.'

Kathy read and re-read the document. This thing was bigger than she had expected. Kulfra was a seaport, the capital of Panavia, a small country on the North African coast from which it was known that drugs found their way into Europe. Interpol had been trying for some years to discover who was behind the trade. It looked as though this might be the break they needed.

Naples. That was another seven days away. Seven days in which she had to find out as much as she could about the two women she had seen with the radio. First of all, she needed to find out who they were. Their faces were naggingly familiar, yet she hadn't been able to place them. She checked her watch. Another three hours before the ship was due to sail. At least then she could stop watching this damned gangplank.

Down below, Les Cargill carefully searched his way through the drawers in Dee's cabin. He was methodical, taking each possible hiding place in turn and checking it thoroughly. By the time he had finished he knew that there was nowhere in the cabin that could possibly conceal the cassette recorder. He sat down on the bunk, cursing silently. All that work for nothing. And he had taken the risk of being recognised.

He had abandoned Dee's bag in a roadside bin on his way back to the ship, being careful to empty the cash from her purse. He wanted to be certain that, should anyone find the bag, they would assume it was just an opportunist robbery. He thought of the naked girl on the beach, wondering what she would do. A grin broke out on his face as he imagined her predicament. She'd be all right, he thought. She had some pretty good assets, and they were all on display. He felt his cock harden as he remembered those gorgeous tits. He wouldn't have minded taking the time to suck those luscious nipples.

He rose to his feet. None of this was helping him to find the diamonds. He must make a new plan. Perhaps he would revert to the original idea of seduction. That little dark-haired guitarist seemed like the best on to try next, if only he could attract her away from the pianist. The two of them seemed inseparable. What he needed was someone else to seduce her friend, leaving the way clear for him.

Les checked about him. Everything was exactly as he had found it. There was no trace of his presence. It was essential that the girls didn't suspect his motive.

He listened hard for anyone outside, then opened the cabin door, slipping out and closing it behind him. He just had time to turn the key in the lock when he heard voices. Just opposite where he stood was a laundry room, the door to which was ajar. He darted inside, pulling the door shut behind him. Then he placed his ear against the wood and listened.

The voices were female, and he recognised them at once as the two members of the band he had been thinking about moments earlier. The footsteps came to a halt just outside where he stood.

'Do you suppose Dee's back yet?' It was the petite brunette speaking.

'No. I don't think she'll be back for a while. She'll be enjoying that sun for as long as she can.'

'I enjoyed the sun today too.'

'And I enjoyed you.'

'Yeah. It was fun. I really love doing it with you, Lisa.'

'Next time we dock, let's you and I go and find a beach somewhere.'

'I'd like that.'

'So would I. Besides, we might find some local talent.'

'What do you mean?'

'Just that maybe a foursome would be fun.'

'You do have some outrageous ideas, Lisa. By the way,

I've booked a sauna for tomorrow afternoon. Care to join me?'

'No. I don't like saunas. Too damned sweaty. I think I'll give it a miss.'

'Suit yourself. I'm going in for a shower now. See you in half an hour?'

'Okay.'

Les heard the cabins on either side of Dee's being unlocked, and the doors opened and closed. He waited a few seconds before slipping out of the laundry room, then set off up the corridor, his mind working fast. The sauna, eh? Perhaps that was his chance.

Dee sat on the bus as it lurched along, heading back towards the ship. It had been quite an afternoon, she mused. Not quite what she had been planning, but tremendous fun for all that. She had managed to visit all six of the cubicles, and in each one she had found a man willing to pay for the use of her lovely young body. She had sucked and fucked her way through them with enthusiasm, giving herself with reckless abandon and coming more times than she could remember.

She might have gone on for longer, had not the shop owner walked through and found her concealing her money between sessions. There was no hiding what she had been up to, so she just stood there, letting him run his eyes over her naked, spunk-spattered body, waiting to see what he would do.

At first he had been rather put out, demanding to know what she was up to, though Dee was unable to explain, since she did not speak the language. However two of the punters heard the noise and emerged from their cubicles. A long conversation ensued, after which the astonished man was left just shaking his head. His attitude soon changed, however, when Dee waved her money under his nose and indicated that she wanted to buy some clothes.

First of all, though, what she needed was a shower. It took a minute or two to explain to the shopkeeper what she required, but eventually he nodded, taking her through the shop and out the back of the counter.

The shower room was small and crude, but it had running water and soap, and that was all Dee wanted at that moment. The water ran cold, but she didn't care.

She didn't even care when the shop owner climbed in behind her. She had been expecting it.

Her first inkling of his presence was the feel of something long and hard pressing into her back. Without bothering to look, she reached behind her and took hold of his shaft. He wasted no time on foreplay, though, forcing her forward against the taps and pressing his cock up between her legs. Dee responded by widening her stance and pressing her bottom back, guiding him toward her love hole. In no time he was shagging her hard, forcing her against the wall and shaking her body with the force of his strokes.

He came quickly, triggering yet another climax in the lascivious young girl as the water cascaded down over her back and down her legs. Then he withdrew, and by the time she had turned round he was gone.

When she came out she found a small towel lying on a chair. She used it to dab off as much of the water as she could, then discarded it and wandered naked into the shop. The man was behind the counter, and he smiled as she came in, indicating the strange items of clothing that were on show.

The choice was not a great one, but certainly interesting. Dee searched long and hard, finally settling on a basque that raised her breasts and exaggerated her cleavage, and a tiny G-string. The nearest the shopkeeper had to a dress was a filmy nightie that only just reached below her crotch and clung tightly to her. Admiring herself in the mirror, Dee couldn't help but smile. It was not exactly what you could wear to Ascot, she thought, but it was better than nothing. And let's face it, that was what she had come in with.

There was sufficient change for her bus fare back to the ship, and Dee left the shop feeling quite buoyed up, her indignation about the theft of her bag almost forgotten.

Now, as she sat on the bus, avoiding as best she could the groping of her fellow male passengers, she smiled quietly to herself. Her afternoon of sunbathing had been a lot more fun than she had expected.

Chapter 16

When Jenny arrived at the changing room of the ship's gym, she found herself alone, the Mediterranean weather having lured most of the customers onto the decks. She had known this would be the case. The gym was hardly ever used at this time of the afternoon, especially when it was warm outside, which was why this was when she chose to visit. She stripped off with enthusiasm, looking forward to a relaxing hour in the sauna.

She had left Lisa on deck, stretched out on a sun lounger, apparently oblivious to all around her. As she undressed, Jenny pondered on her new friendship. She truly enjoyed the time she spent with Lisa, and the revelation of the joys of sex with another woman had really opened up her mind. There was something about the way Lisa caressed her that was totally different from any man she had ever encountered. She had wondered for a while if she was lesbian, but had swiftly dismissed the idea. After all, she still had the desire to feel a cock between her legs, a sensation which no dildo could ever give her.

Jenny paused before the changing room mirror, admiring her own reflection. Life on board the ship was doing her good. Her flesh was, if anything, even smoother, her breasts firm and protruding, her waist slim. Her tan was coming on well, too, though it was hard to tell how well, since she had been doing a lot of her sunbathing nude, resulting in hardly any bikini line at all.

She picked up a towel and slung it over her shoulder. The sauna was just across the corridor from the changing room, and there would be nobody about. She wandered across and let herself in. It was unusually steamy, but she wasn't bothered. She crossed to one of the wooden benches, lay down her towel and stretched herself out on her back, allowing the baking heat of the sauna to wash over her naked body.

'Is it steamy enough for you?'

The voice was so close that it made Jenny start. She looked round and was shocked to realise that she was not alone. A man was sitting on the bench opposite, a towel wrapped about his waist.

Jenny sat up at once, pulling her towel up and draping it over her front.

'Excuse me,' she said. 'I didn't see you there.'

He smiled. 'That's okay. No need to cover yourself up on my account.'

'I didn't expect to find anyone here. The sauna's usually empty at this time.'

'I'll go if I'm embarrassing you.' The man made as if to get to his feet.

'No, that's okay,' said Jenny. 'I was just rather surprised, that's all.'

'You have a very lovely body.'

Jenny blushed. 'Thanks.'

'You play in the band, don't you?'

'That's right. Lead guitar.'

'You're very good.'

'Thanks.' Jenny wished she could think of something more erudite to say. She was at once pleased and embarrassed by his complements.

'Do you come here often?' she asked.

'That sounds like a pick-up line at a dance.'

She laughed. 'I'm sorry. I guess I'm a little embarrassed.'

'There's no need. Let's have some more steam.'

He rose to his feet and walked across to where the hot stones lay, picking up a ladle and depositing some water onto them. The water dissolved in an instant, sending a loud hiss of steam up into the room. Jenny watched him. He was a fine figure of a man, slim and tanned, his hair streaked with blond. She dropped her gaze to his crotch where, even under the towel, she could see a bulge.

He saw her look and smiled. 'What's your name?'

'Jenny.'

'Hi. I'm Les.'

He reached out a hand, but when she went to grasp it her towel dropped away, exposing her right breast. She snatched her hand back, covering it once again, but not before he had been granted a good look. She blushed again.

'Sorry.'

'Nothing to be sorry about, Jenny. I already said you have a lovely body. May I sit with you?'

'If you like.'

He settled on the bench beside her. He was sweating

129

with the heat of the sauna, and giving off a distinctly male aroma that she found somehow arousing.

'So what do you do when you're not playing?'

His conversation was easy, and as they chatted she felt herself beginning to loosen up. He had a good sense of humour, and soon she was laughing aloud at his jokes. After a while she let the towel fall into her lap, finding the way his eyes dropped to her breasts unexpectedly arousing. Normally she would have been far too shy to bare herself like this. She suspected it was Lisa's influence that was suddenly making her so easy-going.

A sudden silence fell between them, and she wondered momentarily if she had offended him by baring her breasts. Then she realised that his eyes had fixed themselves on her own, and for a few seconds the pair of them stared at one another without speaking.

When he leant across to kiss her, it seemed the most natural thing in the world, and she offered no resistance as he placed an arm about her shoulders. His lips met hers and she opened her mouth to him, allowing his tongue to snake inside and intertwine with hers.

He kissed her long and hard, holding her close to him so that her breasts were pressed against his strong chest. When he finally removed his mouth from hers and sat back, her nipples had hardened into brown points. He glanced down at them, lifting a hand and placing it over one of the soft, smooth orbs that jutted so invitingly from her.

'You have gorgeous breasts,' he said quietly. 'So firm, yet soft. May I kiss them?'

Jenny was slightly nonplussed. She was used to her

lovers simply taking the initiative, not asking permission. She reddened once more.

'Well, I . . .'

But he hadn't waited for an answer. He lowered his head and took her nipple into his mouth, sucking at it sensuously.

'Mmm,' she sighed, leaning back against the wall of the sauna. The gentleness of his touch was heavenly, and she closed her eyes, abandoning herself to pleasure as he kissed and sucked her succulent orbs.

For a time he simply concentrated on her breasts, using his mouth and hands to stimulate them deliciously. Jenny remained passive, her hands by her sides, her eyes closed as she revelled in his caresses. Then, with a shock, she felt his hand begin to slide down her body. Her own hand moved to the towel draped across her lap just as his fingers closed on it. For a moment she held onto it, gripping it tightly, but he was too strong for her, pulling it from her fingers and tossing it to one side. Then he put a hand on her knee and began to move his fingers up her thigh.

'No . . .' she murmured, but there was no conviction in her voice, and when he pushed her legs apart she offered little resistance.

His fingers took their time, creeping up the smooth flesh of her inner thigh, moving tantalisingly slowly towards what had suddenly become the centre of her desire. She found herself quivering with anticipation as they inched ever closer to her sex, the muscles inside her love hole convulsing as her juices flowed freely.

'Oh!'

She gave a sudden exclamation as his hand brushed

against her soft nether lips. Then his fingers crept down to her anus and for a second she thought they would penetrate it. But they lingered there only a short time before gently sliding up her slit, making her moan softly as he sought out her love bud. Her hips gave a sudden lurch forward as he found it and he began working his fingers about the hard little nodule, teasing it out and beginning to stimulate it into life.

'Ahh!'

He slid a finger inside her, rotating it as he did so and sending exquisite sensations through her. At once she felt the juices begin to flow anew, her backside wriggling back and forth as he pressed in deeper, the warm wetness enveloping his hand.

He began slowly easing her down into a lying position on the bench. Once again she resisted momentarily.

'What if someone comes in?'

'They won't. Ease up, Jenny, I really want you.'

Once she was on her back he knelt between her open thighs, gazing down at her lovely young body, his fingers still firmly embedded in her love hole. She lay back with her eyes closed, her breasts quivering with every thrust of his hand. She was lost now, and she knew it. She badly wanted to be fucked and she pressed her hips upward against his hand, urging him ever deeper within her.

She heard something drop on the floor and opened her eyes, gazing down between her breasts. He had removed his towel, and his cock was stiff and erect, jutting from his dark pubic thatch like a great pale truncheon. She reached for its tip at once, closing her hand about its bulbous end. She wrapped her fingers round it and slid back the foreskin, staring fascinated as the purple hood was exposed. She ran her hand down its length, feeling it twitch under her touch.

'You're very hard,' she murmured.

'All the better to fuck you with,' he said with a grin.

'Do you normally fuck women you've only just met?'

'Only if they've got gorgeous bodies, like yours.'

'Then fuck me, Les. I don't think I can wait much longer.'

He slipped his fingers from her and moved forward between her wide-stretched thighs. Then he lowered himself onto her. She continued to hold his cock, guiding him to where she wanted him, spreading her legs still wider as his shining tip nuzzled up against her aching hole.

He slipped in easily, making her gasp with pleasure as he forced his way in, plunging his weapon deeper and deeper inside her until she felt completely filled by him. She took his backside in her hands, pulling him even closer, wanting even more of his throbbing penis within her.

'Oh, shit, you feel good,' he muttered, his hands reaching for her breasts once again.

When he began to move, she moved with him, her hips undulating back and forth. He fucked her with an easy grace, his thrusts gentle but positive, each one eliciting fresh moans from the prostrate girl. She kept time with him, pressing herself up at him and matching him stroke for stroke, her whole body tingling with desire at the vigorous shafting she was receiving.

The sauna was very hot, and it wasn't long before the sweat began to pour from both of them, running in rivulets from his back and dripping down onto her. Soon both their bodies were soaking wet, their skins sliding against one another as they screwed. Jenny could feel the wetness trickling down between her breasts and covering her belly. His hair hung down lank and shining, his face glistening with perspiration as he gasped for breath in the close, humid atmosphere.

Yet still he went on, relentlessly sliding his cock in and out of her, making her grunt and groan, her backside slapping against the bench as she responded with enthusiasm.

He ejaculated suddenly, with a grunt of satisfaction, his cock twitching violently as he pumped his seed into her. She came almost simultaneously with a keening cry, writhing ecstatically beneath him as the exquisite pleasure of his orgasm filled her.

They went on for another full minute, their hips grinding together in mutual passion until at last he collapsed onto her, their bodies slapping wetly together. She held him close, wanting him to stay inside her for as long as possible, but at last he pulled away.

He rose to his feet, still panting with exertion, and looked down at her shining body, a smile on his face.

'I think we both need a shower,' he said.

She smiled back. 'Next time, maybe we should find somewhere a little cooler.'

'Is there going to be a next time?'

'I hope so.'

'When?'

'Tonight? After the show? You could come back to my cabin.'

'Sounds great.' He picked up his towel and made for the door. When he reached it, he turned back.

Jenny was still stretched out across the bench, her body glistening with sweat, her legs spread, a slow trickle of white semen escaping from her vagina. He paused, and she felt his eyes caress her.

'Till tonight, then,' he said.

Then he was gone.

Jenny stretched her limbs languidly, a smile on her face.

One thing was for certain. She wasn't a lesbian.

Chapter 17

Kathy Prender looked down at the woman stretched out on the sun lounger in the brief bikini, her head face down on the pillow. She's got a gorgeous figure, thought Kathy. She hadn't really managed to get a good look at Lisa when she had come across her on the little deck behind the funnel. Now, as she ran her eyes over her womanly curves, she recognised what a beauty she was.

It was not until she had entered the Entertainment Lounge the night before that Kathy had remembered who Lisa and Jenny were. The sight of them on the stage with the other two band members had suddenly jogged her memory, though, and the discovery that there were four of them had set all kinds of new trains of thought in motion.

Were they a team, or was it just one of them that was involved in the smuggling? And what about the robbery itself? Was the whole thing carried out by one of them, or were they merely couriers employed to get the loot out of the country? Whatever the truth was, Kathy had acted fast, going straight to the ship's purser and getting details of the girls' names and addresses. This information she had telexed to London at once, and now she was once again awaiting their reply.

But Kathy wasn't prepared to do nothing whilst she waited. She was a policewoman, and above all a detective, and it was her job to glean as much information as she could on the four girls. And who better to start with than one of the pair who had actually been in possession of the cassette player in the first place? Thus, when she had spotted Lisa alone, without her usual companion, she had been quick to act, hurrying down to her cabin and changing into her bikini.

Kathy wasn't one to care too much about the way she dressed, and the bikini had been something of an impulse buy during her frantic shopping trip before boarding the ship. It was very brief, the bottoms forming a vee shape, with the waistband running high over her hips and dipping down to barely cover her public mound. The top too was somewhat daring, cut low over her full breasts, lifting them and accentuating her cleavage. Even Kathy had been surprised by the effect. The nature of her job meant that she had to keep herself fit, and her body was slim and lithe. The bikini gave her the opportunity to show it off, and she paused before the mirror in her cabin, struck by the sexy girl who gazed back at her. Now, as she strode across the deck, she could feel the men's eyes follow her as she walked along, and it felt very good indeed.

But she knew she had no time to consider shipboard romances. It was time to become professional once more, and as she eyed the girl stretched out on the sunbed, her mind was racing with ideas that would allow her to strike up a conversation.

Beside Lisa was a low table, on which was placed a long, cool-looking drink. It was barely started, the ice cubes still unmelted. Kathy narrowed her eyes. The simplest plans were the best, she mused, so why not use one?

She began picking her way through the other sunbathers to where Lisa lay. Then, as she passed the prone girl, she allowed her towel to brush against the glass on the table. The drink rocked once, then fell on its side, its contents spilling out onto the deck.

'Oh no, I've spilled your drink,' she said.

Lisa, who had sat up and grabbed at the glass just too late, watched in dismay as the liquid flowed across the

'And it was a full one too,' went on Kathy. 'I must replace it.'

'That's not necessary,' said Lisa. 'It was an accident.'

'But I insist,' said Kathy. 'It was a full glass. Waiter!'

She waved her hand in the air at a passing steward, who came over to them.

'What was it?' she asked.

'Look, you really don't have to,' said Lisa.

'Yes, I do. It was very clumsy of me to spill it like that. Now, what were you drinking?'

'It was a margarita actually,' said Lisa.

'A margarita,' she said to the man. 'No, on second thoughts, make that two. It looked rather nice before I managed to spread it across half the ship.'

'That's really very kind,' said Lisa.

'Not at all.' Kathy screwed up her eyes. 'Don't I know you?'

'I don't know. Do you think you do?'

'I'm not sure. You seem familiar somehow.' She pretended to think for a moment. 'I know!' she said suddenly. 'You play in the band, don't you?'

Lisa smiled. 'That's right.'

'You're very good. I've been down in the lounge quite often in the evenings to listen to you.'

'And to dance?'

Kathy shook her head. 'No partner, I'm afraid. I'm cruising on my own.'

'But surely an attractive girl like you could pick up a guy? After all, there's plenty of hungry wolves out there.'

'But not Mr Right,' said Kathy. Then an idea hit her. 'Anyhow,' she went on. 'Who says it has to be Mister?'

Lisa stared hard at her, and she knew the remark had hit home.

'What's your name?' Lisa asked.

'Kathy. What's yours?'

'Lisa. Say, Kathy, why not join me for a while? It's not much fun lying here on my own.'

'If you're sure I'm not imposing.'

'Anything but. It's boring lying here by myself. Drag up a sun lounger.'

Kathy pulled one of the spare loungers up beside Lisa and stretched herself out on it. At the same time the waiter arrived and placed their drinks down side by side on the table. Kathy took a sip of hers. She had never tried a margarita before and was pleasantly surprised by the refreshing taste.

The two girls began to chat, Lisa telling Kathy about the band and how it had formed, whilst Kathy listened with interest. She was concerned to find if there were any obvious flaws in the girl's story, but if there were she could detect none. Kathy was used to listening to suspects' stories and was well-trained in spotting a lie. Nothing she heard from Lisa suggested that the girl was telling anything but the truth.

Lisa began to ask her about her own situation, and she spun a yarn about being a civil servant and having come into a small inheritance that she had blown on the trip. She tried to steer the conversation back to Lisa and her friends, but once more could glean nothing that made her suspect Lisa of lying. There was nothing else for it, she decided. She would have to escalate her relationship with Lisa to a new level. Then Lisa inadvertently gave her the opportunity she needed.

'You don't look as if you've been doing much sunbathing, Kathy,' she said. 'I bet you've hardly got any bikini line.'

'No, you're right,' replied Kathy. 'I should have got out in the sun earlier, but I never seemed to get around to it. Actually, the trouble with bikini lines is that you have to go on wearing the same bikini for the entire holiday, or they show.'

'I suppose you're right. You really need to tan all over.'

'Chance would be a fine thing, aboard a ship like this.'

'I know a place.'

Kathy looked up, trying to keep her face expressionless. This was just what she had wanted Lisa to say.

'What, on board ship?' she said in mock surprise. 'Surely not.'

'Do you want me to show you?'

'I'm not sure.'

'Come on, Kath. It was your idea.'

'Yes, but—'

'Yes but nothing. It's the perfect place. And it'll give us the chance to get to know one another much better.'

'Well, all right then. If you're sure it's private.'

'One hundred per cent sure. Now, finish your drink and we'll be off.'

Kathy swigged down the last of her cocktail, hoping it would give her a little dutch courage. Now that the suggestion had been made, she found her heart beating hard. She simply couldn't free her mind of the image of Lisa and Jenny on that small private deck behind the funnel.

The two girls picked up their towels and Lisa led the way. It was soon clear to Kathy that their route was taking them precisely where she had expected, and before long they were standing at the foot of the funnel.

Lisa indicated the ladder.

'It's up there,' she said.

'What, up the ladder?'

'Don't worry. It's quite safe. I've been up lots of times. Come on.'

Lisa began to climb. Kathy stood at the foot of the ladder and watched. She found herself fascinated by Lisa's pert behind as it swayed up the ladder above her. There was no doubt that the girl was stunningly beautiful, and very sexy with it. She thought for a moment about what was going to happen when they reached the deck above, and a strange knot formed in her stomach. This is above and beyond the call of duty, Kathy Prender, she told herself.

Lisa had reached the top now and was looking down.

'Come on, Kathy,' she called. 'It's all clear.'

Kathy grasped the ladder and began to climb, her heart beating fast. As she neared the top, she gazed guiltily about her to ensure that she hadn't been seen. Then her head came over the edge, and all thoughts of discovery were forgotten as she caught sight of Lisa.

The girl had discarded her bikini and stood facing her, completely nude, her legs placed apart and her hands on her hips. Kathy found herself swallowing hard as she took in the girl's naked beauty. In the bikini Lisa had been extremely lovely. Naked she was stunning. Despite the nude stints with Jenny, her breasts were still quite white compared to the rest of her skin, the dark brown teats showing in marked contrast. A similar white line ran from her crotch across her thighs, drawing attention down to the dark triangle of curls at the top of her legs. Her stance, with legs akimbo, afforded Kathy an uninterrupted view of her sex, the thick lips parted slightly.

'Up you come,' she said, laughing. 'And stop gawping at me. Haven't you seen another girl's tits and cunt before?'

Kathy blushed. 'Of course,' she said, though in her heart she knew that it was not strictly true. She may have been aware of what little girls looked like, but she had never before been in the presence of a mature woman in such a state. And the sight was kindling odd desires within her. Desires of which she would not have thought herself capable.

Kathy hauled herself over the edge and stood up on the small deck.

'You're right,' she said to Lisa. 'This is a really quiet spot.'

'Well then, what are you waiting for?' said Lisa. 'Get your kit off.'

Kathy hesitated. This really was outside her normal duties. She'd heard of plain clothes, but no clothes? She wondered how it would look in her official report, if she chose to include it. She hoped she wouldn't have to. With a deep breath she reached up behind her back for the catch on her bikini top.

Lisa's eyes were on her as she flicked the catch undone. The bra dropped away and Kathy blushed hotly as her breasts were revealed. She gazed down at them. They were nothing to be ashamed of, she reasoned. In fact they were lovely, plump and perfectly shaped with large nipples which hardened to points as Lisa's eyes fixed on them.

'And your knickers,' said Lisa. 'Don't be shy now.'

Slowly Kathy dropped her hands to her bikini bottoms. She ran her thumbs round the waistband, then looked across at Lisa. The girl had an intense expression on her face as she watched. Was it desire that Kathy detected in her eyes? She couldn't be sure. She dropped her eyes again and tugged down the brief pants.

Kathy kicked aside the scrap of material, then straightened, staring back at Lisa, her hands held by her side whilst the girl took in her prominent mound, thatched with dark curls, a hint of pinkness showing beneath.

'Say, you're quite something,' said Lisa. 'A real peach. I still can't understand why you don't pick up more guys.'

'I told you,' said Kathy quietly. 'I'm not interested in guys.'

'What about this?'

Lisa stepped forward an reached her hand out, closing it over Kathy's breast. She squeezed it, rubbing the nipple between her thumb and forefinger.

Kathy stood stock still, making no move to encourage or discourage Lisa's advances. Inside, though, her mind was whirling. She had never been touched by a woman so intimately before, and was amazed at the desires that were being kindled in her by Lisa's caresses. It had been ages since she had had any kind of sexual encounter, let alone with another girl, and the emotions that were awakened by Lisa's bold move were very strong indeed.

She continued to stand still when Lisa moved a pace closer to her, and made no attempt to back away when the girl placed her lips on her own. She felt Lisa's mouth open, then, with a shock, the sensation of a tongue trying to force its way between her lips. She resisted for no more than a second, then opened her mouth.

With one hand still on Kathy's breast, Lisa slid her other arm about her neck and pulled her close. Their bodies touched, and Kathy felt the roughness of Lisa's public hair brush her thigh.

For a few seconds more she stood rigidly, afraid to respond to the other girl's caresses. Then, all at once, she let herself go, wrapping her arms about Lisa and pulling her close, feeling the hard buds of her nipples pressing against her own as she sucked hungrily at the other girl's tongue.

The kiss was as long as it was passionate, the two practically eating one another as their bodies writhed together. Kathy felt Lisa press her sex against the top of her thigh, raising a leg to wrap it round her as she rubbed herself up and down.

When the pair of them broke the kiss, Lisa immediately dropped her head to Kathy's breasts, making the police-woman gasp with pleasure as she closed her lips about the nipple and started to suck.

'Mmm.'

Kathy threw back her head and pressed her breasts forward against Lisa's mouth. She had expected to have to put on an act when she had decided to let herself be seduced, but she wasn't acting now. She was genu-inely aroused by the way Lisa was treating her, and was afraid she might lose her self control as she felt her companion's hand slide down her stomach towards her groin.

'Ah!'

Once again the intensity of her arousal surprised Kathy as she felt the fingers touch her clitoris. Suddenly it was the most delicious sensation in the world to have a woman's fingers caressing her sex, and she wondered how she had gone for so long without the exquisite pleasure that Lisa was now giving to her. She widened her stance, pressing her hips forward against the girl's hand whilst she instinctively reached down for Lisa's own breasts.

The skin was soft and pliant under her touch, feeling silky smooth. She sought out the nipple. It was hard and rubbery and she rolled it between finger and thumb, giving Lisa cause to gasp with pleasure.

Lisa raised her head from Kate's breast, leaving it shiny

with her saliva. She looked up into the other girl's face whilst she continued to work her fingers back and forth over her slit.

'How does that feel?' she murmured.

'Good. Oh, so bloody good,' gasped Kathy.

'I want to taste you, Kathy,' she said. 'Lie down on the deck and spread your legs.'

It was a suggestion that fifteen minutes earlier would have received a shocked refusal. But that was fifteen minutes earlier, before this extraordinary girl had watched her strip naked, and had caressed her so intimately. Now Kathy did not hesitate. She prostrated herself on the hot, hard boards of the deck and spread her legs wide, bending her knees and raising her sex up to her companion. She gazed down between the twin mounds of her breasts as the naked girl knelt before her, her eyes fixed on the glistening wetness of Kathy's sex.

'Ohhh!' The touch of Lisa's tongue on her clitoris sent a shudder of pleasure through Kathy's frame. She writhed about as she felt the girl's lips close over her love bud and suck it to erection. She began to toy with her own breasts, squeezing and kneading them as her body tingled with pleasure, the fire that Lisa had kindled in her loins threatening to overwhelm her.

Lisa's hands held Kathy's thighs apart as her tongue lapped back and forth over her glistening clitoris. Kathy could no longer keep her backside still, gyrating it wildly at the delicious sensation. When she felt Lisa's tongue slip deep into her vagina she thought she would die of pleasure.

'Ah! Ah! Ah!'

Kathy's backside slapped down against the hard wood of the deck, her head thrown back, her eyes closed as the passion within her built until she thought she could stand it no longer. Then, with a hoarse moan, she was coming, her juices flowing copiously from her to be lapped up by the enthusiastic Lisa.

Kathy couldn't remember a more satisfying orgasm. It seemed to release all the pent-up tension inside her, her body quivering with sheer pleasure as spasm after spasm wracked her. Lisa kept her tongue working back and forth inside her until Kathy felt her body finally beginning to relax, the arch of her back decreasing until at last she was prone on the deck, still breathing heavily. Only then did Lisa raise her head, her chin shiny with moisture, and stare down at Kathy.

'Feel better?' she asked with a grin.

'Mmm.'

'Good.'

Lisa rose to her feet and began pulling on her bikini once more. Kathy sat up, an expression of dismay on her face.

'You're not going?'

'Got to. We've got a rehearsal in twenty minutes, and I'm supposed to be there.'

'Oh . . .' The disappointment in Kathy's voice was genuine. 'I was hoping—'

'Hoping what?'

'Well, to return the compliment.'

'Come and see me after the show tonight. We'll go to my cabin and take it up from there. Okay?'

'Okay, Lisa.'

'Good. See you later.'

And with that she vaulted over the rail and began climbing down the ladder.

Chapter 18

Les Cargill followed Jenny down the corridor, her hand held firmly in his. He watched her as she walked, admiring the way her petite frame moved so sensuously, her pert little behind wiggling as she hurried along. He thought of the fucking he was about to give her and felt his cock stiffen as he did so. Losing the cassette recorder had a real pain, but getting his cock inside the young guitarist made it slightly less painful. Besides, this was an opportunity to see if she was the one with the machine. Definitely a good way to mix business with pleasure.

She stopped outside her cabin and turned to face him. 'This is it.'

He moved forward, wrapping his arms about her and kissing her hard on the lips, his tongue snaking into her mouth. She responded eagerly, pressing her body against his, so that he knew she could feel the bulge at his crotch.

She pulled back and gazed into his eyes.

'God, I want you,' she said.

'And I want you. Let's go inside.'

She fumbled in her bag and produced the key, then inserted it in the lock and turned it. Once inside, she flipped the light switch and Les stared about him with interest. The cabin had a very feminine feel to it. It smelled of scent, and everything was neatly in its place. The bed was made, a tiny negligee spread over the pillow, a box of tissues on the table beside it.

Then something else caught his eye. Something that held his attention completely. Something that made him draw his breath in.

There, on a shelf at the far end of the cabin, was the cassette recorder. His heart beat fast as he eyed it. He had found it at last! He only hoped and prayed that the diamonds were still inside.

So intent was he on the machine that he barely noticed Jenny drop to her knees before him. He was soon brought back to his senses, though, when he felt her unzip his fly.

The feel of her cool little hands against the heat of his penis was wonderful and he gave a sharp intake of breath as she freed him from his pants, the full length of his rod jutting from his groin. She wasted no time, going down on him at once, sucking hard at his cock, her hands gripping the shaft and wanking him back and forth.

'Oh, Christ. Steady, Jenny, you'll have me off before I'm ready,' he gasped.

She looked up at him, smiling. 'Sorry, Les,' she said. 'I just had to taste your cock. It's beautiful.'

He took her by the hand, pulling her to her feet. She offered no resistance as he began to strip her, unzipping her tight little dress and pulling it over her head. Her bra followed, along with her panties, and soon she was clad only in her hold-up stockings, which rose to about four inches below her crotch, somehow seeming to accentuate her nudity as he ran his eyes admiringly over her firm young body.

He reached for her at once, pulling her close, his cock pressing against her stomach as he ran his hand down her back and over her backside, cupping the firm globes of her behind and squeezing them. She pressed her young breasts against the hairs of his chest, the solid little nipples like small rubber buttons pushed against his skin. She raised her head, and he lowered his so that their lips met in a long and amorous kiss, his fingers sliding down the crack of her backside and seeking out the heat of her vagina. By the time they broke away, his rampant tool was twitching violently and she gazed down at it, taking it in her hands and caressing it.

'Let's fuck, Jenny,' he murmured.

'Can I just have a quick shower first?' she asked. 'It's just that I'm a bit sweaty after the gig.'

'You'll be even more sweaty in a minute.'

She giggled and broke away. 'Just two minutes, Les, then you can have me. Wet and willing.'

She skipped into the bathroom and closed the door.

'There's a bottle of scotch in the cupboard,' she called. 'Why not pour us both one?'

But Les was not interested in the drink. The moment she was out of sight he headed across to where the tape recorder stood on the shelf. He picked it up and shook it. There was no sound, but that didn't surprise him, since the bag of gems had been well packed. He peered through the crack where the small piece had been broken off. There, inside, he could just see the grey velvet bag in which the stolen jewels were held. He reached into his pocket and pulled out a penknife. Now if he could just . . .

Rat-a-tat!

The bang on the door made him start so much he almost dropped the machine. He put it hastily back on the shelf and quickly tucked his still-hard cock into his trousers.

Rat-a-tat!

'Jenny? You there?'

Les stood frozen to the spot, unsure of what to do next. Then the bathroom door opened and Jenny emerged, still naked and dripping with water.

'Aren't you going to open the door?' she asked.

'I think it's for you.'

Jenny went to the door and opened it. There, outside, stood Lisa, clad in a bathrobe.

'Do you always answer your door starkers?' she asked. 'I might have been anybody.'

'Sorry,' said Jenny, blushing. 'But I knew it was you.'

'You got somebody in there?' Lisa peered over her friend's shoulder.

'Well, yes, actually.'

Lisa caught sight of Les. 'Sorry to disturb,' she called. 'You weren't already fucking, were you?'

'Lisa!'

'Sorry, Jenny. But you're not exactly dressed for a game of Scrabble, are you?'

'Listen, Lisa, what was it you wanted?'

'The tape recorder. Mind if I borrow it? Only I'm entertaining too, as it happens, and we fancied some music.'

'Oh, take the damned thing.'

Jenny pushed past Les, and he watched with consternation as she picked up the machine and took it to her friend.

'Thanks, Jenny. Sorry to be a pain.'

With that Lisa departed, carrying the precious machine and leaving Les staring after her in dismay.

Jenny caught his expression. 'What's up?' she asked. 'You didn't want to listen to it, did you?'

'Where did you get it?'

'It was on the shelf. You saw it.'

'No. I mean, where did you get the machine in the first place?'

'It's Trixie's.'

'Where did she get it?'

'She found it, I think. I don't know. This some kind of twenty questions?'

'No. I'm a detective and that machine's stuffed with stolen diamonds.'

He watched her face carefully as he said this, searching for any sign that his words held any significance for her, but she just giggled.

'Don't be silly, Les. There's no stolen diamonds here.'

'Not any more.'

She laughed again, wrapping her arms about him.

'Come on,' she said. 'Where's that drink? On second thoughts, I'll get it. You strip off. I need your cock inside me as soon as possible.'

Les watched her as she poured the drinks. He had said what he had on the spur of the moment, to test her reactions. Well, either she was a very good actress or she was completely innocent of the presence of the diamonds. Either way he at least knew they were still intact, though he cursed his misfortune in being unable to secure them when he had had the machine in his hands.

Jenny turned and handed him a tumbler, then held up hers. They clinked glasses and both took a drink. Then Jenny took his glass from him and put both down on the table.

'Now,' she said, taking him in her hands once more. 'How would you like me, missionary or doggy?'

'I've got the machine,' called Lisa as she pushed open the door. 'Jenny had it, as I'd suspected. She also had a rather dishy guy in there, so I didn't stay long. Now, what kind of music was it that you wanted to hear? After all, you asked for it.'

Kathy Prender lay stretched on the bed, clad in bra and panties. She looked up as Lisa re-entered the room, her eyes lighting immediately on the tape recorder. Like Les, she found herself mesmerised by the sight of her goal, so close, yet so far away.

'I don't know, something slow and sexy.'

Kathy was feeling quite self-conscious as she watched her new-found friend place the machine down on the table beside the bed. She still couldn't quite reconcile herself with this new situation, nor with the intense pleasure she had gained from their encounter that afternoon. She felt herself torn two ways. On the one hand there was the tape recorder, in which she believed the gems to be stashed. On the other was this beautiful woman to whom she felt so physically attracted. She had not intended to become emotionally involved, but somehow it seemed to be happening to her.

'I'll see what I've got.'

Lisa pulled a suitcase from under the bed and began rummaging in it. Kathy took her opportunity and picked up the tape recorder. Like Les, she was anxious to see whether the gems were still inside it. Possibly even to get them in her hands. She checked round the seam between the back and the front of the machine. There was the missing chip of plastic, as she had expected. She held it to the light and squinted inside. Then her heart leapt. There, jammed hard into one corner, was a grey velvet bag, identical to that in which she knew the gems had been kept by the jeweller. So they were still there!

For a second she contemplated blowing her cover right then and there and confiscating the machine. The trouble was, she still didn't know enough about who had actually stolen it. The more she saw the casual way in which the tape recorder was treated by the girls, the more she was uncertain that they were the thieves. The whole thing was very puzzling. One thing was for sure, though. She had to try to get the diamonds back without raising the suspicions of the band members. And she had an idea how she was going to do it. In fact she had sent a telex to London that very morning requesting what she needed.

'You can't get the tapes in there. They go in the front.'

Kathy looked up in surprise to see that Lisa was watching her. She put down the machine, her face reddening.

'I . . . I was just looking at it.'

'What's to look at? It's just an ordinary cassette.'

'Yes . . . Yes, I suppose it is.'

'Then stop hugging it and pass it over here. You wanted some music, remember?'

'Yes . . .' Reluctantly Kathy handed over the precious machine to Lisa, who placed it down on the table and slipped a cassette inside. A smooth Latin rhythm sounded from the speaker and she began to shimmy back and forth, as if lost in the music. Her hand dropped to the sash on her robe, pulling it undone and allowing it to fall to the floor. Beneath she was naked apart from a pair of high-heeled shoes, and Kathy felt her mouth go dry as she ran her eyes over her companion's delicious curves.

'Come and dance.'

Kathy rose slowly to her feet and approached the swaying girl, watching in fascination as her breasts bounced up and down with her movements.

'Strip first. Here, let me help.'

Lisa moved close to Kathy, wrapping her arms about her and reaching for the catch on her bra. She flicked it undone easily, pulling it down Kathy's arms and off. The panties followed just as quickly, and in no time Kathy was as naked as her companion. Then they began to dance, their two slim forms moulding together as the beat took them.

Almost at once Kathy experienced the curious magnetism that she had felt on the deck that afternoon, and her nipples hardened as they pressed against Lisa's. She slid her hand down, tracing the long curve of her partner's spine, then feeling the soft contours of her buttocks, pulling her close so that the roughness of her pubic mound rubbed against her own. They kissed, a long and sensuous kiss, their bodies pressing even closer as they moved to the beat of the music.

Suddenly Lisa broke away.

'I've got something to show you,' she whispered in Kathy's ear.

Kathy watched, puzzled, as the girl opened a drawer and pulled something out, holding it up for her to see. When she saw what it was, Kathy gasped.

It was a dildo, with the end shaped exactly like a man's erect penis, thick veins running down its length. But it was no ordinary dildo. For a start it was more than two feet long. And it was double-headed, each and similarly shaped like a thick, hard male organ.

Lisa offered the object to Kathy and she took it tentatively. She ran her fingers down its length, marvelling at its rubbery texture. Then she looked up questioningly at Lisa.

'Lie on the floor and spread your legs,' ordered Lisa.

Kathy obeyed at once, stretching out on the soft carpet at her companion's feet, then gradually spreading her thighs apart and opening up the leaves of her sex.

Lisa stood staring down at her, then held out a hand. Kathy passed her the dildo, and watched as the girl lifted it up to her face. She took it into her mouth, closing her lips about the end and sucking, as if on a man's cock. Kathy felt a thrill course through her as she watched, her eyes travelling from the head of the object, now running with saliva, down to Lisa's breasts, and further to the pink slit that looked so inviting between her legs.

Lisa dropped to her knees between Kathy's thighs and, taking the penis from her mouth, guided it towards Kathy's vagina. Realising at once the girl's intention, Kathy dug her heels into the floor and raised her backside, pressing her sex forward to accept the thick object.

'Oh!'

She gave an involuntary cry as she felt herself penetrated. Lisa pressed the dildo into her, twisting it as she did so, pushing it deeper and deeper inside until Kathy felt certain it could go no further. Then she began working it back and forth, the rough surface sliding in and out of Kathy's vagina in a way that set her passions alight. She began to writhe her hips back and forth, pressing herself upwards against the object that had suddenly become the centre of her desire, encouraging Lisa to push it ever deeper as she lost herself in the pleasure it was giving her. This was the first time she had felt a genuine sex toy inside her, and she couldn't believe the delicious sensation it gave her.

Suddenly the movements stopped, and Kathy raised her head, looking questioningly at her companion.

'My turn now,' said Lisa.

She lay down on her back so that Kathy was staring straight at her open sex. She allowed one leg to rest over the top of Kathy's left leg whilst she pushed the other underneath her right. Then she manoeuvred herself closer.

Suddenly Kathy realised Lisa's intention. She was going to insert the other end of the dildo in her own vagina, so that both of them would be penetrated simultaneously. Sure enough, Lisa took hold of the thick tool that projected from her partner's cunt and pressed it against her own, all the time inching closer and closer.

Kathy watched spellbound as the girl's sex lips enfolded the bulbous end of the dildo, then swallowed it, each movement sending a thrill through her own body. Lisa pressed herself forward, enveloping more and more of it until their crotches were only inches apart. Then Lisa began to move, thrusting her hips back and forth and making the object fuck them both simultaneously.

'Ahhh!'

'Ohhh!'

The girls groaned in harmony as they writhed about on the floor, mutually impaled on the object of their pleasure. Kathy was in raptures, the diamonds forgotten momentarily as she revelled in the sensation the dildo was giving her, her hips jabbing down on it urgently.

'Oh shit, I'm going to come any minute,' gasped Lisa.

'Me too.'

'Gotta have more sensation.'

So saying, Lisa reached down and took hold of the centre of the dildo's shaft in her fist. She began working it back and forth, the movement just like that of a man wanking, her hand flying up and down whilst Kathy simply screamed with pleasure.

They both came together, their cries echoing about the cabin as each one revelled in the pure ecstasy of the moment, their juices flowing over the surface of the shaft and covering Lisa's fingers. She continued to work the dildo back and forth until Kathy felt she could take no more and collapsed back, gasping for breath, her sex lips still twitching about the shaft. Only then did Lisa relax too and the pair of them lay prostrate, gasping for breath.

Lisa raised her head and looked at her red-faced companion.

'I think we're in for quite a night,' she said.

Chapter 19

Jon Howland sat staring at the empty seat opposite him in the restaurant, shifting uncomfortably in his seat. He wasn't sure whether he wanted his dinner companion to turn up or not. It seemed so strange to him to be here at all. Even the location was outside his normal orbit, a part of Naples he had never previously visited, though the menu seemed excellent. He took another nervous sip at his drink and pondered the circumstances that had brought him here.

He had known Svetna for more years than he cared to remember. Ever since he had begun working as entertainments manager aboard the *SS Diana* he had had to deal with her on an almost daily basis. He had always found the Purser's secretary extremely attractive. She was a mature woman, in her early forties he guessed, making her a good ten years older than him. But had the body of a twenty-five-year-old, with firm breasts, a slim waist and long, shapely legs. She dressed well too, in well-cut clothes that showed of her body to perfection. Many was the time Jon had speculated on what she would be like in bed. Somehow the idea of an encounter with such a mature and experienced woman seemed very attractive to him.

It wasn't just her looks, though. There had always been something of a sensuous air about the woman. Her voice was a smooth purr, the mid-European accent lending an undeniable sexiness to everything she said. Her eyes were large and dark, and when they caught your own there was an intimacy in her gaze that was enough to accelerate the heartbeat of any red-blooded male. To be near her was to sense a latent and irresistible sexuality.

Despite this, there was something in her demeanour that seemed to make her unobtainable. Svetna was the epitome of efficiency in everything she did, and her professionalism was legendary, but he had never thought of her as anything but a business colleague. Somehow, despite her pleasant and cordial manner, she always seemed to hold others at arm's length. She never gossiped about herself, even to her girl friends, and people who had worked with her for years knew virtually nothing of her private life. Jon, whilst he had long admired her, had never even considered making a pass at her. Indeed he knew, somehow, that such a gesture would be futile. Svetna did everything on her own terms, including choosing her men.

That was why her invitation for that evening had taken him by surprise. It simply wasn't like her to suggest any change in her routine without some purpose. Jon couldn't help feeling that there was such a purpose to this rendezvous, though what it could be he scarcely dared think.

If Svetna's demeanour in the workplace was legendary, that was as nothing compared to the legends surrounding her sex life. These had circulated the ship for years, and Jon knew them well. Yet they remained legends. He had never met anyone who claimed to be able to substantiate a single word of them.

There was the legend that the entrance hall to her flat in Naples was hung with nude photos of her. There was the legend that she had a collection of steamy pornographic movies that she used to get her and her partner into the mood. And there was the legend that she gave the best blow job in town, but only if you washed your cock first. All these things were whispered amongst the crew, yet nobody had ever been given the opportunity to verify them. And now here was he, Jon Howland, about to dine alone with the strange and beautiful woman who was their subject.

Jon removed the letter from his pocket and read it once more. Its contents were simple:

'Dear Jon. I want a chance to show you the Naples the tourist never sees. Meet me at the address below at eight o'clock.'

Just that. No signature, no explanation. Simply those few words and the unmistakable whiff of her perfume.

'Hello, Jon.'

The words were spoken close to his ear, and he started as he turned to face the speaker. She looked stunning, in a simple black one-piece dress that hugged her curves beautifully. Her legs were clad in fine-denier stockings and on her feet she wore elegant high heels. He stared at her for a few seconds, quite unable to speak, so taken aback was he by her arrival.

Remembering his manners suddenly, he began to rise to his feet, but Svetna had already pulled back the chair opposite and sat down. She had never had much time for British formality, he reflected.

'Jon, you're staring,' she said. 'Is there something wrong?'

'Yes. I mean no. Sorry, Svetna,' he croaked. 'It's just that you're looking so . . . so gorgeous.'

She smiled. 'Flatterer. Now tell me, have you ordered yet?'

'No. I was waiting for you.'

'Good. Because I know exactly what's good here. Call the waiter over.'

Svetna took charge, ordering for both of them. When the waiter had gone she sat back in her chair and gazed across at him.

'Sorry I was late, Jon. There's a bit of a crisis on the ship. For a while I thought I would never get away.'

'What's up?'

'Well, it's all very exciting. Especially for an innocent little thing like me.' She threw him a look that had all the innocence of a Bengal tiger eyeing its prey. 'We have a jewel thief on board.'

'A jewel thief?'

'That's right. They are saying that five million pounds' worth of diamonds was stolen just before we sailed from Southampton, and the police believe they're on our ship.'

'Tell me more.'

She pouted. 'The purser is not telling me much. But I listen, and read the notes. They think the diamonds were brought on board by a woman, but she might not be the thief. The real thief might have planted them on her to avoid Customs.'

'And where are the stones?'

'The British police put an officer on board before we sailed. This officer knows where the diamonds are, but wants to wait for the woman to, how do they put it? Make a move.'

At this moment the waiter arrived at the table and served the food, forcing Svetna to break off her story. The meal was excellent, the wine equally good, though his offer of dessert and brandy afterwards was refused. This he took as further evidence that she hadn't asked him out simply for the food, though what else she had in mind he hardly dared to speculate. He watched as she swallowed her last mouthful, then brought her back to the subject of the robbery.

'So if this policeman knows where the jewels are, why not arrest the girl in question?'

'I told you. They cannot be sure that she's the right one. They're waiting for her to show her hand.'

'But surely she could just jump ship here in Naples?'

'No. It seems there's a connection with Kulfra, in Panavia.'

'Kulfra?'

'Yes. That is where the police think the diamonds are going.'

'And that's our next stop after Naples.'

'Correct.'

'So, this copper, what does he look like?'

'Copper?'

'The policeman. Maybe I'd recognise him.'

'That's the trouble,' she said. 'I don't know. I have seen the messages and the telexes, but who the detective is I don't know.'

'Pity. Still, it's a great story. You must see all kinds in your job, Svetna.'

She smiled. 'You'd be surprised, Jon.'

'I'd like to hear more.'

'Why not come back for coffee? You know I have a flat here in Naples?'

He swallowed. She had made the invitation casually, and yet its significance was not lost on him for a moment. He knew her flat to be on the other side of town. If she was suggesting he go that far, it seemed unlikely that they would stop at just coffee.

'What kind of coffee?' he asked, trying to sound nonchalant.

'The type of coffee is important?'

'Not really.' Howland wondered if he was handling this very well. 'It's just that I have a preference for Kenyan.'

'I have Kenyan and Brazilian. Will that be all right for you?'

He nodded. 'Fine.'

'Good. Pay the bill.'

The words were spoken as an order. Jon realised that she was taking charge again, as she had in the ordering of the meal. It was as if she was controlling the evening. Jon made no complaint, though. He simply raised his hand and beckoned to the waiter.

'Lisa!'

Dee rapped on the door of her friend's cabin as she called out. There was the sound of someone stirring inside, then the door opened.

Lisa was wearing a long, sheer nightdress. It was

transparent, the dark circles of her nipples prominent as they pressed against the sheer material. She looked slightly taken aback when she recognised Dee.

'Sorry, Lisa,' said Dee. 'I hope I'm not interrupting anything.'

Lisa shook her head. 'It's all right. I'm waiting for someone, but they haven't arrived yet.'

'Not coming up on deck? It's a lovely evening.'

'No. Like I said, I'm expecting someone.'

'Jenny?'

'No. She's found a new friend. That guy called Les.'

'Not jealous, are you?'

Lisa laughed. 'Hell no. Jenny's really sweet and I love her. But we're both free to do what we want. There's no obligation.'

'Good. Anyhow, the reason I'm here is to borrow the cassette player, if that's okay. Some of us are having a little party on deck, and we want some music.'

'I'd have thought that on our night off you'd have wanted to avoid partying.'

'This is just a small affair. You can come and join us later if you want.'

'Thanks, but no thanks. I've got my own plans.'

'Okay. Is it all right to take the tape?'

'Sure. Help yourself. It's on the shelf over there.'

'Thanks.' Dee crossed the cabin and reached for the machine.

Dee was never sure how the accident occurred. One minute she thought she had hold of the cassette player, the next it was crashing to the floor, striking the ground hard and flying apart. The two girls gazed down in dismay at the machine as it lay on the floor in two parts, the back having been completely detached.

'Oh shit,' said Dee. 'That's torn it.'

'I don't think it's too bad,' said Lisa, stooping to retrieve the parts. 'The back's just come off, that's all.'

'Wait a minute. What's that?'

Dee indicated the grey velvet bag that lay on the floor beside the tape recorder. She picked it up.

'It's a bag with something inside. It must have come from the recorder.'

'What's in it?'

'Hang on. The knot's a bit tight. Now let's have a— Oh!'

Dee stared in surprise at the handful of glittering stones that tumbled into her palm.

'Jeez. Look at that,' gasped Lisa. 'They can't be real, can they?'

'I don't know. They look real enough to me. How do you tell?'

'See if they'll scratch glass.'

'What?'

'A real diamond will scratch glass. My mother told me that. Here, give me one.'

Lisa took one of the stones from Dee's hand and went across to the mirror. Grasping it between finger and thumb she ran it across one corner of the glass. When she withdrew, a small, neat scratch was left.

'Wow!'

'They must be worth a fortune. How do you suppose they got into the recorder?'

'Somebody must have stashed them there,' said Dee.

'A smuggler?'

'What else? Where did this machine come from, anyhow? It's not mine.'

'Nor mine. I think it's Trixie's.'

'Trixie? You mean she's the smuggler?'

'I don't know. It's all so bizarre. Maybe we should ask her.'

'Well, we can't ask her tonight. She's gone ashore clubbing. She won't be back till the early hours.'

'Do you think we should hand them in?' Lisa sounded doubtful.

'Hand them in to where? The Italian police? We'd spend the next six months in prison whilst they argued over what to charge us with. Besides, we have to talk to Trixie first.'

'Yeah. I guess you're right. So what do we do with them meanwhile?'

'Put them back in the bag for starters. We'll stash them in your drawer until tomorrow. Then we'll see what Trixie has to say.'

At that moment there was a knock at the cabin door.

'Oh hell,' exclaimed Lisa. 'That's Kathy. Quick, get those things out of sight.'

Dee hastily pulled the drawstring on the bag closed whilst Lisa went to the door. She dropped the bag into the top drawer of Lisa's chest and turned just in time to see Kathy enter the room.

'Hi,' she said, trying to sound unconcerned.

But Kathy seemed scarcely to hear her. Her eyes were fixed on the two parts of the tape recorder lying on the table.

'Had a bit of an accident,' said Lisa brightly. 'But I think it can be fixed.'

'But it's come apart,' said Kathy in dismay. 'What happened to—' She checked herself, putting her hand over her mouth.

'What happened to what?'

'Er . . . The machine. What happened to it?'

'I dropped it, that's all. It's not the end of the world, you know. It'll go back together.'

'Anyhow,' said Dee. 'I've got a party to go to. I'll take this to my room and try and fix it.'

'Can I help?' asked Kathy.

'Hey, Kathy, I thought you were with me tonight,' said Lisa.

'Yes. Of course. I just wondered—'

'Don't. Just leave Dee to it. I've got some champagne on ice, and we're going to enjoy it.'

'Have fun, then,' said Dee. 'I'm off.'

And she set off, slamming the door behind her and leaving Kathy staring after her in confusion and dismay.

Chapter 20

Jon Howland's heart was beating fast as he stood outside Svetna's flat waiting for her to unlock the door. In the taxi they had conversed quite intimately, and for the first time Svetna had revealed to him some of the details of her past life. To the idle observer it might have appeared a perfectly innocent conversation, but all the time Jon had sensed that there was something more significant passing between them. He had had the distinct impression she was opening up to him, bringing them closer together. It was as if the conversation was a form of foreplay, a kind of dropping of the veils to reveal the true Svetna beneath. Jon couldn't help wondering whether this might be a prelude to a more physical undressing to follow, and he had found himself growing ever more aroused as the journey progressed. Now, as he awaited admission to her flat, he sensed once again that she was in control, and that everything that had happened since they had met that evening had been part of a preordained plan.

She pushed open the door and stood back.

'Come inside, Jon,' she purred.

He stepped into the hallway and she followed him. She

clicked on a light and made her way past him. Jon stopped short, gaping at the pictures on the wall.

They were all photographs of Svetna, and in all of them she was nude. They were not cheap snaps, though. These were professional shots of an extremely attractive model. Erotic they certainly were, pornographic even, but great shots all the same, and clearly designed to arouse, an effect they were certainly having on him.

Legend number one confirmed!

He moved down the hallway, studying each picture in turn, taking in the contours of her lovely body, his eyes lingering on her breasts and crotch so delightfully displayed. By the time he reached the kitchen the coffee pot was already coming to the boil.

He stood and watched as she prepared the cups, her fingers lingering on them as if to stroke the fine china. Even making coffee was an erotic act where Svetna was concerned.

She seemed to feel his eyes on her and turned to smile at him.

'Thirsty?' she asked.

'Mmm,' he mumbled absently.

'Soon be ready.'

She pressed past him into the bedroom next door, her closeness sending a thrill through him. He cast his eyes over the room, with its wide bed and silken sheets. It seemed almost made for seduction. She busied herself briefly in the room, then made to leave again. This time when she came to pass him he blocked the doorway, staring down at her.

'What is it?' she asked.

174

'I'm just wondering which room I'm going to kiss you in first,' he said.

She did not reply, simply remaining where she was, the ghost of a smile on her lips. Jon felt clumsy and inept before her svelte coolness. He reached blindly for a line.

'I suppose the bedroom is as good a place as any,' he said, and pulled her close.

They kissed, but almost at once she pulled away. For a moment Jon was confused. Surely he hadn't misread the situation? Then he realised she was smiling.

'No kissing until my makeup is off,' she said.

'Ah,' said Jon. Then, still testing the waters: 'I just wanted to be sure that's what you wanted.'

'Oh yes. I want you . . .' She raised her eyes and stared intently into his. '. . . Desperately.'

Then she pushed past him into the kitchen

She carried their coffee cups through into the small sitting room. The room was furnished in a modern and tasteful way, with a low couch at one end. She settled on it and he sat down next to her. For a few seconds there was silence as each sipped the coffee.

'You like to watch a video?' she asked.

'What kind of video?'

'A sexy video?'

'If you like.'

She opened a cupboard beside the television and extracted a cassette. She slid it into the machine and pressed a button. Almost at once the image of three people appeared on the screen, two men and a woman. All three were totally naked, the girl down on all fours sucking one of the men's penises whilst his companion rogered her from behind.

There were no discreet camera angles. The action was for real.

Legend number two confirmed!

They finished their coffee and he placed his cup down beside hers. The images on the television screen had made his cock hard, and he knew that she had noticed. When she leaned back he inclined his body toward her and she made no move to stop him. He began to stroke her body, running his hands up the sleek nylon of her stockings.

'Mmmm.' She slid closer to him, resting her hand in his lap, where he knew she could feel the throbbing of his organ.

Suddenly she twisted away from him and sat up.

'Time to take my makeup off. You wait here.'

She sprang to her feet and danced out of the room. Jon remained where he was, his eyes fixed on the video screen, where two girls were licking one another's cunts with relish.

'That's better.'

When she returned she was still dressed as before. Only the slightly paler lips betrayed the fact that her face was now free of cosmetics. She settled down next to him once more and turned her face to his.

He leaned forward, and their lips met, their mouths opening and their tongues intertwining. She wrapped her arms about his neck, pulling him down against her and crushing her lips against his. He felt as if he would be swallowed by her passion as the kiss went on and on and she ground her body against his, her soft breasts crushed hard against his chest.

When at last he broke away, both were breathing heavily

and he could tell that she was as aroused as he was. He reached for the zipper at the back of her dress and pulled it down all the way to her bottom, then slipped it from her shoulders and off. Beneath she wore matching black bra and pants, along with a lacy suspender belt supporting her stockings. He pulled her to him once more, kissing her with passion as he reached for the catch on her bra.

It came undone easily, and she allowed him to pull it from her and drop it on one side. He sat back to admire her breasts. They were plump and firm, jutting forward with hardly any hint of sagging. Her nipples were dark brown in colour and stood out like small, hard knobs. He took her breast in his hand, running his finger over the silky skin and massaging the soft flesh in his fingers.

Her hand sought out the bulge in his trousers, rubbing against his crotch and caressing him there. He felt her reach for his fly, her fingers finding his zipper easily and sliding it undone in a single movement. He shivered slightly as he felt the coolness of her hand against his erection, easing it from his pants until, with a gasp of relief, he felt it spring from the constriction of the garments and stand proudly erect.

She began to caress him, running her hand up and down his shaft, her fingers tracing the contours of the bulging veins. At the same time her other hand was at his shirt, undoing the buttons one by one. When she had freed the last one she pulled the shirt aside, revealing the dark mat of hair on his chest. She leaned forward and closed her mouth over his nipple, sending an immediate thrill through Jon's already excited body.

They kissed again, she manipulating his erection whilst

he slid his hand downwards to her brief panties. He hooked a finger under the gusset and pulled the flimsy material to one side. He felt her stiffen as he slipped a finger into her vagina. It was hot and wet and the muscles squeezed about his finger as he pressed it into her.

She pulled away. 'In the bedroom,' she said. Yet another order.

By the time he reached the bedroom, shedding clothes as he went, she was totally nude, stretched out on the bed, her legs spread lazily apart. He ran his eyes over her form. She had the most gorgeous body he had ever seen, with slim waist and long, tapering legs. The hair on her pubic mound had been carefully trimmed into a thin triangle, and that about her sex removed completely. Her slit was wide and pink, the lips spread open as if in invitation. Jon stood over her, his cock firmly to attention, his heart pounding.

She reached up and took his hand, pulling him down onto the bed. He lay over her, their bodies pressed together, their mouths joined in another ardent kiss. When their lips broke apart she rolled him onto his back and once again her mouth found his nipples. It was the most extraordinarily arousing thing he had ever imagined, and he gasped aloud at the delicious sensation as she sucked and nibbled at each one in turn. Then, just as he feared he might come without even entering her, she rolled onto her back again.

'Now,' she said. 'We fuck.'

She reached down for his erection, guiding it towards the centre of her pleasure. There was no sense of urgency in her movements, but he could tell she was as aroused as he was. He eased himself up slightly, entirely in her control, and allowed her to position him where she wanted him.

He gave a grunt of pleasure as he felt himself slip inside her, the hot moistness of her sex enveloping him like a purse. She wrapped her arms around his backside, pressing him down and forcing his cock ever deeper within her until it was totally buried.

He began with slow, gentle movements, his hips working back and forth as he slid his cock over the smoothness of her inner walls. All the time she was contracting and relaxing the muscles inside, giving him a delicious massage within her.

Somehow, even when he was on top, she seemed to be in charge, the movement of her hips dictating the pace at which they screwed. Any attempt on his part to increase the rate brought a squeezing of the fingers on his buttocks, a clear signal to moderate his thrusts once more.

'Not too fast,' she murmured. 'Make it last.'

Jon wasn't certain that he could make it last. His senses were filled with the softness of her body and the tingling excitement within her that transmitted itself to him almost telepathically. His body was demanding that he thrust even harder. Never before had he fucked so sensuous a woman. There was no ambiguity about her attitude now. She knew what she wanted and was taking it from him. It was almost as if he was being used by her for her own pleasure, but used in a way about which he had no complaint. He strained to moderate his tempo, despite the fact that he could feel his own passion building with every stroke.

For a time their lovemaking continued at this steady rate, Jon savouring Svetna's body and the enthusiastic way she responded to him. He was surprised at his ability to restrain his own passion. Once again he had to put it down to Svetna's control over the whole situation. She would allow him to come when she herself was ready.

Suddenly her movements stopped, and he looked down at her in surprise.

'From behind now.' Once more she was in charge.

He rolled off her, his cock glistening with her juices, and watched as she hoisted herself up onto all fours in the middle of the bed. Then she pressed her breasts down onto the covers and raised her backside high, affording him perfect access to her sex and anus.

'Fuck me, Jon.'

He rose to his knees and positioned himself behind her, his prick in his hand as he guided it towards her vagina. Then he was inside her once more and fucking with passion.

This time she grunted with pleasure as he thrust his hips against her backside, a new urgency filling him.

'Now, your finger.' Orders again. He reached round her waist and slid his hand down over her pubic mound, seeking the hard little button of her love bud. He teased it out and began to run his fingers over it, causing her to redouble her moans as he did so. This time he sensed that she was ready, and for the first time she was allowing him to have his rein. He pumped his hips back and forth with an ever increasing tempo, feeling his orgasm build inside him.

He came with a shout, his balls suddenly unleashing a gush of spunk into her. She responded with her own orgasm, her face buried deep in the pillows so that the cries were reduced to muffled squeaks, her backside pumping back and forth as she milked the sperm from him.

He went on thrusting until his semen was spent. Then he held her, his finger still teasing her clitoris as he felt the stiffness slowly ease from her body. At last she collapsed forward onto the bed and he fell beside her, panting for breath.

It was some time before either of them spoke. Jon was the one who finally broke the silence.

'Why me?' he asked. 'And why now?'

'Because I wanted you.'

'I don't understand.'

She propped herself up on one elbow, facing him.

'Just that. Sometimes I see a man and think, this is a man I want to fuck.'

'You mean a sort of notch on the bedpost?'

'I beg your pardon?'

'A name on the list. Another Svetna conquest.'

'Do you feel conquered?'

'Not really.'

She reached out and ran her fingers across his chest.

'There's no conquest,' she said. 'This is for pleasure. I love to fuck, and I need a man who can perform for me. I decided you were such a man. You enjoyed it, didn't you?'

'Yes.'

'Then stop trying to analyse when there's nothing to analyse. Pleasure for you, pleasure for me. That's all there is.'

Jon rolled onto his side. She was an extraordinary woman. Like none he had ever met. But now he was exhausted and the bed was comfortable. He closed his eyes.

When he awoke he had no idea what time it was, only that the sky outside the window was still dark. He blinked up at the lovely naked woman who stood over him, urging him to his feet.

She took his hand and led him across the hallway to the bathroom. The sink was filled with warm soapy water and she made him stand close to it.

Her hands dropped to his genitals and she began slowly and carefully to soap them. She was very thorough, cleaning them all over with a light caressing touch that soon had him erect once more. Then she towelled him dry and took him back to the bedroom, sitting him down on the edge of the bed and kneeling between his thighs.

'Now I give you something to remember,' she said.

She dropped her head down and took his cock between her lips.

Legend number three, he thought ecstatically as his rampant tool began to throb once more.

Chapter 21

'There's a parcel for me, I believe.'

Kathy Prender stood at the ship's reception area, leaning against the counter and addressing the young clerk who sat behind it. The message had come through from London that morning that the package she had requested had been despatched by diplomatic bag. Now she reached eagerly for the small packet that the man handed to her.

Kathy had had a sleepless night since her encounter with Dee and Lisa the night before. The sight of the tape recorder in two parts had been a shock to her, and still she was confused as to what the girls were up to.

There could be no doubt now that the gems were no longer in their former hiding place, but where could they be? Both Dee and Lisa seemed to be claiming that the machine had been damaged by accident, but if that were true they would surely have found the bag of gems. In which case, why on earth hadn't they handed them in? Surely the fact that they had kept hold of them was proof that they were involved in the robbery?

She made her way down to her cabin, still clutching the parcel tightly in her hand. Once inside she locked the door, then sat down and began undoing the wrapping. When she finally had it open, she withdrew a small velvet bag from within. She undid the cord around the neck of the bag and emptied the contents into her palm.

The gems were very good imitations, glittering in the light from her table lamp in a most convincing way. She turned them over in her fingers, admiring the way they had been cut. They would certainly be good enough to fool anyone at first glance, though she knew that the moment an expert had the opportunity to examine them he would see through the subterfuge.

She spread them out on the table and sat staring at them. The trouble was, her plan to substitute them for the genuine articles was no longer as simple as she had thought. Previously she had known exactly where to find the gems. Now she was not so sure. What if they had already left the ship? What if some Neopolitan jeweller was already examining them in some back street shop?

She shook her head. It seemed too unlikely. All the intelligence from London suggested that the contraband was headed for Panavia, and they wouldn't be there for some days yet. The diamonds had to be still on board, in which case she would find them.

She scooped up the glittering baubles and placed them back in the bag. Then she slipped it into her pocket. She would have to search the girls' cabins, starting with Lisa's. All she needed was an opportunity.

She unlocked the cabin door and let herself out. Then, with a purposeful step, she set off toward the upper decks.

Dee Masters paused outside the door to Jon Howland's

cabin and raised her hand to knock. Then she hesitated, unwilling to disturb him. She checked her watch. Eleven o'clock. It was late enough. She was slightly puzzled. It wasn't like Jon to sleep in like this. Normally he was up in time for breakfast. She knew he had had a date the night before, but even so, to see him remain in bed this late was unusual.

She grasped hold of the doorhandle. It turned, and the door opened a crack. Beyond was darkness and silence. She slipped inside, closing the door behind her. She blinked, trying to accustom her eyes to the gloom. She could hear the sound of heavy breathing and, as her vision cleared, she discerned the body on the bed.

Jon was naked, lying face down on top of the bed, his face buried in a pillow. His breathing was deep and even and he was clearly fast asleep. Dee sat down beside him on the bed and stroked his back, admiring the firmness of his body.

She had not had sex with him since the day of the audition. In fact she had been celibate since her encounter in the back of the sex shop, and now, seeing his athletic form, she suddenly felt the stirring of desire for a man's body close to her and a man's cock penetrating her.

'Jon.'

He made no response.

'Jon!' This time she spoke slightly louder, but still he did not stir.

Then Dee did something she couldn't fully explain herself. On a sudden whim she began to strip.

She unzipped the light summer dress she was wearing and dropped it onto the chair beside Jon's crumpled suit

185

from the night before. Then she quickly unhooked her bra and placed it on top. Finally she slid her knickers down her legs and tossed them aside.

She paused to admire her body in the mirror on the wall. She knew she had a lovely figure, and she ran her eyes over her jutting breasts and pert behind. Then she looked down at the prostrate male body on the bed and licked her lips. She'd wake him up all right!

She lay down on the bed beside him and moved close, pressing her pale young body against his. He gave a snort and stirred slightly, then relapsed into slumber.

Dee eased a hand under his body and wormed it down between his legs. When she found his cock, it was soft. She took it in her hand and squeezed it gently.

He stirred again.

'No, Svetna,' he mumbled. 'No more.'

Dee suppressed a giggle. Svetna! So that was who his mysterious date had been! No wonder he hadn't told anyone. She squeezed his cock again and he gave a grunt, suddenly flopping over onto his back.

Dee propped herself up on her elbow and let her eyes rove over him. He had a good, strong body, and the tan he had acquired since leaving England made him appear even more handsome. She took his cock in her hand and toyed with it gently. It had stiffened slightly under her ministrations, but it was still far from hard. With an impish grin on her face she lowered her head over it.

She took him into her mouth, enjoying the smell of his manhood as she sucked gently at him. He moaned softly, his eyes half opening, then closing again. She caressed his balls, sucking harder as she felt him harden in her mouth.

She took his shaft between finger and thumb as she did so, working his foreskin up and down, her nipples brushing against his thigh.

'Svetna,' he gasped.

By now he was fully erect, and Dee sat back to admire her handiwork. She had forgotten how long and thick his cock was and, seeing it now, wet with her saliva, she felt her own arousal increase.

Jon was flat on his back and obviously still fast asleep, though what sort of dream he was having Dee could only imagine. She lay beside him, wanking him slowly and watching the pleasure on his features.

She moved a hand down to her own crotch, sliding her index finger the length of her slit and finding the hard little button of her love bud. She began to frig herself in rhythm with the hand that was working Jon's foreskin. It felt good to be naked with a man again, and she pressed herself against his strong body, her flesh tingling at the sensation. She lay for some time, stimulating them both in a lazy, careless way. Inside her, though, the passion was beginning to mount, and suddenly she needed more stimulation than she could manage by herself.

'It's no good, Jon,' she murmured. 'My fingers aren't enough. I need that cock of yours inside me right now.'

She rose to a kneeling position, then straddled him, staring down at his prostrate body and at his erection, which rose almost vertically, twitching slightly beneath her fingers. She manoeuvred herself over it, spreading her legs as wide as she was able. Then she began to lower herself, giving a suppressed cry of pleasure as she felt his thick glans make contact with her slit.

She was wet now, very wet, and ready to be penetrated. She began to press downwards, still holding his rod against the entrance to her vagina.

With a gasp she felt it penetrate her, forcing the walls of her sex apart as she squatted lower, enveloping him with her body until her sex lips were pressed against the base of his shaft, and he was all the way in.

Dee began to move, raising herself from him, then dropping back again, moaning with the sensation as his erection slid over the tightness of her sex. It felt wonderful to have a cock inside her once more, and she revelled in the exquisite sensation of the fucking.

Her fucking.

She was fucking him. He was simply providing the instrument of her pleasure, the thick, meaty pole on which she was taking her pleasure.

'Ahhh!'

The cry came from Jon's lips, betraying the fact that, though he was asleep, he was still able to sense the ministrations of the naked young girl who was astride him. She wondered what he was dreaming about. Was it Svetna? Or was it another girl? Herself even? Whoever it was, the expression on his face told her how much he was enjoying it.

She began to move faster, carried on by the lustful desire that filled her. She bounced up and down on his cock, her breasts shaking in the most delightful way as she rode out her pleasure on him. She wanted to laugh aloud at the joy of feeling an erect prick inside her once again, even if its owner was dreaming of someone else. In a way she almost preferred it thus, since it allowed her own imagination to run free. It was a very short time before she felt her climax approach, making her redouble her efforts, her head thrown back, her body arched.

'Ohhh!'

She hadn't expected him to come, but the sensation of hot, thick semen pumping into her from his twitching cock told her that he had been every bit as aroused as she, and seconds later she too was climaxing, the walls of her sex convulsing as the waves of intense pleasure rolled over her.

'Svetna, Svetna, Svetna.'

Jon cried the name aloud as his body rocked back and forth beneath her. Dee didn't care, though. She was lost in her own pleasure, small mewing sounds escaping her lips with every thrust until, her body drained, she flopped down on top of him.

He opened his eyes.

'Shit, you're a hell of a girl, Svetna,' he gasped.

She reached down and took his balls in her hand, then placed her face close to his.

'If you mention that woman's name again, Jon Howland,' she muttered, 'you won't be much good for fucking for a month.'

Chapter 22

'I tell you, it's not my machine,' insisted Trixie. 'It turned up in my luggage when we came on board. I thought it must belong to one of you.'

'What, it just appeared and you didn't question where it came from?' asked Lisa incredulously.

'Yes. I just put it to one side, meaning to ask you guys about it later. Then I guess it slipped my mind.'

'What's so important about it, anyhow?' asked Jenny. 'Nobody's asked for it back, and it's not as if we've been hiding it or anything.'

Lisa looked hard at Trixie, then at Jenny. She had convened this meeting of the band in Trixie's cabin in the hope of finding the truth about the machine and about the gemstones inside. So far, though, she seemed to be getting nowhere. All they were doing was arguing. She wished Dee was here. The singer had insisted on going to get Jon to join them before they started, but that had been more than half an hour ago. Lisa couldn't understand what was keeping her.

'Surely it it can't have just appeared in your bag, Trixie,' she insisted. 'Someone must have got access to it somehow.'

'Yes,' said Jenny. 'Think, Trixie.'

'It's you who should be doing the thinking, Jenny,' replied Trixie.

'What do you mean?'

'Well it was you and Lisa that took all the bags through Customs. That was the only time the bag was out of my sight.'

'Trixie's right,' said Lisa. 'The bags were unattended for quite a while. Anybody could have slipped the tape recorder into Trixie's luggage whilst we were occupied with those two bogus Customs men.'

'But why would they want to?' insisted Jenny. 'What's so important about some crummy cassette player? After all, you can buy one in the ship's shop if you want to.'

Lisa looked at the two girls. They seemed genuinely puzzled by her cross-examination. Besides, Trixie's story was perfectly plausible. Anyone wishing to sneak the machine into the bags had had ample opportunity to do so whilst she and Jenny had been fucking the men in the Customs shed. She took a deep breath.

It was time, she decided, to come clean.

'Listen,' she said. 'It's not the machine itself that's so important. It's what was inside it.'

'Inside it?'

'Yesterday Dee knocked the thing onto the floor and the back fell off. Inside was a bag of diamonds.'

'What . . . ?' The two girls stared open-mouthed at Lisa.

'That's right. Somebody was using it to smuggle diamonds out the country.'

'How many diamonds?'

'Well, I'm no expert, but I reckon they're worth a few million.'

'Wow!'

'Where are they now, Lisa?' asked Trixie.

'In my cabin.'

'What are we going to do?'

'Well, first of all I wanted to talk to you two. Make sure you're not the culprits.'

'Surely you didn't think—?'

'I didn't know what to think. Nor did Dee. That's why we're having this meeting. That's why Dee was supposed to be bringing Jon along. We want to see if he's got any ideas.'

At that moment there was a knock at the cabin door.

'Who is it?' called Lisa.

'It's me, Dee. And I've got Jon with me. Let me in, quick. It's important.'

Lisa moved across and unlocked the door, standing aside to allow the couple in. Lisa noticed the flush in Dee's cheeks and stared hard at her, then at Jon. Dee blushed at the stare, and Lisa guessed at once what had made her so late. She smiled and winked at her friend, raising her eyebrows quizzically.

Dee hesitated, and the redness in her cheeks intensified. Then she smiled too, thus effectively confirming Lisa's suspicions.

'Have you told Jenny and Trixie what we found?' she asked.

'Yes,' replied Lisa. 'And they know nothing about it.'

'You sure?' asked Dee.

'Absolutely,' said Trixie vehemently.

'Definitely. I had no idea,' put in Jenny.

'We think the machine was planted in Trixie's bag,' said Lisa. 'Probably whilst the luggage was in the Customs shed.'

'That sounds pretty plausible,' replied Dee. 'Because Jon's got some really interesting news. I told him the whole story, and he actually knew about the diamonds.'

'What? You knew they were in that machine?'

'No. Not exactly. But I knew they were on board.'

'Tell us.'

Jon went on to tell them the story he had been told by Svetna. How the gems had been stolen in a London robbery and somehow smuggled on board, and about the undercover police detective who was seeking them.

'And do they know anything about the guy who stole them?' asked Trixie.

'They don't even know if it was a guy,' replied Jon. They think it might even be a woman.'

'So whoever it is, they're going to be trying to get the diamonds back?'

'That's right. And this detective is going to try and intercept them.'

'Wait a minute,' said Jenny.

'What is it?'

'Just something Les said to me the other night.'

'What?'

'He said he was a policeman. And he was after some stolen diamonds. I didn't believe him at first, but maybe he was telling the truth.'

'But surely he wouldn't just come out and say it like

that,' said Trixie. 'What kind of detective would admit what they were up to so openly?'

'Unless it was a test,' said Jon.

'What do you mean?'

'Had he seen the tape machine?'

'Well, yes,' replied Jenny. 'He was looking at it when Lisa arrived to borrow it. That's when he made the remark.'

'So he might well have known that was where they were concealed?'

'I guess so. What are you getting at, Jon?'

'Well, suppose he wanted to see how you would react? After all, he knew you had access to the machine, and that made you a suspect.'

'Yeah. How did you and he meet up, anyhow?' asked Dee.

'In the sauna. You know I always go when there's hardly anyone there. He was the only other person.'

'He got himself into my cabin on the first night, as well,' said Trixie.

'That's hardly evidence,' said Dee. 'There's not many men haven't since we left home.'

'No, but he was the first one,' said Trixie defensively.

'And come to think of it, he was taking a pretty close look at the tape recorder,' said Jenny. 'In fact he looked quite put out when Lisa said she wanted to borrow it.'

'I think we might be onto something here,' said Dee. 'Maybe we should take Les into our confidence. At least he'd stop suspecting us and set off after the real thief.'

'Perhaps we could help him,' said Jenny. 'After all, this is a big ship. He can't possibly watch everybody at once.'

'I think Jenny's right,' said Jon. 'Where abouts is this Les, Jenny? I think we should have a word with him as soon as possible.'

'Not today you won't,' said Jenny. 'He's gone into town to meet a business associate who's joining the ship here. They won't be back on board until just before we sail.'

'Business associate, eh?' said Trixie. 'Could be reinforcements.'

'Whatever, we need to talk to him as soon as we can,' said Jon. 'Meanwhile we say nothing. I don't fancy spending the next six weeks in an Italian jail.'

'What about the diamonds?' asked Jenny. 'Are they safe?'

'They're in my drawer in the cabin at the moment,' said Lisa.

'Can we get a look at them?'

'I don't see why not. Come on, I'll show you.'

'And at the same time, we'd better find a better hiding place,' said Jon. 'Your top drawer is hardly the place.'

The five of them made for the door. Lisa was first out, and the others went to follow her, only to crash into one another. Lisa had stopped short in the doorway and was staring down the corridor.

'Kathy? What the—'

Kathy had been crouching at Lisa's door, apparently fiddling with the lock. Now she straightened up, her face crimson.

'What the hell were you doing?' asked Lisa as the others spilled out behind her.

'I . . . I was just checking to see if you were in.'

'But I told you I was going ashore this morning.'

'Yes, well . . . I was just making sure. I mean, you hadn't gone, had you?'

'No. And I'm beginning to feel glad I hadn't.'

'What's she got in her hand?' asked Trixie. 'It's a piece of wire, isn't it?'

'It's a hairpin. It fell out of my hair and I was picking it up.'

'You were trying to pick the lock.'

'Don't be silly. Why on earth would I want to do that?'

'She was,' put in Dee. 'She was breaking into your room, Lisa. She thought you were ashore so she was taking her chances.'

'Is that true, Kathy?' asked Lisa.

'No. Of course not. Listen, I can see you're busy. I'll come back later.'

She began to back away from them.

'Wait a minute,' called Lisa. 'I want a word with you.'

But it was too late. Kathy had turned and was fleeing down the corridor and round the corner.

Lisa made a move to follow, but Dee put a hand on her arm.

'Leave her,' she said.

'What on earth was that about?' asked Jon.

'I don't know,' said Dee. 'But I think we'd better get into Lisa's cabin and make sure the diamonds are all there.'

'You don't think—' gasped Lisa.

'I don't know what to think. I'd just like to check on those gems.'

Together they crowded round Lisa as she unlocked the door, then flooded into her cabin. Lisa yanked the drawer open and reached inside. Then she gave a sigh of relief.

'It's all right,' she said. 'They're here.'

'Better check they're the same ones.'

Hurriedly Lisa undid the neck of the bag and emptied the stones into her hand. Then she took them across to the mirror and tested one on the glass as she had before. A second scratch appeared, parallel to the first.

'They're the ones, all right,' she said. 'But what do you think Kathy was up to?'

'I'd have thought it was obvious,' said Trixie.

'You don't mean—'

'That she's our jewel thief? I certainly do.'

'But she can't be. Can she?'

'Tell us how you met, Lisa.'

'It was pure chance. She knocked my drink over, then bought me another. Then we went up to the private deck and . . . Well you know the rest.'

'How did you know she was lesbian?'

'She as good as said so. Although . . .'

'Although what?'

'Well, she didn't seem very experienced. I mean, for one who took the initiative like that, she seemed not to know the first thing.'

'And what about her behaviour yesterday,' said Dee. 'When she came in and saw the tape recorder broken.'

'That's right. She did seem very preoccupied by it. It was as if it was her own machine we'd broken.'

'If you ask me, that's all the proof we need,' said Trixie. 'She's our jewel thief, I'm sure of it. She's just been trying to gain our confidence and then, as soon as she thought we were off the ship, she decided to get her booty back.'

'And to think I fell for it,' said Lisa. 'What a fool.'

'Don't worry,' said Dee. 'It could have happened to anyone. The thing now is, what do we do next? Should we hand her in?'

'That'd be as bad as handing in the diamonds,' said Jon. 'We'd be material witnesses and we'd spend the night in interrogation whilst the ship sailed for Africa.'

'Jon's right,' said Dee. 'We daren't do anything while we're in port.'

'I think we should wait until Les gets back,' said Jenny. 'After all, he knows all about the diamonds. He'll be able to tell us what to do.'

'I think that's sensible too,' said Trixie. 'We can put the whole thing in his hands.'

'Meanwhile we've got to put the diamonds somewhere safe,' said Dee. 'Before Kathy tries her hand again.'

'Give them to me,' said Jon. 'I'll get Svetna to lock them in the ship's safe.'

'But what if she looks inside?' asked Lisa.

'I've got a lockable jewellery box,' said Dee. 'We can put them in there. Then she'll just think they're ordinary jewellery and put it with all the other passengers' stuff.'

'Do you think they'll be safe?' asked Dee.

'In Svetna's hands?' replied Jon. 'Safe as houses. She guards that safe as if it's her own.'

'Let's do it, then,' said Lisa. 'The sooner those gems are locked away the better. Then we'll just have to wait until Les gets back.'

Chapter 23

Les Cargill pushed back his chair and let out a loud belch.

'That's the best tagliatelle I've had in years, Akran,' he said.

'I told you this place was good,' replied his companion. 'And the best is yet to come.'

Les grinned across the table at his dinner partner. Akran was good company, and was, he had to admit, an extraordinarily handsome young man, his dusky features well-chiselled and framed by long, jet-black, wavy hair that hung down to his broad shoulders. Les guessed that the man must be extremely popular with the fairer sex, a surmise that was confirmed by the way in which women entering the restaurant stared at him as they passed.

Along with the good looks, though, there was an intangible air of cruelty about the man from North Africa. His smile, when he showed it, somehow lacked real humour and his dark eyes glittered in the low lights of the restaurant. Les wondered about his background. He had heard that the man was the son of an Arab prince and his Italian mistress, and there was no doubt that his features showed traces of both sides of his ancestry.

The two of them had met for the first time that night, though the rendezvous had been arranged before Les had left London, indeed before the robbery had even taken place. He had been approached in a pub one night by a man who had heard of his visits to fences to ascertain interest in the prospective haul from the robbery. It was this stranger's suggestion that he escape aboard the *SS Diana*, and it was he who had provided the finance Les had needed to carry out the job. Les had asked no questions. Now here he was, face to face with his contact at last, and enjoying his hospitality.

All of a sudden, a small band in the corner of the room struck up, and a spotlight fell on the stage. As the two men watched, a girl sprang from the shadows. She wore an impossibly short black dress, so tiny that the suspenders that held up the fishnet stockings encasing her legs were in plain view. Les licked his lips as he watched her begin to dance.

'So tell me now.' The dusky young man leaned across the table toward him and lowered his voice. 'The diamonds are safe on board?'

Les tore his eyes away from the figure on the stage. 'They are on board, certainly,' he said.

'But safe?'

'I believe so.'

The man's eyes narrowed. 'You believe?'

'There were problems when I boarded. The Customs. I had to hide the gems.'

'Where?'

'In someone else's luggage.'

On the stage, the girl was removing her dress, pulling

apart the small bows that fastened it down the front one
by one. It fell open, revealing black bra and pants and
black suspender belt.

'Whose luggage?'

Once again Les was forced to turn his attention to his
companion.

'A fellow traveller. But don't worry, I know exactly
where they are.'

'And you can get them back?'

'Of course.'

'Then why have you not already done so?'

'No reason to raise suspicions. After all, these girls aren't
going anywhere.'

'Girls?'

'That's right.'

Les went on to describe the circumstances that had left
the gems in the hands of the Kool Kittens. Akran listened
carefully, occasionally interjecting a question. And all the
time the lovely young woman on the stage continued
to strip, rolling down one stocking, then the other and
discarding them on the stage.

When Les had finished his tale, Akran sat back, his
face grim.

'I still do not like it,' he said. 'You know how important
those gems are to my boss. We plan to use them to finance
an extremely lucrative deal. Without them our business
will be in difficulties.'

'Just what is your business, Akran?'

'Let's just say that we need a means of spreading revenue
in a way in which it can't be traced. Revenue to finance
certain export details.'

'I see.' Les didn't need to ask more. It was clear to him that the exports must involve illegal substances. Anyhow, what did it matter to him? All he cared about was the payoff he was due to receive.

Les fixed his eyes on the stage once more as the stripper reached behind her for the catch on her bra. It came undone at once and she held it to herself, a hand placed over each cup, rubbing around in circular movements as if stimulating herself. Then she let it drop, revealing a pair of sumptuous breasts, the nipples large and hard.

'So.' Akran leaned forward once more. 'You understand why the gems are so important?'

'Sure. Don't worry, Akran. I'll get them back tonight if you wish. Even if it means breaking into Jenny's room.'

'Who is Jenny?'

'One of the band. I've been fucking the little airhead in order to keep tabs on the stuff.'

'And she'll let you into her cabin?'

'Sure. I can wrap the little bitch round my finger.'

'Then maybe we don't want to get the gems from her just yet.'

'I don't understand.'

'Listen. I am known in my country. When I go ashore in a few days I'm bound to be searched. You too, possibly, if anyone who knows me in Naples has seen me with you. There are spies everywhere. So maybe we get your Jenny to take the gems through Customs, then we take them back afterwards.'

'Hmm. I see what you mean.'

'You think she'd do it?'

'I could find a way.'

'Good. But you seem distracted. Is there a problem?'

'Distracted, yes. But it's not a problem.'

Les nodded in the direction of the stage. Akran turned in time to see the stripper pull down her panties, kicking them to one side. She stood, totally naked but for her high-heeled shoes, her hands on her hips and her legs spread wide. The bright spotlight revealed her shaven sex lips and she began to revolve her pelvis in a lewd dance, thrusting her pubis forward at the whistling crowd.

'Hmf,' snorted Akran. 'Kids' stuff. In my country I own clubs where the entertainment is more explicit, and the girls not merely on show. Come through the back. I have arranged a preview for you.'

He signalled to the head waiter, who approached their table at once.

'Is the entertainment prepared?'

'Yes, sir. If you'd like to follow me.'

The man beckoned, and Les rose, following the two of them across the room. They made their way to a door marked 'Private'. The waiter opened it and they went through. As they did so, Les threw a final glance over his shoulder at the stripper. She was lying on her back, her legs spread wide, two fingers deep in her vagina.

The room into which they were led was much smaller than the one in which they had eaten, with only two or three tables, none of which was occupied. At the front was another stage, similar to that in the restaurant, but with a wooden frame in the centre hung with gleaming chains. Les and Akran were shown to seats just in front of this stage and drinks brought to them. Once they were settled, the waiter clapped his hands. At this a curtain opened and three girls appeared. All were identically dressed in small bikinis. They were all Europeans, a small brunette in the centre flanked by two taller blondes. They hurried to centre stage then stood in a line, their eyes cast down.

'Very pretty, yes?' said Akran. 'These girls are special. Their families or husbands want to get rid of them. They need money, you see. So they sell them to my organisation, where we train them to bring pleasure.'

'You mean sex slaves?'

Akran tutted. 'Such an emotive word, slave. Certainly we have paid an indenture which obliges them to do as we say. But when their time is up they will be free to do as they wish.'

'And you can keep them even here?'

'We have to pay a few people off, but yes. Then, when the time is right, we ship them to my country where their work really begins. These three have only just completed their basic training, and this is their first time on stage.'

Les ran his eyes over the trio. Each was stunningly beautiful, the two blondes having the high cheek bones and aristocratic pose of Scandinavians, whilst the dark-haired girl's beauty was more that of the English rose, her large almond-shaped eyes giving her a truly innocent look. All three had magnificent bodies with large breasts, slim waists and long, elegant legs.

'Now,' Akran went on. 'They will play out a little tableau for us. One of them is due for punishment, and you may choose which.'

'Punishment?'

'Yes. A stiff cane across the backside is normally

what is administered. Unless you have something more imaginative in mind?'

Les stared anew at the three beauties before him. All three looked extremely nervous, but none attempted to protest. He swallowed. The prospect of watching one of the three being punished was already causing his cock to harden.

'No,' he said. 'A caning is fine. Who will administer it?'

'Why, the other two, of course.'

'Of course.'

'So which one is it to be.'

'The dark-haired one, I think.'

'An excellent choice. It will provide symmetry, after all.'

He signalled to the head waiter, who crossed to their table. Akran said a couple of words to him and the man nodded, then beckoned to the girls. The three followed him silently from the room.

'Now,' he said. 'Enjoy your drink. They will be back soon.'

It was ten minutes before the lights on the stage went up again. Les looked on eagerly as the curtain at the back swung open and the three came into view.

What he saw did not disappoint. The two blondes had changed into black leather leotards, cut low at the bosom and high up the thigh and cinched tight at the waist. Their legs were encased in long boots with jangling spurs at the heel, and each wore an elegant eye-mask which gave their faces a cat-like appearance. The third girl, in contrast, was clad in a short, dowdy dress that barely covered her thighs.

The material was stained and holed, and through the rents her bare, pale skin could clearly be seen. Her hands were fastened behind her with rope, and she wore a leather collar at her neck to which was attached a chain. It was by this chain that she was being led.

The women dragged her forward and pushed her down to her knees before the two men. She stared up at them, her eyes wide. Les studied her features carefully. Was he mistaken or was there, mixed with the fear, a hint of excitement in her expression? He turned to Akran, who smiled.

'I told you they were trained,' he said. 'Perhaps now you can see what I mean.'

'Your methods must be extremely good.'

'But of course.' He turned to the girls. 'Why have you brought her here?'

'If you please, my lord, she is to be punished.'

'For what reason?'

'Lewd behaviour, my lord. She was caught servicing two of the waiters in the restaurant, one with her vagina, the other with her mouth.'

'And have you anything to say in your defence, young strumpet?'

The girl hung her head and said nothing.

'Ten strokes,' said Akran. 'And see to it that she is well marked.'

'Yes, my lord.'

The two girls dragged the third to her feet and pulled her across to the wooden frame that Les had noticed on entering the room. They turned her to face the men, then each took hold of her dress at the shoulder and pulled.

The cloth tore as if it was rotten, the dress simply coming apart in their hands. Each of the guards was left holding a ragged remnant which she tossed aside. Beneath the rags, the girl was quite naked, her face glowing as she stood helpless before the leering men.

They left her like that for a full minute, allowing the two to drink their fill of her vulnerable beauty before she was finally turned to face the frame.

The top of the device was a flat sheet of wood about eighteen inches wide and three feet high. They bent her forward over it so that her breasts hung down on the far side. Then they took the chain on her collar and fastened it to the floor in front of her. Once this was secure, her captors took hold of her ankles, stretching them wide apart. Set into the floor were iron shackles, and one of these was attached to each of the girl's legs. Finally they took a chain that hung down from the ceiling over the centre of the frame and attached it to the rope that held her wrists behind her, hauling them up, forcing her arms back until her position looked extremely uncomfortable. Only then did they stand back to admire their handiwork.

The girl was totally helpless, bent over the frame, her legs spread wide apart so that the pink of her sex showed clearly to the watching men. Les felt his cock stiffen still further as his eyes took in her helpless situation. Akran had been right. This made the striptease he had witnessed earlier seem tame by comparison.

One of the blondes went to a chest that stood at the back of the stage and extracted something, bringing it across to where the two men sat. As she laid it on the table Les saw that it was a long, narrow box, not unlike the sort that a pool cue might be kept in. Akran opened it and showed its contents to Les. It held not a cue, but a pair of thin bamboo canes. He watched as the man removed one after the other from the box and flexed it in his hands.

'Good,' he said. 'Be sure and use them properly, or your own arses will suffer.'

'Yes, my lord.'

The girl took the canes from him and went back to the stage. She held out both to the other blonde, who selected one. Then they moved round in front of the hapless captive and held their canes up to her face, one after the other. As they did so, the girl inclined her head as best she could and planted a kiss on each.

'Five strokes each,' said Akran. 'And be sure you make them tell, or you will be next.'

A silence descended over the room as the first of the blondes tapped her cane against the captive's bare behind.

Swish! Whack!

The cane came down hard against the white flesh, cutting a thin white diagonal stripe that immediately darkened to red. No sound came from the victim, but Les could sense the tenseness in her body as the second punisher raised her cane.

Swish! Whack!

The second stripe fell across the first, forming a large X on the soft skin.

Swish! Whack!

Hardly had the second girl pulled her cane away that the first struck again, the crack of cane on flesh ringing about the room.

Swish! Whack!

Les leaned forward in his chair, watching eagerly as the punishment was meted out. The two leather clad beauties were showing no restraint at all. It was obvious that they took Akran's threat seriously and were in no hurry to change places with the naked girl so cruelly stretched across the frame.

Swish! Whack!

Swish! Whack!

The girl's backside was red all over now, and her body danced with every blow that fell, her arms tugging at the restraints in a vain attempt to prevent the stinging stripes that burned so brightly. As Les watched the lovely plump behind pump back and forth, he was reminded of nothing more than somebody fucking and his rampant cock strained against his pants as the thought entered his mind.

Swish! Whack!

Swish! Whack!

A light sheen of sweat had formed over the girl's flesh that glistened in the lights of the stage, a small puff of spray rising up every time one of the canes fell. There was another source of moisture too, though. One that held Les's attention much more. It was a small, silvery trail that had leaked from the girl's vagina onto her inner thigh and was trickling slowly down her leg. Les stared in amazement. Surely this couldn't be turning her on?

Swish! Whack!

A whimper came from the captive, the first sound she had made since the punishment had begun, and Les held his breath as the cane rose for the final time.

Swish! Whack!

The last blow fell with the same force as the first, leaving not an inch of the girl's backside unmarked as it crashed down, eliciting, at last, a cry of pain from its victim.

The two blondes stood back from the writhing girl. There was now no mistaking the overt sexuality of her movements, her hips jabbing against the edge of the frame, the moisture between her legs shining brightly.

Akran turned to Les.

'You see how well trained these sluts are?' he said. 'We have her beaten and all she wants is to fuck. Perhaps you would like to let her taste your cock?'

He snapped his fingers and the two blondes rushed across to stand in front of the table. Akran motioned to the open case and the pair both placed their canes inside.

'The miscreant must pay homage to our visitor,' he said. 'See to it.'

The women took Les by the hand, one on each side, and pulled him to his feet. They led him around in front of the captive. Les studied her features. Her face was dripping with sweat, her hair hanging lank and matted. She was panting hard, her dangling breasts swaying back and forth as she did so. She raised her eyes to him as he came closer and once again he saw the spark of excitement in her face as she met his gaze.

Les felt a hand brush his erection through his jeans as one of the blondes began loosening his belt. She pulled it undone, then unfastened his waistband and dragged down the zip. At the same time her companion reached inside and freed his cock from the confines of his pants. It sprang up, stiff as a flagpole. The girls began to run their hands over its length, making him gasp with pleasure.

The beauty on his left then wrapped her fingers round his shaft and pulled it forward. He saw then that the captive had her mouth open and was ready to receive him. With a grunt of pleasure he thrust himself between her lips and she started to suck greedily at him, her tongue darting back and forth over his glans as she pulled him deep into her mouth.

He began to fuck her face, his hips pumping back and forth, forcing his rampant cock into her mouth with enthusiasm. Then he gasped again as he felt the most exquisite sensation about his balls. He looked down to see that one of the blondes had dropped to her knees and manoeuvred herself beneath him, taking his scrotum into her mouth and licking and sucking with enthusiasm.

A moan from the captive made him look up. The second blonde had returned to Akran, and Les watched with interest as his erection too was freed from his pants and guided towards the helpless girl.

Akran wasted no time, thrusting his rampant tool deep into the warm wetness of the girl's vagina, making her moan once more. Les wondered whether it was the pain of Akran's wiry pubic hair rubbing against the inflamed flesh of her rear that made her moan, but when he studied her eyes again he could detect nothing but pleasure.

The two men began fucking the girl in earnest, shaking her small frame as each rammed his cock deep into her body whilst their handmaidens continued to suck and caress them. Les knew that, after the show he had just witnessed, he would not be able to hold back for long, and sure enough he soon felt his balls tighten as they prepared to unleash their load.

Les came with a grunt of pleasure, his cock twitching violently as it squirted thick, creamy semen into the mouth of the captive. At the same moment he heard a shout from Akran and realised that he was simultaneously filling the girl with his spunk from the other end. The girl's body tensed for a moment, then she too was groaning with what Les knew could not be a faked orgasm.

The three of them rocked back and forth in unison as each was overcome with the pleasure of their climax, the two blondes manipulating them expertly to ensure that their satisfaction was total. When at last Les knew there was nothing more left in him he withdrew, gazing down at the panting girl, two trails of white spunk dribbling down from the edges of her mouth as she struggled to swallow his seed. He raised his eyes and looked across at Akran, who was standing quietly whilst his blonde servant licked him clean.

'You guys certainly know how to entertain,' he grinned.

Chapter 24

The knock at his cabin door took Les by surprise. He wasn't expecting any visitors. In fact just at the moment visitors were rather unwelcome. He glanced across at Akran, who was sitting on a chair across the table from him, a sheaf of papers open in front of him.

'Who the hell's that?' the dark-skinned man asked. 'I thought you said we wouldn't be disturbed.'

'I don't know. Wait here.'

Les and Akran had returned late to the ship on the previous evening. The session in the private club had gone on for some time, with the girls all joining in to provide their entertainment. Les had had both the blondes after his session with the dark girl, and such had been his enjoyment, he and Akran had come close to missing the ship.

Now they were together again, finalising the details of their deal with the gems. The money was to be paid to Les on delivery of the diamonds, and he had been giving Akran the number of his Swiss bank account when the knock had sounded. He made his way to the door and stopped just behind it.

'Who's there?'

'It's me, Jenny.'

'Can you come back later, Jenny?'

'I need to see you now.'

'I'm in a meeting. A colleague joined the ship last night. We've got business to discuss.'

'I think this might interest your friend as well. It's about something I've got. Something that I think you want.'

The two men glanced sharply at one another.

'What do you mean?'

'Let me in and I'll tell you.'

Les raised an eyebrow, and Akran nodded.

'If she knows something, we'd better find out now,' he murmured.

'All right. Just for a minute, then.'

Les turned the key in the lock and opened the door. Outside stood Jenny, her face flushed.

'Now, what is it?'

'Aren't you going to let me inside?'

He stood aside and allowed her to enter. She stopped short when she saw Akran, who rose to his feet, a smile upon his face.

'Akran, this is Jenny,' said Les. 'She plays in the ship's band.'

He took her hand and planted a kiss on the back of it.

'Charmed, I'm sure.'

Jenny blushed as she looked into his handsome face, clearly captivated by his appearance. 'How do you do,' she said lamely.

'Come on then, Jenny,' said Les. 'Get to the point. Akran and I really are busy.'

'I think you're going to want to hear what I have to say,' said Jenny 'It's really very important.'

'Go on, then.'

'Well,' she began. 'For a start, I don't believe you're who you say you are.'

Les stiffened at these words, but his voice remained calm.

'How do you reach that conclusion?'

'A number of things. Bits of information, things that I've been able to piece together to give me the true picture.'

'Go on.'

'Well, it all started with the tape machine.'

'Tape machine?' Now Les was really interested.

'You know,' she went on. 'The one that was in my room the other night. Don't tell me you didn't notice it, because I know you did.'

'Oh, *that* tape machine.'

'Yes. Well, the odd thing is that none of us know where it came from. It just sort of appeared with our stuff when we came aboard.'

'And have you any suspicions?'

'We think it was planted in our bags at Southampton. We think someone wanted us to bring it aboard.'

Akran's eyes darkened. 'An extraordinary story,' he said. 'But why would anyone want to do such a thing?'

'Because they didn't want to take it through Customs.'

'I see. But what was so special about this machine? Surely there are no laws against exporting such things?'

'That was the problem. We couldn't understand that either. But don't you know the reason, Les?'

Les stared at her, his heart beating fast. There was no

217

doubt in his mind that they had discovered something. Something that could prove extremely dangerous to him. For a moment he wasn't sure what to do. Should he admit all and throw himself at Jenny's mercy? He looked at Akran and knew at once that his companion would never agree to such a plan. But if Jenny knew what they were up to, the only alternative would be to silence her, and he was very reluctant to take such extreme measures. Buy her off? That too seemed a dangerous option. He forced a smile.

'I'm not sure that I do know what you mean,' he said. 'Tell me more, Jenny.'

'All right. If you insist. But there's really no need to be so coy. The truth is that we might never have guessed what was going on if we hadn't had the accident.'

'Accident?'

'Yes. It was Lisa and Dee. They managed to knock the machine onto the floor by mistake, and it fell apart.'

Les took a deep breath. 'Go on.'

'That was when we discovered something inside it. Something I think you were after.'

'What made you think I was after it?'

'Oh, come on, Les. All those diamonds. You're not going to deny it, are you?'

'It's your story. What happened next?'

'That was when we heard about the robbery.'

'Who told you?'

'We found out through the purser's clerk. She told our boss that someone had smuggled a stash of hugely expensive diamonds on board, and that there was a policeman on the ship trying to find them.'

'A policeman?' Les stared at her. That was the first he

had heard of a policeman being aboard. He glanced across at Akran, whose face had creased into a frown as he heard the words.

Les clenched his fists, trying his best to stay outwardly calm. It looked like the game was up, then, unless he could do something to silence the girl. He turned to Jenny once more.

'Who else knows about this?'

'Just the other girls. And Jon, the entertainments man.'

'And you haven't gone to the authorities yet?'

'We thought it best to come to you first. You see we've worked out who you are. That little clue you gave me the other night was just to test me, wasn't it?'

Les, now thoroughly confused, shook his head.

'Test?'

'That's right. Listen, Les, we know you're the policeman. Once we'd heard you were on board, the whole thing fitted into place.'

'I'm . . .' Les was at a loss for words.

'Don't worry. Your secret's safe with us. And the diamonds are safe too. Once we realised what they were, we stashed them in the ship's safe. Nobody knows what they are. So you see, you've got nothing to fear. What about Akran, though? Where does he fit in? Interpol?'

Les's mind worked faster than he had believed possible. 'Interpol?' he stammered. 'Oh, er, yes. That's right. Clever of you to suss that. Wasn't it, Akran?'

Akran, who had been listening open-mouthed to the conversation, simply nodded dumbly.

'Well,' said Les, beginning to gain control of the

situation once more. 'That was an extremely clever piece of detective work on your part.'

'And there's more. We think we know who the thief is.'

Jenny went on to recount how Lisa had been befriended by Kathy and how they had caught her trying to break into Lisa's room.

'So you see,' she concluded, 'we think that Kathy is the one you're after.'

'This Kathy,' said Akran. 'What cabin is she in?'

'Cabin 254.'

'I see,' said Akran, making a mental note of the number.

'So what comes next?' asked Jenny. 'Are you going to arrest her?'

'Er, not just yet,' said Les. 'I'm waiting for her to lead me to her accomplices, you see.'

'You mean you knew about her all along?'

'Of course. After all, I am a detective.' For the first time since Jenny had entered the room, his voice had a note of confidence.

'But why couldn't you tell us what you were up to?'

'All far too hush-hush. Besides, I didn't want to implicate you. I mean, this is a very serious business. That's why Akran's involved. There are people in his country, Panavia, who want to use those diamonds to arm an uprising against his government.'

'Gosh.'

'So you can imagine how grateful we are to you for your efforts,' put in Akran.

'So what shall we do? Do you want me to get the diamonds for you?'

'No,' said Akran. Les darted a quizzical glance at him.

'No,' he said again. 'Leave the diamonds where they are for now. After all, nobody's going to take them from there. And the least attention drawn to them the better. The safest thing is to take them off the ship when we get to Panavia. And that's where you could help us once again, Jenny.'

'I'll help in any way I can.'

'There are people in my country who will recognise me. Unscrupulous people. They may try to get the gems from me when I disembark. However, if someone unknown carried them ashore—'

'An innocent tourist—' put in Les.

'Then they wouldn't suspect. Once they were safely on shore, I could make certain that they went to the right people.'

'And you want me to do it?'

'That's right. If you feel you're up to it. We won't force you.'

'Of course I'll do it.'

'But can we trust your friends?'

'Naturally. They're on your side.'

'Good. But they must be discreet.'

'They will be. What shall I tell them?'

'Simply say that they mustn't blow our cover, and they should keep out of the way of the Kathy woman. We'll do the rest.'

'You've done a good job, Jenny,' said Akran. 'With your continued help, perhaps we can wind this whole thing up.'

Jenny looked from one man to the other. She was feeling

very pleased with herself indeed. She saw Les in a new light now. The idea of him as an undercover detective thrilled her, and her mind went back to the James Bond stories she had read when she was younger. All of a sudden she felt a great physical attraction between herself and both the men. She moved closer to Les.

'Will I be able to see you?' she asked.

'Once we're ashore, yes. Until then, perhaps we'd better stay apart.'

'But that's three days.' She took his hand. 'I'm not sure I could wait that long.'

He pulled her close to him, his muscular body towering over her petite form.

'Perhaps I should give you something to be going on with.'

'Mmm.'

His fingers went to the buttons on her shirt and he began to undo them one by one. She pulled away, glancing across at the other man.

'Don't worry about Akran,' said Les. 'He's very broad-minded.'

He resumed unfastening her top, flicking the buttons swiftly undone, allowing it to fall open and reveal the brief laciness of her bra beneath. It was bright red, and lifted her small, plump breasts beautifully, making the bright creaminess of her flesh bulge above it.

Les's fingers were fumbling with the catch of her skirt now, undoing it and yanking down the zip. It fell to the floor. Beneath she wore a pair of briefs that matched her red bra. They were very skimpy indeed, tufts of her pubic hair visible over the waistband. She blushed as she saw

Akran running his eyes over her scantily-clad body with obvious interest.

Les pulled her to him and pressed his lips to hers. She opened her mouth, allowing his tongue to snake inside and seek out her own whilst his hands roved over her skin. He found the fastener that held her bra on and took it between finger and thumb.

'No.' She drew her head away and tried to wriggle free, but he held her too tight. 'We can't do it here,' she muttered.

'Why not? I told you Akran won't mind.'

'But I'm not . . .'

But even as she spoke she felt him snap the catch on her bra undone. She tried to clutch it to her but he was too strong, and the colour in her cheeks deepened as her breasts were fully revealed to Les and his companion. She tried to turn and press herself against Les, but he would have none of it, taking hold of her shoulders and swivelling her so that she stood with her back against his shirt, facing Akran.

'What do you think?' he asked.

Akran smiled. 'Very pretty,' he said. 'Your modesty becomes you, my dear.'

Jenny dropped her eyes, partly due to her embarrassment, partly because she did not want Akran to see the desire in them as the whole situation began to turn her on. Somehow it suddenly seemed terribly exciting to be exposed like this, her breasts bared before this stranger. A thrill ran through her as she felt Les's hand reach round and cup her soft mammaries from underneath, his fingers brushing against the puckered flesh of her nipples. She wanted to be fucked now, and she knew he wanted to fuck her. But here? In front of his friend? A fresh shudder of pleasure shook her as she considered the prospect, a pleasure that was redoubled as she felt his fingers hook into the waistband of her panties.

He pulled them down in a single movement, crouching to free them from her slim, high-heeled shoes. Then he straightened, holding her hands to her sides whilst his friend perused her nakedness.

'Here.' He tossed the fragment of lace that had been the last vestige of Jenny's modesty across to the dark man. Akran caught them and held them up to the light. Jenny knew he was looking at the traces of wetness that had come from her, and her face continued to glow as he observed the extent of her arousal, a slight smile on his face.

Les's hand slipped down her stomach.

'No . . .'

Once again she protested, but once again without conviction, her body belying any reluctance as she widened her stance to allow him access to her warm honeypot.

'Ah!'

The cry was one of pure lust as he fingered her, his strong digits sliding over the wetness and penetrating deep into her vagina. All decorum forgotten, she began to thrust her pubis forward against his hand, willing him to probe deeper into her.

He began to toy with her breasts, all the time keeping her facing Akran, who watched with obvious interest, his eyes travelling up and down her body. Despite her embarrassment Jenny found herself gasping and moaning under his caresses, suddenly and perversely wanting Akran to see her wantonness, her whole being concentrated on the pleasure that Les's hands were giving her.

All of a sudden Les let go of her. She turned to see that he had sat down on the edge of the bed. He opened his legs and looked down at his crotch, then up at Jenny.

She needed no further bidding. At once she dropped to her knees in front of him and reached for his fly, dragging down the zip and delving inside. Her hand closed around the thick shaft of his cock. It seemed to pulsate under her fingers and she dragged it out from his underpants, already salivating as she contemplated its taste.

The moment it was free she closed her mouth over the end, sucking greedily at it, her hand caressing his balls as she did so. She knew Akran was watching her every move, but she no longer cared. Her one desire was to give pleasure to the man in front of her and to receive pleasure from him in her turn.

She sucked on, her head bobbing up and down now as she allowed him to slide in and out of her mouth. She wondered if he would come in this manner, and her desires increased as she thought of his semen filling her mouth and dribbling out onto her chin. But he had other ideas, as she realised when he took hold of her hair and pulled her face up to his.

'Straddle me, Jenny,' he ordered. 'Get that cunt of yours round my dick. I wanna fuck you, Jenny.'

Eagerly she rose to her feet and positioned herself over him. She took his glistening cock in her hand and guided it toward her vagina.

'Oh!'

The sensation of his thick glans pressing against her sex

sent a new wave of pleasure through her, and she began to press down, spreading her legs as wide as she was able in order to accommodate him.

All at once she felt him enter her, his cock sliding deep inside, stretching the walls of her sex and filling her wonderfully. She sank down as low as she could, taking him further and further in until she was settled in his lap. She wrapped her arms about his neck and planted her lips over his. As she did so she began to move, working her slim little body up and down on his erection, gasping aloud at the wonderful sensation of being fucked, her breasts bouncing up and down with every thrust.

Les too wrapped his arms about her, then he flopped back, dragging her with him so that she lay over his prostrate body, her backside moving up and down as she worked her pubis against his crotch.

The sensation of something thick and hard pressing against her backside made her start. She lost her rhythm for a moment as she swung round to see what it was. Then she drew in her breath with surprise. There, standing behind her, naked from the waist down, stood Akran, his long brown cock standing stiff as a pole. The end was wet with spittle, and even as she watched, he spat on his fingers and reached down for the crack of her backside.

'No!'

She tried to pull away, but Les held her fast whilst his companion lubricated her anus, letting his finger slide inside her rectum and rubbing his saliva into her flesh. Then she felt him press his cock against the tight hole of her behind.

For a second she almost panicked. She had never been

taken in her nether hole before, and she wasn't at all sure if she could accommodate the thickness of Akran's manhood. At the same time, though, a surge of excitement swept through he as she contemplated what she was being asked to do.

To service two men at once! To allow them to simultaneously penetrate her front and rear! It was the most extraordinary thing that had ever been demanded of her. Yet here she was, her cunt full of Les's cock whilst Akran continued to press against her rear.

'Relax,' murmured Les. 'Let him in.'

Using all her willpower, Jenny fought her instinct, and felt the muscle of her sphincter ease. Then she gave a cry as Akran's cock slid into her, just the glans at first, then more and more as he pressed his hips forward until she knew he was buried as deep as he would go.

'Now move, Jenny,' said Les. 'Fuck us both.'

Jenny did as she was asked, working her hips back and forth, and at once was almost overwhelmed by the sensation she was experiencing. Never before had she felt so fully penetrated. It was as if she was overflowing with thick erections, and wave after wave of pleasure swept through her as her movements increased.

From behind she felt Akran's arms encircle her, taking her breasts into his palms and squeezing them whilst Les gripped her backside, pressing his hips against hers and urging her into still more frantic movement. She began to moan aloud, unable to suppress her wanton reaction to what was happening to her, sandwiched between two men, their massive penises spearing her lovely young body.

Jenny's mind was a whirl. It had been enough that Les

had wanted to fuck her in front of Akran. But to have the dark stranger inside her too was beyond her wildest imaginings, and the sensation of their arousal was more than she could take. She began a low keening moan of lust as she gave herself to them, no longer caring about the sluttishness of her behaviour and simply intent on enjoying the orgasms she could feel building in both.

Les came first, his body stiffening momentarily before his cock began to spurt jet after jet of semen deep into her. She gave a shout of pleasure as his cock twitched and jerked inside her, loving the sensation of the hot spunk filling her sopping vagina. Moments later, Akran too tightened his grip upon her breasts, then let himself go, his ball unloading still more creamy sperm into the wanton girl.

Jenny simply came and came, a new spasm of orgasmic pleasure overwhelming her with every spurt of come into her vagina and rectum. She screamed aloud with the sheer pleasure of it, her body dancing up and down between the two men as she extracted every last vestige of their orgasms from them.

At last, though, they were still, the three of them panting in unison. Akran withdrew first, his cock sliding easily from her rear that was now so well lubricated by his sperm. Once he was out she rose to her feet, giving a little gasp as Les's tool slipped from her. Then she collapsed back onto the floor, her legs still spread, thick white semen oozing from her sex and backside, a smile of satisfaction on her face.

Chapter 25

Kathy Prender stood, leaning on the rail and looking out at the thin blue strip of land that had become visible on the horizon during the last hour. That it was the coast of Panavia, there could be no doubt. They were due to dock there later that day, and the closer they came to the shore the more imminent became the decision she knew she would have to make.

Since her encounter with the band outside Lisa's cabin two days before, she had had no contact at all with the girls. In fact she had avoided them as best she could, uncertain how to react to them after being caught so blatantly red-handed. The encounter had put her in something of a dilemma. On the one hand they had to remain her prime suspects. After all, they had been in possession of the gems since boarding the ship in England, and no other possible criminals had come to light. For a while she had wondered if they had been the unwitting carriers of the contraband, but since the tape machine had been broken open she knew that they must be aware of the presence of the diamonds. Why, then, had they not handed them in? Surely the most likely course of action would have been to take them to the authorities aboard the ship. Their failure to do so seemed yet another piece of evidence that pointed to their guilt.

And yet she couldn't bring herself to believe they were guilty. She had had much experience of criminals during her career, and the girls simply seemed to lack the necessary guile. The way they had allowed the tape machine to be carelessly carried about the ship, despite the fact that it contained a king's ransom in jewellery, simply didn't fit with the image of the sophisticated burglar who had stolen the gems in the first place.

Kathy turned from the ship's rail and began walking slowly down the deck. She checked her watch. They were due to dock in Kulfra in four hours. Four hours! That was how long she had to reach a decision.

But in her heart of hearts she had already reached that decision. There was nothing else for it. She would have to turn the girls in. She couldn't afford to let them get ashore in Panavia with the gems. As long as they were at sea, there was no danger, but once they docked it would be all too easy for them to get the jewels off the ship. And once that happened the game was almost certainly lost.

If only she had been able to plant the artifical gems in Lisa's cabin. Then, with the real gems secure, she would have been free to watch what happened when the fakes were handed over, and perhaps would have netted an even bigger fish than just the original thief. But to take such a risk with the real ones was unthinkable. She had the interests of the owner to consider. She sighed. It was a very unsatisfactory ending to the case, but she had to retrieve the stolen goods before they docked. And that meant having the band arrested and searched whilst they were still at sea. Slowly, reluctantly, she turned in the direction of the Captain's cabin.

'Oh, sorry.'

She hadn't seen the man as she turned and had walked right into him, causing him to spill the cup of coffee he was carrying down the front of his shirt.

'I'm awfully sorry,' she repeated. 'I didn't see you there.'

'That's all right. Don't worry. It wasn't hot.'

The man smiled at her, a wide smile of perfect white teeth that contrasted with the darkness of his skin. For a second Kathy was captivated, taking in his strikingly handsome face, his long dark locks and his tall, slim body.

'Is something wrong?'

She shook her head, as if emerging from a private reverie.

'No. It's just . . . Your shirt. It's probably ruined.'

'It's not important,' he said, flashing her that smile again. 'I have others.'

'But even so, it wants soaking before it stains. I should put it in some water. Is your cabin nearby?'

'Yes, but . . . No, it doesn't matter.'

'What do you mean?'

'Well, just at the moment I'm unable to use it.'

'Why not?'

'It is slightly delicate, I'm afraid. You see, I share it with my friend and he is, well, entertaining at present.'

'Entertaining?'

'A young lady.'

'Oh, I see.' Kathy found herself blushing, though she wasn't sure why. 'Even so, you must get that shirt into soak as soon as you can. It would be a shame to ruin it.'

The man spread his arms. 'What can I do?'

Kathy considered for a moment. She really should be on her way to the Captain's cabin, but at the same time she felt guilty abandoning this handsome young man with the brown stain on his shirt.

'I'll tell you what,' she said. 'Come back to my cabin and I'll soak it for you.'

'But I couldn't impose.'

'You're not imposing. After all, it's my fault the shirt got covered in coffee in the first place. Come on, it's not far.'

She took him by the arm and guided him towards a doorway that led into the accommodation section of the ship. His arm was strong, with bulging biceps, and she felt a thrill at his closeness to her. She threw him a sidelong glance, admiring his strong profile.

She led him down two flights of stairs and along a passageway to the door of her cabin. She unlocked the door and led him inside, then indicated the bathroom.

'Take off the shirt,' she said. 'I've got some soap powder in the cupboard. I'll just give it a quick soaking.'

'This is really very kind.'

'Not at all.'

She watched as he unbuttoned the shirt and pulled it off. His chest was broad and muscular, the same dark brown as his face, with black hairs matting it. In the confined space of the cabin he seemed even larger than he had on deck, and once more she felt a thrill as she admired his body.

He held the shirt out to her and she accepted it.

Then she went into the bathroom and began to fill the sink.

'There's a bottle of scotch in the cupboard,' she called. 'Help yourself. And pour one for me whilst you're there.'

She heard the clink of glasses as she placed the shirt in the warm soapy water and began to wash out the coffee. It was still wet and came out easily, so that soon she was rinsing the soapsuds down the drain.

He moved in behind her in the small bathroom, reaching round and placing her glass on the shelf above the sink. She expected him to leave her, but he remained where he was, standing so close that she could smell him. When she took hold of her drink, she was surprised to see that her hand was shaking. She took a large swig, then coughed as the liquor burned her throat.

'You okay?' he asked, patting her back gently as she choked.

'I think so. Just took too much, that's all,' she gasped.

He took the glass from her and replaced it on the shelf. He stood for a moment, not moving, his arm still draped over her shoulder. Then he drew her to him.

Kathy made no attempt to resist, simply melting into his arms, allowing him to pull her close until her face was buried in his neck. Then he inclined his head and she raised her face to him.

His lips closed over hers and his tongue forced its way into her mouth. Kathy hadn't felt a man this close for as long as she could remember, and she responded eagerly to him, wrapping her arms about his neck and pulling him to her, her eyes closed as the sensuousness of his embrace overwhelmed her.

His hands travelled down her body, tracing the curve of her hip and closing about the plump firmness of her behind, pressing her hips against his so that she could feel the hard lump at his crotch.

He broke off the kiss and held her at arms' length, his eyes drifting down her body. She wore a short dress over her bikini, the neckline cut low so that the bulge at the top revealed a large expanse of smooth skin. She reddened slightly at his frank inspection, dropping her eyes.

'What's your name?' His voice was deep and husky.

'Kathy. What's yours?'

'Akran. You're a very beautiful woman, Kathy.'

'Thank you.'

He reached forward and ran his hand over the mound of her breasts, squeezing them through the thin fabric.

'I want to fuck you, Kathy,' he murmured. 'Does that shock you?'

'No. I mean . . . Well . . .'

'Do you want to be fucked, Kathy?'

'I . . . We've only just met.'

He took her chin in his hand and held her face up to his.

'You do want to be fucked, don't you?'

She blushed. 'Yes.'

'Will you do it my way?'

'Your way?'

'I have certain preferences. You won't be disappointed.'

'What kind of preferences?'

'Have you ever been tied up, Kathy?'

'No. That is, not for—'

'Would you like to try it? I think you'll like it. Every woman I've ever done it to has enjoyed it.'

'I'm not sure.'

'Let me show you, Kathy. I won't hurt you, I promise.'

'Well . . . All right, then.'

There was something about him that made her want to surrender to him. A certain air of authority that she found impossible to disobey. When he smiled at her she felt a tremor run through her entire body.

'What are you going to tie me with?' she asked.

Taking her hand he led her back into the cabin, where he looked about him. The window to the cabin had velvet drapes that were hung with nylon cords, apparently for decorative purposes. He unwrapped them and tested them. They were about the thickness of a pencil and seemed extremely strong.

'These will do,' he said. 'Please strip off, Kathy.'

'What, everything?'

He inclined his head, leaning back against the window and folding his arms.

Kathy's head was buzzing with strange thoughts and emotions. Ten minutes earlier she had been up on the deck about to visit the Captain. Now here she was, ensconced with this stranger and being asked to strip off for him. It all seemed crazy, and yet she knew she wanted to do it. Sex with Lisa had been good, but now she realised that it was a man that she really craved, and a finer specimen than Akran would be difficult to find.

Slowly her hand went to the neck of her dress. It was fastened by a zipper that ran all the way down to the hem, and she took the tab between finger and thumb and began to slide it downwards, her eyes fixed on Akran's.

She shrugged the dress from her shoulders and dropped it onto a chair. Then she paused for a second to allow him to take her in. The bikini was brief, a strapless top that lifted her breasts beautifully and a skimpy pair of bottoms that plunged down in a deep vee threatening to expose her pubic mound at any minute.

She reached behind her, unhooking the bra and letting it fall away. Freed from its restraint her breasts projected proudly, the nipples already long and hard. At once she reached for her briefs, peeling them off in a single movements. Completely naked now, she straightened up to face him, hands at her sides, her legs placed slightly apart.

For a full minute neither of them moved, she trembling and naked whilst he admired her lovely body. His eyes were almost like a physical caress, lingering on her contours and she began to feel a warm wetness between her legs as he took in her beauty.

'What now?' she said at last.

'Lie on the bed, and place your arms above your head.'

She crossed to the bed, lowering herself into a sitting position, then stretching out, her hands reaching up for the metal bedhead behind her. She spread her legs slightly, aware of the wetness that glistened on her sex lips.

He came and sat beside her on the bed. She longed for his caress on her body, pressing her breasts forward to encourage him to handle them, but he paid no attention, concentrating on her arms. He took her left wrist and lifted it, wrapping the cord half a dozen times about it before securing it with a knot. It was quite tight, but the rope was soft so that there was no pain.

He dragged her wrist up to the metal bar at the corner of the bed and tied it there with a few turns of the cord. Then he stretched the end across to her right wrist and began securing that in a similar manner.

When he had finished she was quite unable to move her hands. They were completely immobilised, leaving her feeling both vulnerable and excited. Once again she longed for his touch on her body, but clearly he was not yet finished.

He moved to the foot of the bed and began wrapping the second of the two cords about her ankle. This he tied as tightly as her wrists, then dragged it down toward the bottom corner of the bed, pulling her body taut as he fastened it to the bed. It only remained to immobilise her other leg in the same manner and she was totally at his mercy, her body stretched wide, her breasts pulled slightly oval by the tension in them, her sex lips parted to reveal the pink wetness inside.

'How do you feel, Kathy?' he asked.

'Helpless. And turned on. Touch me, Akran, please.'

He smiled, settling down on the edge of the bed beside her. He reached out and took hold of her breast, running his fingers over the smooth skin and rolling the nipple between his fingers. She gave a little moan of pleasure as he did so, her body writhing slightly despite the restrictions on her movements.

He slid his hand down, over her belly, combing her pubic hair for a moment before sliding his fingers into the heat of her crack.

'Ah!'

Her hips suddenly jumped forward as he found her love bud and began rubbing it with his fingers. Kathy was extraordinarily aroused now, the bondage somehow increasing her sensitivity to the gentleness of his touch. He watched her as he stroked, clearly pleased with the control he had over her.

'Oh Akran,' she gasped. 'You've got to fuck me. I'm going mad like this.'

'And to think it was all so easy,' he said quietly.

'What do you mean?'

'Well, I would have thought a trained detective like yourself would have been too clever to end up in a situation like this.'

Kathy felt a cold feeling at the pit of her stomach. 'I don't understand,' she said.

'I think you do, Detective Inspector,' he replied.

'Wh-what are you saying? I told you, my name's Kathy.'

'I'm sure it is,' he murmured, still toying with her clitoris. 'But I also know you to be a member of the British police. And that is not good for me.'

'The police? But that's rubbish!'

'Not rubbish, I think. That's why I have to ensure that you do nothing to hinder me and my partner until the goods are safely off the ship.'

'You can't do this to me,' she protested. 'This is kidnap. It's against the law.'

'Against whose law? You are not on British territory now. Right now you're nowhere, and pretty soon you'll be in Panavia. And there the laws on keeping a woman captive are very different.'

Kathy stared. 'You don't mean I'm . . .'

He shook his head. 'Don't worry,' he said. 'Delectable though your body is, it would be too much trouble to smuggle you ashore and into one of our Pleasure Houses.'

'Pleasure Houses?'

'They are places where indemnified women are kept for the pleasure of their masters.'

'But surely that's against the law?'

'Of course there are laws governing how they are treated. But in Panavia a man's house is his castle, as I think you English say. Any girl would have to escape from the place in order to make a complaint.'

'But that's terrible.'

'Why? The men are happy and the women are given all the pleasure they might crave. Anyhow, you are safe from such a fate, unlike the young ladies who were carrying the jewels.'

'The ladies who. . . What do you mean?'

'The pop group. Those delectable young fillies have been the unwitting carriers of the gems since the ship left England. Later today they will hand them over to us in the misguided belief that we are policemen. After that, their fate will be in our hands.'

'You can't mean you're going to keep them in Panavia against their will?'

'Naturally we couldn't allow them back once we've got the gems. Besides, they will make very pretty adornments to my master's collection.'

'You swine. You won't get away with it.'

He sighed. 'I had hoped for a less clichéd response from you I must say. Now I must put this on you.'

He ceased toying with her love bud and reached into his pocket, pulling out something black with straps hanging from it. He held it up, and Kathy realised with a shock that it was a ball gag. She shook her head from side to side, trying to hold her mouth shut, but he was too strong for her and soon had it between her teeth, the straps fastened behind her head.

'There,' he said. 'That's much better. I don't think you'll be moving from there in a hurry.'

'Mmff!' She glared at him.

'Now,' he went on. 'What about that fuck you were asking for just now?'

Kathy's eyes widened. He surely wasn't going to take advantage of her now? It seemed impossible. And yet she was completely unable to prevent him, trussed and naked as she was. She stared down between her breasts as his fingers found her vagina once more.

'Mmmm!'

The sound was half protest, half groan of pleasure as he felt for her still swollen clitoris. Despite herself, Kathy was still extremely turned on, and the crudity of his caress did nothing to decrease her arousal, nor to stem the flow of wetness which was leaking from her onto her thigh.

'You do still want it, don't you?' he asked with a grin.

Kathy shook her head in denial. But at the same time she knew he was right. Deep down her body craved penetration, and when she saw him reach for the zip on his fly she felt the muscles of her sex twitch in anticipation.

His cock seemed huge. She wondered if it had been such a long time since she'd seen one that she'd forgotten. But no, she was certain it was the biggest she had ever seen, thick and rampant with a bead of moisture shining on the tip.

He straddled her, settling down on her stomach, his brown, hairy body a stark contrast to her pale and smooth skin. Her eyes were fixed on his cock as he sat astride her, and on the heavy balls that hung down beneath his thick black mat of pubic hair.

He started to move up her body.

At first she thought he wanted her to suck him. But how could she with the gag filling her mouth? Then, to her surprise, he placed his cock down her cleavage and, taking one of her breasts in each hand, pressed them together, trapping his erection in between.

He began to move, working his hips back and forth as he screwed her breasts. Kathy lifted her head, watching in fascination as his thick penis slid in and out of the valley between them. The glans was wet and shining now, and she could feel his massive weapon throb as he pleasured himself.

It was an extraordinary sensation, being tit-fucked. The exquisite feel of his hard rod against the softness of her mammaries, the chafing of his hands against the sensitive flesh of her nipples and the sight of his erection so close to her face all combined to stimulate her wonderfully. For a moment she thought he would come like that. Squirting his spunk over her face and breasts. The idea excited her somehow, and she braced herself in anticipation as Akran continued his smooth thrusts.

All of a sudden, though, he released her breasts and sat back.

'Time to fuck you properly,' he said. 'After all, that's what you asked for.'

Once again she shook her head, but her body answered for her, her nipples stiff and upward-pointing, her sex still wet, her hips undulating as if she was already being taken.

He manoeuvred himself back until he was kneeling between her legs looking down at her outspread body. Then he lay forward, his hand holding his cock as he guided it towards her open thighs.

'Mmmm.'

Once again she could manage nothing more than a muffled grunt as he penetrated her, his massive weapon sliding ever deeper into her until their pubises were in contact and she could feel the weight of his balls against her skin. Then, with a slow and easy movement, he began to work his hips back and forth, bringing yet another muffled groan from his captive.

For Kathy, it was hell and heaven all at once. On the one hand she hated this man for taking advantage of her as she was, but on the other the sensation of being penetrated was wonderful, and she writhed about beneath him, pressing her hips upwards against his as he began to fuck her hard.

Akran used her as another man might use an inflatable doll, except that Kathy was very real indeed, as were her desires. He took her with gusto, his backside pumping up and down, pounding her body so that her breasts shook with every stroke. All at once Kathy ceased to care about anything but the pleasure he was giving her, abandoning herself to the sheer gratification that the sex was bringing.

When he came, she came too, her body fairly dancing beneath his as her cunt accepted his spunk. Somehow the bondage served only to increase her pleasure and her muffled screams of passion betrayed her enjoyment to him.

Akran continued to thrust into her until his ardour was spent. Then he withdrew, leaving her groaning on the bed, her stretched cunt dribbling his sperm onto the bedspread. He rose to his feet, smiling down at his conquest as she lay panting and helpless on the bunk.

He gave her a kind of mock salute.

'Farewell, Detective Inspector,' he said. 'Let it never be said that you failed to get your man.'

And with that he left her, still trussed and immobile, and closed the cabin door behind him.

Chapter 26

'Mmm. This place is heavenly,' said Lisa.

'You're not kidding,' replied Jenny. 'It's so secluded. Nobody would ever know we were here.'

She stretched her body languidly in the warm sand, her face turned up towards the deep blue sky. Beside her Jenny was applying more suntan oil to her legs, rubbing it in with a smooth, lazy motion.

'What's the time?' she asked.

'Does it matter?' replied Lisa. 'In a place like this, time seems meaningless.'

'I know what you mean,' said Jenny. 'It's just that Les and Akran must be due quite soon.'

Lisa propped herself up on one elbow and stared down at her petite companion.

'Do you think we should be more decent?' she asked.

Both girls were totally naked, their clothes long since confined to their beach bag. Now, as she stared at Jenny's lovely young breasts already browned by the sun, Lisa felt a familiar stirring within her.

'They won't mind,' said Jenny, lying back, oblivious to her friend's gaze. 'I expect they'll quite like it.'

So far the afternoon had gone exactly as planned.

The ship had docked at lunchtime, and by two o'clock the passengers were filing ashore. Jon had retrieved the jewellery box from the safe and had brought the precious bag to Lisa's cabin, where the girls had gathered. They had watched in silence as Lisa had emptied the bag's contents onto the table and counted the gems. Once they were satisfied that none was missing, they had replaced them and stowed them in the bottom of the beach bag.

'Right,' said Lisa. 'Let's go.'

Dee shook her head. 'Sorry, Lisa,' she said. 'You and Jenny will have to go it alone. Trixie and I want to do a bit of work on that new number for next week, and Jon's got a new act joining the ship this afternoon.'

Jenny pouted. 'That's a pity,' she said. 'I thought you'd all want to be in at the final act.'

'We would, Jenny,' said Dee. 'But duty calls. Anyhow, you two should be able to manage okay on your own. Les has given you a map, hasn't he?'

'Yes. Apparently we're to meet him at a quiet beach just outside town. Akran's even given me the cab fare.'

'Well then, I guess you'll cope. After all, there's two of you, and two of them. That seems a pretty good equation.'

'You trying to pair us off?' asked Lisa.

'From what I hear of Jenny's experience with them, they don't need a pair,' said Trixie.

Jenny blushed. 'It was just something that happened on the spur of the moment, that's all,' she said.

Lisa put her arm round her friend. 'Don't be embarrassed, Jenny,' she smiled. 'I thought the whole thing sounded a lot of fun.'

And so Lisa and Jenny had left the ship on their own that afternoon. As they passed through the Customs shed, almost unnoticed by the men who manned it, they spotted Les and Akran being led into a separate room.

'Looks like Akran was right, Jenny,' said Lisa. 'It's a good thing they entrusted the goods to us.'

The cab had dropped them off on a quiet piece of road about five miles from the port. There they had followed Akran's instructions and found themselves on a small secluded beach lapped by the warm waters of the Mediterranean. Jenny had stripped off at once, eschewing her bathing costume and plunging naked into the waves. After a swift glance about her, Lisa had followed, and soon the pair of them were splashing happily in the surf. Now, as they lay sunning themselves on the sand, Lisa found time to contemplate her lovely young friend's body.

Jenny was lying gazing out to sea, her back half turned to her friend. Lisa stretched out a hand and placed it on her flank, tracing the curve of her waist and running her fingers up to her breast, which she took in her palm and squeezed gently. She was rewarded with the sensation of her friend's nipple puckering to hardness at once.

Jenny looked back at her.

'What are you up to?'

'Just having a little feel,' said Lisa, smiling mischievously.

'A little feel, eh?' Jenny returned her smile. 'I know you, Lisa Smythe. A little feel usually leads to a much bigger one.'

'I haven't heard you complaining.'

'Maybe you haven't been listening hard enough.'

Lisa's face fell. 'Hey, Jenny. I know you've got this thing going with Les. It's not that serious, is it?'

Jenny laughed. 'It's okay, Lisa,' she said. 'I still feel the same about you.'

'Even so, if this thing with Les is special . . .'

Jenny turned over, so that she was facing her friend.

'Listen, Lisa,' she said. 'I've got no illusions about Les. He's not the type to get serious.'

'And are you?'

'Are you kidding? Okay, Les is good fun. And he's got a fantastic cock. But I told you about Akran, and the way they both fucked me together. Now does that sound like the way a couple who were serious about one another would act?'

'So you think there's no future to the relationship?'

'Hell, no. Once we leave Panavia I'll be history to him. And him to me. Besides, I've got some serious fucking to do before I think about settling down. Anyhow, what about you and Kathy?'

'What about us?'

'Well, you two were seeing quite a lot of each other for a while. Was that serious?'

'What, after she turned out to be after the diamonds?'

'But you didn't know that before.'

'No. You're right. And she really did seem to enjoy being with me. I guess she's a good actor, that's all.'

'So neither of us is about to get hitched, then,' laughed Jenny.

'I guess you're right. Hey, come here.'

Lisa placed a hand behind Jenny's head and pulled her

close. Jenny did not resist, nor did she complain when Lisa placed her mouth over hers.

The kiss began tentatively, their lips barely touching, nibbling gently at one another. Jenny placed her hand over Lisa's breast, caressing it in her palm. Lisa did the same to Jenny, her hands running over the soft globes. Then she pulled her friend closer, and they began kissing in earnest, their tongues meeting inside their mouths. Lisa dragged Jenny on top of her, their breasts crushed together. She forced her knee up between Jenny's legs and began rubbing her crotch with her thigh. The smaller girl reacted with a gasp. She pulled her face away.

'Not here, Jenny,' she said, almost in a whisper. 'Someone might see us.'

'Like who?'

'I don't know. Anybody. We don't know who might pass by.'

'And what if they did? You afraid of something?'

'Of course not. It's just . . .'

'Just nothing. I want you to lick my cunt, Jenny. And I don't care who sees. I'm so randy right now I'll bring myself off if you're not interested.'

Jenny frowned for a moment, then her face broke into a grin.

'You're incorrigible, Lisa,' she said. 'So it's a sixty-niner is it?'

'You're damned right it is. Wait a minute, though. Try this.'

Jenny watched as her friend rummaged in her beach bag, at last emerging triumphant with a bottle of red wine in her hand.

'What, you're planning to use a bottle?' she asked incredulously.

'Not a bad idea,' laughed Lisa. 'But actually, I've got an even better one. Hang on whilst I open this.'

She pulled a corkscrew from the bag and began to twist it into the cork. Then she levered it out with a pop.

'Fancy some?' she asked.

'What, straight out the bottle?'

'Better than that. Just watch.'

So saying, Lisa stretched herself out on her back and planted her legs as wide apart as she was able. Then she raised her backside from the sand. Jenny looked on, puzzled, as she picked up the bottle again. Then her jaw dropped as her friend pulled apart her sex lips with finger and thumb and inserted the neck of the bottle inside. She carefully upended it, and with a glug, a quantity of the wine came out of the bottle. Lisa removed it with equal care, a dribble of the red liquid escaping from her vagina and running down the crack of her backside.

'Care for a drink now, Jenny?' she asked, raising an eyebrow.

Jenny moved between her friend's wide-stretched thighs and gazed down at her open sex. It was brimming with wine, and as she watched the muscles contracted, allowing yet another drop to escape.

'Come on Jenny,' urged Lisa. 'Drink up.'

Tentatively, Jenny lowered her head. The aroma that reached her nostrils was an odd mixture of wine and feminine arousal. She protruded her tongue and lapped at the liquid. It tasted dry and fruity. As she drank, a shudder ran through her friend's body.

'More,' gasped Lisa.

Jenny went down again, this time licking deep inside, slurping up the delicious liquid as it came to the surface. She pressed her face against Lisa's crotch, sucking hard and swallowing the wine down. Then her tongue was inside once more, licking out the last dregs from Lisa's vagina. Lisa gasped and wriggled as she did so, pressing her crotch upward into her face, her eyes tight shut, her expression a picture of pure lust.

Jenny raised her head. Her mouth was covered in wine, a drop of it trickling down her chin and making a narrow rivulet between her breasts.

'Shit, I didn't know wine could taste that good,' she said. 'Do it again.'

Once more Lisa filled her love hole with the fluid and once more Jenny slurped it from her, making the girl groan aloud with the sensation as she lapped at her. This time Lisa came very close to orgasm, and by the time Jenny had finished she was crying aloud with sheer lust.

'My turn,' said Jenny. 'Do it to me.'

'Okay,' panted Lisa. 'Lie on your back, baby, and show me your cunt.'

Jenny did as she was asked, raising her pubis as high as she was able. The neck of the bottle felt hard and cold against the sensitive flesh of her sex, and the sensation as the cool liquid poured inside her made her start.

'Steady, Jenny,' said Lisa. 'The best is yet to come.'

Jenny stared down between her breasts as Lisa lowered her head over her open crotch.

'Oh!'

She was quite unable to suppress the cry as she felt her

251

friend's tongue make contact with her slit. Moments later her cries turned to ones of ecstasy as every drop of the wine was lapped from her. Even after it was finished Lisa continued to tongue her, each touch sending her into new paroxysms of pleasure.

Between them the two wantons finished the bottle of wine, taking it in turns to drain one another's vaginas, each bringing the other to the point of coming until, as Jenny lapped the final drops from Lisa, the girl finally let go, her screams ringing out as her orgasm overcame her. Jenny continued her licking, prolonging her friend's climax for minute after minute until at last she was spent, flopping back on the sand with a blissful smile on her face. Only then did Jenny stop, collapsing on top of her prostrate friend and kissing her on the lips.

'Oh, wow, that was something else, Lisa,' she said. 'I'll never think of red wine in the same way again.'

Lisa smiled. 'You're the best, Jenny,' she said hugging her. 'I'd do anything for you.'

'How about giving me an orgasm then?' Jenny replied, giggling.

'Your wish is my command. Besides, it seems a shame to waste that bottle.'

'The bottle?'

'Sure. Why not? Lie on your back, Jenny, and show me that delectable little cunt of yours.'

Jenny did as she was told, prostrating herself on the warm sand, her legs spread wide. Lisa knelt down beside her and began massaging her firm breasts, flicking at her nipples so that they stood proud and hard from her.

'Mmm. That's nice,' murmured Jenny.

Lisa bent forward to take one of the protruding teats in her mouth, whilst at the same time sliding her hand down Jenny's belly, through her pubic hair and round to the gaping slit of her sex. Jenny gave a shudder of pleasure as she felt the fingers penetrate her, pressing her hips upward against Lisa's hand, her face a picture of arousal. She could feel her juices flowing more strongly with every movement of Lisa's hand, and the heat in her love nest was becoming almost unbearable.

It was clear that Lisa could sense her friend's urgency, because at that moment she reached for the bottle.

The sun had warmed the glass considerably, and when Jenny felt it touch her sex she was both surprised and gratified by the sensation. Lisa rubbed it up and down her slit, teasing her clitoris with the rough area about the neck. Jenny could barely keep still, her hips gyrating wildly as her friend teased her expertly.

'Oh God, Lisa,' she cried at last. 'Put it in me. Please!'

Lisa slid the bottle down until it was at the very entrance to Jenny's vagina. Then she began to press and twist.

'Ah!'

Jenny shouted aloud as she felt the hardness of the glass slide into her in the most intimate way possible. The bottle was long, tapering from the neck to the body evenly, so that every push stretched the young wanton wider and wider until she felt she could take no more. But it was not until she felt the cap pressing at the very entrance to her uterus that her friend relieved the pressure.

Lisa began to move the bottle back and forth, mimicking the motion of a cock inside the girl. She did it slowly at first, watching as Jenny groaned with pleasure at every stroke. As she moved it in and out she turned it slightly, aware of the extra stimulation this would afford her little friend. At the same time her hands returned to the prostrate girl's breasts, her fingers roving over the trembling flesh.

Any qualms Jenny had had about being discovered on the little beach were forgotten as she revelled in the treatment her cunt was receiving from her companion. All that mattered to her now was the long, hard object that was embedded so intimately inside her and was giving her so much pleasure. Her heels dug into the sand as she raised her crotch high in the air, her body clear of the ground all the way to her shoulders as she gave herself up to lust. She could feel her orgasm building from the very depths of her womb, and she tensed as it arrived.

'Ah! Ah! Ah!'

Jenny's cries rent the air as her orgasm overcame her, her body held rigid whilst her friend pumped the bottle in and out of her sex with gusto, each stroke sending a new spasm through her. She shut her eyes tight, her hands clenched in fists as the onslaught went on and on, until she thought she could take no more. Then, at last, she was coming down, her body slowly relaxing, her backside sinking towards the sand until she lay panting there, the bottle still projecting from her, the wetness from inside her dripping onto the sand.

'Well, well, well,' said Les. 'You two have been keeping yourselves amused, haven't you?'

Chapter 27

Lisa and Jenny were completely taken by surprise by the arrival of Les and Akran, who had come round to the cove from the back. So engrossed had the two girls been in their lovemaking that they had totally failed to notice their male company until they were right on top of them. Now both leapt to their feet, their hands instinctively covering their breasts and sex as they faced the new arrivals. Jenny was at a special disadvantage as she was obliged to ease the bottle from her vagina as the two men watched, expressions of amusement on both their faces.

'W-we didn't hear you coming,' said Jenny, her face scarlet as she dropped the bottle onto the sand and placed her hand flat over her pubic mound.

'But we heard you all right,' said Les. 'I'm surprised half the country didn't, the noise you were making.' He picked up the bottle, still dripping with Jenny's juices, and held it up to his friend. 'Looks like we missed the party, though.'

Akran grinned. 'I think we might have seen the best bit.'

'Yeah. Say, did you girls forget to bring your swimming costumes?'

'They're in the bag,' said Lisa. 'Come on guys, cut the crap.'

She stepped forward and reached for the beach bag, but Les snatched it up before she could do so.

'Not so fast,' he said. 'Where's your friends?'

'They couldn't come,' said Jenny. 'There's just us two.'

Akran frowned. 'That's a pity. Do you think they'll cause trouble?'

'Why should they?' asked Jenny. But he ignored her, turning to Les.

'There's no problem,' said Les. 'It would have been nice if all four were here, but there's not a lot the others are going to be able to do. After all, they've got to find them. And the authorities here aren't going to be too bothered about a couple more European girls.'

'What are you talking about?' asked Lisa.

'Nothing,' said Les. 'Akran was just concerned about whether your friends trust you on your own.'

'Of course they do,' said Lisa. 'Now can we have our clothes back, please?'

'Not just yet,' smiled Les. 'Why not take your hands away and give us a proper look? After all, there's nobody else about.'

Jenny looked at Lisa, who gazed back at her, then shrugged. Slowly both girls let their hands drop to their sides, revealing their charms fully to the appreciative stares of the men.

'That's better,' said Les, his eyes drinking in Lisa's full breasts and thick sex lips. 'Now, where are the goods?'

'At the bottom of the bag,' said Jenny. 'Take a look.'

'I will.'

Les reached down to the bottom of the beach bag. He fumbled around for a few seconds, then a smile crossed his face and he withdrew his arm. Akran moved closer to him as he held up the small velvet bag.

'Is that it?' he asked.

'I think so. Let's just check inside.'

He undid the neck of the bag and emptied the contents into his palm. In the bright sunlight the diamonds' sparkle was almost dazzling and the four of them stared at the gems in fascination.

'That's them,' said Les triumphantly. 'Millions of quid just held in one hand. And all ours.'

'All the owner's, you mean,' said Lisa. 'Although I guess there'll be a reward.'

Akran turned to her, a strange smile on his face. 'Well, you'll get what's coming to you, anyhow.'

'That's for sure,' said Les, slipping the bag back into his pocket.

'So what now?' asked Lisa. 'Do we go back to the police station?'

'No hurry,' said Les. 'After all, it's a lovely day. Why don't we enjoy the sunshine a bit?'

'Sounds good,' said Akran. 'What do you say, girls, fancy a swim?'

'But what about the jewels? Shouldn't we hand them in?' asked Lisa.

'All in good time,' said Akran, placing his arm round Jenny's waist. 'What about some fun first?'

Jenny looked across at Lisa.

'Well, I guess it won't do any harm,' said Lisa.

'After all,' said Les. 'It's not as if you girls aren't dressed for a swim.'

'Undressed more like,' said Akran with a smirk. He slid his hand up Jenny's ribcage and caressed her breast, making the nipple harden instantly.

'Come on, then,' said Les, stripping off his shirt. 'Last one in's a cissy.'

The two men quickly pulled off the rest of their clothes whilst the girls watched. Soon all four were naked and running down into the waves.

There followed a ridiculous game of tag, in which the four chased one another through the surf, shouting and laughing as they splashed about. They romped for a full half hour before Jenny, exhausted, hauled herself out of the water and flopped down on the beach. She lay there for a while, watching the others continue to play. Then Akran detached himself from the group and wandered up the beach toward her.

She eyed him as he approached, admiring his slim, brown body and muscular chest. Her eyes dropped to his cock. It was long and thick, dangling down in front of a large scrotum, his balls bulging. He was certainly a fine specimen, she mused.

Akran sauntered up and stood over her, his body casting a shadow over her face.

'Had enough?'

She nodded, her eyes still fixed on his penis. 'You too?'

'I fancied some other kind of fun.'

'Like what?'

He dropped down to his knees in front of her, then

reached out for her hand. She allowed him to take it, and he immediately guided it to his crotch.

Jenny took his scrotum in her palm, manipulating it between her fingers and feeling the heavy testicles inside. She stroked his shaft and was rewarded by a slight swelling in its girth.

'Suck it, Jenny,' he ordered.

He sat back onto his heels and she pulled herself forward until her face was above his lap. Then she lowered herself to his crotch, lifting his penis up and placing it in her mouth. It felt soft and warm, and she began to suck it, sensing it begin to stiffen almost at once. She sucked harder, her hands still manipulating his balls as she did so. With every suck he became larger and stiffer, forcing her lips wider apart until he completely filled her mouth, his cock standing rampant and hard from his thick patch of pubic hair.

Jenny sucked hungrily at him, her hair falling down over her eyes and into his lap as her head bobbed rhythmically up and down over his shaft. He took hold of her breasts once more, squeezing them in his large hands. She raised her head and stared into his face.

'That feel good?' she asked.

'Great. Looks like Les and Lisa have had enough of swimming too.'

She glanced across in the direction he was looking. Sure enough Lisa was stretched out on her back at the edge of the water, her legs spread wide apart whilst Les sucked at her nipples, his fingers buried deep inside her sex.

Jenny wanted to watch for longer, but she found her head being pressed down in Akran's lap once more, so she dutifully continued fellating him, her fist closed about his shaft, working his foreskin back and forth as she did so. At the same time he fondled her breasts clearly fascinated with the way they bounced up and down in time with the motion of her head.

All of a sudden he pushed her away once more.

'On your hands and knees, Jenny,' he said. 'I fancy having you from behind.'

Obediently, Jenny scrambled up onto all fours, eager to feel Akran's cock inside her. Her sex was extremely wet now, and she suddenly found herself needing desperately to be fucked. He placed a hand on the back of her neck and forced her head down. She complied at once, thrusting her backside high in her air and opening her legs as wide as she was able. When she felt his hand on her behind she gave a gasp of pleasure, her sex lips pulsating, forcing a bead of moisture to escape onto her inner thighs.

He knelt down behind her, and she felt the heat of his swollen glans as it sought out her love hole. For a second she thought he was about to bugger her once more as the wet tip of his erection lingered close to her anus. Then he slid it downwards and with a cry of pleasure she felt him press it against the portal of her pleasure hole. She opened herself to him, lowering her breasts onto the warm sand and presenting her sex to him, as if inviting him inside. Akran grunted, then shoved his hips forward and he was in her, sliding his cock all the way into her vagina.

'Ohhh!'

Jenny's cry was one of pure lust as she felt the wet walls of her sex forced apart by his rampant organ. She cried even louder as he ran his hands about her waist and his strong, hard fingers found her swollen clitoris, rubbing it hard as he began to thrust into her.

Jenny raised her head and looked across at where Lisa and Les were locked together. They were in a sixty-nine, with Lisa's lips wrapped about the cock that penetrated her mouth from above whilst Les thrust his tongue deep into her open sex.

'Oh shit, that's good.'

Jenny's words were barely intelligible, her voice alternating between a murmur and a shout as Akran pounded against her backside, shaking her small frame violently with every stroke, so that she had to brace herself hard against the sand to avoid toppling over. There was something intensely erotic about the way he was taking her. Something about his animal passion that was arousing her more than she had thought possible. This was no meeting of lovers in a romantic encounter, this was a randy little wanton being fucked hard by a rampant stud, their only aim to give one another pleasure. This was sex at its most basic, and Jenny loved it, her entire body given up to the lust of herself and her man.

Akran's orgasm came suddenly, almost catching her by surprise as she suddenly found her cunt being filled with gushing semen, squirting in copious amounts from him and jetting against the very entrance to her uterus. Seconds later the muscles of her sex gave a violent contraction and she too was coming, shouting her pleasure to the world, her body shuddering with lust as the spasms overcame her. She dug her hands deep into the sand, her face contorted with desire whilst Akran continued his violent thrusts, his thick cock sending spurt after spurt into her. At that very moment she heard Lisa's voice give a cry and she glanced across in time to see a great gob of spunk fly from Les's erection onto her friend's face as the girl struggled to close her lips about his thick rod.

Jenny had no time to concentrate on Lisa's pleasure, however. Her own orgasm was the thing at the front of her mind, as the sensuality coursed through her in waves. She squeezed the muscles of her cunt about Akran's rod, milking him for every drop of spunk, determined to keep him inside her until he had no more to offer. It wasn't until she felt him begin, at last, to relax that she did the same, slumping forward onto the sand, his heavy body resting on top of her, the pair of them struggling to regain their breath.

She felt him slip from her and straighten up. She rolled onto her back, her eyes closed, a satisfied smile on her face. She lay back in the warm sand, her legs still spread wide, allowing his thick semen to escape from her vagina and trickle from her thighs.

All of a sudden a shadow fell across her face and she opened her eyes to see Les standing over her, his cock still hard and glistening with Lisa's saliva. Beside him stood Lisa herself, her face and hair spattered with spunk, a rivulet running down her neck and between her breasts.

'Hi,' said Lisa. 'You okay?'

'What do you think?' said Jenny. 'Looks like you've just run off with my guy.'

'You don't seem to have done too badly yourself.' Lisa turned to Akran, who was already pulling on his pants. 'What do we do now?'

'The jewels have to be taken to where they belong.'

'You're handing them in to someone?'

'You could say that.'

'Will we get a reward?' asked Jenny, climbing to her feet.

'Of a kind,' said Les, who was also dressing as he spoke to them.

'What kind?'

'Well let's just say this whole incident will change your lives. And make me and Akran pretty rich at the same time.'

'Hang on, Les,' said Lisa. 'What the hell are you talking about? How's this going to make you rich?'

Les turned to Akran. 'I guess we can tell them now,' he said.

'Sure,' replied Akran.

'Listen, guys,' said Lisa slowly. 'Just what are you getting at?'

'Well,' said Les. 'You know your story about the jewels being stolen, and the thief being on the ship, as well as a copper from London?'

'You mean to say it wasn't true?' asked Jenny, her eyes wide.

'Oh, it was completely true. Every word of it.'

There was something in his tone that sent a cold feeling down Jenny's spine. 'So what's the problem?' she asked slowly.

'The problem,' laughed Akran, 'is that you backed the wrong horse.'

'I don't understand.'

'Let me spell it out for you, then. The copper isn't a man at all. It's a woman.'

Jenny gulped. 'A woman?'

'A woman who you both helped to put completely off the trail.'

Jenny stood staring at the men. Then turned to her friend. As she did so, a look of comprehension slowly spread across Lisa's face.

'Kathy!'

Les grinned. 'Detective Inspector Kathy Prender, to be precise. One of London's finest.'

Jenny's jaw dropped. 'But we thought—'

'You thought she was the baddie. That gave us a lot of amusement, Akran and me.'

'Hang on,' said Lisa. 'If Kathy's the police, then you two must be—'

'The crooks. Yes, I'm afraid it's true,' said Les. 'And you two have performed exactly as was required of you.' He patted his pocket. 'Everything delivered safely. And Akran and I didn't even have to go through Customs.'

'You bastards,' said Lisa.

'Oh shit,' said Jenny.

'So you can see now why Akran and I are going to be rich.'

'Wait a minute,' said Lisa. 'What was it you said about this incident changing our lives?'

'Well you didn't expect just to go back to the ship, did you?'

Once again a chill ran down Jenny's spine. Suddenly she felt very naked and vulnerable, and instinctively she covered her nudity with her hands.

'W-what do you mean?' she asked.

'You'll find out soon enough. Suffice to say that there are places in this country that will pay a great deal of money for a pair of beauties like yourselves.'

'You don't mean . . .' Jenny turned to her friend, who was looking similarly aghast.

'I'm afraid I do,' went on Les. 'After all, you're both so good at satisfying men. This simply means you'll be making a career of it.'

Suddenly Jenny felt her hand grasped by Lisa.

'Come on, Jenny. We're getting out of here.'

But it was too late. Barely had she spoken the words than the men stepped forward and grabbed the two girls. Jenny struggled hard, but Akran was too strong. There was a flash of metal in the sunlight and she felt something cold and metallic close about her wrist. A moment later her arms were pulled behind her and a similar band was attached to her other wrist. With her hands cuffed behind her she could only watch helplessly as her friend received the same treatment from Les. Soon the pair were standing side by side, naked and manacled, whilst the two men held them fast.

'You won't get away with this,' shouted Lisa.

'I think you've been watching too many gangster films,' replied Les. 'That's what the good guy always says.'

'I'll scream the bloody place down.'

Les spun her round to face him, reaching for her breast and caressing it as he spoke.

'There's nobody to hear you,' he said. 'Besides, if you make a racket we'll gag you, and that'll make you even more uncomfortable. Now we're leaving, and you're coming with us.'

Jenny watched as her friend stared defiantly into Les's eyes, and for a second she thought the girl was going to scream. Then she saw Lisa's eyes drop, and she knew they were beaten. Akran started to walk up the path at the back of the bay and Les motioned them to follow. Lisa hesitated a second, then complied. Jenny simply sighed and set off behind her across the warm sand.

They followed the path through the bushes and up onto a narrow track. Then Lisa stopped suddenly and Jenny almost ran into her. She stared over the girl's shoulder and her heart sank. There, parked beside the track, was a van painted dark green. Beside it stood two men, both clad in khaki and carrying light machine guns.

Jenny felt a push at her back.

'Come on,' said Les. 'We haven't got all day.'

Jenny followed Lisa up to the van, her face glowing red as the two guards regarded her naked body frankly. She knew that evidence of the fucking she had received on the beach was visible in a silvery streak that ran down from her cunt almost to her ankle, and that Lisa's face was still smeared with Les's spunk, and she saw the men grin and nudge one another as they drew closer.

'Stop there.'

The pair of naked beauties came to a halt beside the van. Akran said something to the guards that elicited a deep chuckle from both. Then one of them went around the back and opened the doors.

Jenny watched as Lisa was led inside. She was left with Les and Akran for a short time, then the guards came back for her.

It was dark and warm in the back of the vehicle, and she

blinked, trying to accustom her eyes to the gloom. Then she discerned the figure of Lisa. She was standing against the side of the van, with her hands still cuffed, but now held high above her head and attached to a ring in the wall. Her ankles too were shackled, her legs held about eighteen inches apart. She looked very vulnerable indeed.

Scarcely had Jenny taken this in than she felt the cuffs on her own wrists undone and her hands pulled above her. They bound her in a similar manner, standing her opposite Lisa. She stared across at her friend, her eyes questioning. Lisa gave her a reassuring wink, but said nothing.

The two guards pulled the rear doors closed and fastened them. Then they sat down on small seats near the rear of the vehicle, their eyes still fixed on the girls' bodies. At once there was the sound of the front doors slamming and the engine coughed into life.

Jenny struggled to maintain her balance as the vehicle lurched forward. Then they were gathering speed down the track.

Chapter 28

'Any sign of them?'

Dee made her way along the deck to where Trixie was leaning against the rail looking down at the dockside. As she approached her the redhead shook her head. 'Not a thing,' she said.

'Are you sure they couldn't have boarded without you seeing?'

'Quite certain. I've been standing here for nearly two hours now, and I've seen everyone who's got on or off. There's no way I could have missed them.'

'But it's nearly dark. They should have been back hours ago. What do you think's keeping them?'

Trixie shook her head. 'I haven't a clue,' she said. 'It's not like them to be so late.'

'Perhaps they've gone somewhere to celebrate or something.'

'Surely they'd have let us know?'

'You're right,' said Dee. 'You don't suppose something went wrong do you? Like maybe the authorities got hold of them?'

'If they had I'm sure we'd have heard by now. Where's Jon?'

'He went ashore. Svetna was going to show him the sights.'

'I bet she was. She hasn't got an apartment here as well, has she?'

'I don't think so, though I wouldn't put it past her. Anyhow they're not here.'

Dee sighed. It really wasn't like Jenny and Lisa to go missing like this. She couldn't help feeling a nagging worry about what might have happened to them. The thought of either of them being accosted with all those diamonds didn't bear thinking about. She wished now that she had agreed to go with them. After all, they weren't playing tonight. A visiting band had taken over whilst they were in port, so the rehearsal she had attended that afternoon could have been postponed. She gazed out over the empty dock, searching in vain for a familiar figure, but there was nobody.

'You don't suppose it's that bitch Kathy?' she asked.

'I can't see how. I know the guy at the top of the gangplank and I asked him to keep an eye out for her. He says she hasn't been ashore all day.'

'Well, I haven't noticed her about the ship. Have you?'

'That's a point,' mused Trixie. 'She wasn't at lunch. And I haven't seen her by the pool.'

'Don't you think that's rather strange?' asked Dee. 'After all, she must know we're handing over the diamonds today. You'd think she'd want to know what's going on.'

'I suppose so.'

Dee frowned. 'You know, the more I think about this, the odder it seems. You don't suppose she slipped ashore somehow without us seeing?'

'It seems unlikely. But if she didn't, whereabouts is she?'

'If she's aboard, we'll be able to find her. Come on, Trixie, let's search the ship.'

'What about watching the gangplank?'

'I think we've watched it long enough. I reckon it's time for action now. Let's go, shall we?'

Dee led the way to the upper deck.

'Where do we start?' asked Trixie.

'The public rooms. We'll go through all the bars, lounges, discos and the rest until we find her. Come on.'

The two girls began a methodical search of the ship, making their way from the top to the bottom and not missing a single room to which passengers had access. When they reached the final one, a small intimate bar in the stern of the vessel, they collapsed onto bar stools and Dee ordered them a drink each. They sat, sipping at them in disconsolate silence. At last Trixie spoke.

'She must have got ashore without our knowing,' she said. 'There's no other explanation. She doesn't seem to be anywhere on board.'

'Unless she's in her cabin.'

'What, all day? And with all this sunshine? Surely not!'

'Well, it's the only place we haven't tried.'

'But surely she'd come out for meals at least.'

'Even so, we ought to take a look. Just to be certain.'

'Well, all right then. Let's finish our drinks first, though.'

The two of them sat for ten more minutes over their glasses. Then Dee rose to her feet.

'Come on, Trixie,' she said. 'One last try. Then maybe we'll have to get some help from somewhere.'

They left the bar and headed to where they knew Kathy's cabin to be. The corridors were empty and their footsteps sounded unnaturally loud as they made their way along. When at last they reached the door they hesitated.

'What shall we do?' asked Trixie.

'Knock, I suppose.'

'What are we going to say if she answers?'

'We just ask her straight where Jenny and Lisa are.'

'But what if—'

'Oh, never mind that,' said Dee impatiently. 'She's probably not even in there.'

She raised her fist and rapped three times on the door.

The two girls waited silent and expectant. Thirty seconds passed. A minute.

'There's nobody there,' said Trixie.

'I guess you're right. Still, let's try once more.'

Dee knocked on the door again and they listened.

'Nothing,' said Trixie. 'We're flogging a dead horse Dee.'

'Shh!' said Dee. 'Do you hear something?'

'What?'

'A thumping sound. Listen.'

Both girls held their breath and strained their ears.

'There!' said Dee. 'Did you hear it that time?'

'I think you're right. There *is* a thumping noise. Perhaps it's the ship's engines.'

'What, in port? Get real, Trixie. No, I think there's somebody in there.'

'Who, Kathy? And if it is her, why doesn't she answer?'

'I'm not sure. But we've got to find out.'

Dee grasped the doorhandle and turned. The door stayed firmly shut.

'Damn, it's locked,' she said.

'Now what?'

'We've got to get hold of a key.'

'But how?'

'Are you still fucking that cabin steward, Trixie?'

'Occasionally. Why?'

'He's bound to have a skeleton key to all the cabins. He'd need it in his job. Do you think you could get it from him?'

'I'm not sure.'

'Well, you've got to try. Where will he be right now?'

'In the laundry room. He's on duty tonight, he told me so.'

'You've got to get the key off him. Go up now and see if he's there.'

Trixie hesitated. 'I don't know,' she said. 'He's probably not allowed—'

'Well, persuade him. Use your charms. Both of them.'

Trixie grinned. 'Well, now you come to mention it, he is quite fond of them.'

'Good. I'll wait here. Be as quick as you can.'

It was another ten minutes before Trixie returned, triumphantly bearing the key.

'Nice work, Trixie,' said Dee. 'He was agreeable then?'

Trixie smiled wryly. 'You should hear what I had to promise him. I'll be up all night. Or rather he will.'

'I'm sure you'll manage. Meanwhile let's get this door open.'

Trixie inserted the key in the lock and turned it. Then

she twisted the handle and pushed. It swung open. The two girls stepped into the cabin, which was in complete darkness. Dee fumbled for the light switch and pressed it.

'What the—'

'Oh my God!'

They stopped short, staring at the figure stretched out on the bunk. There lay Kathy, just as Akran had left her, stark naked and secured to the four corners of the bed. The two girls' jaws dropped.

'What happened to you?' gasped Dee,

'Mmff.' Kathy shook her head from side to side, the gag still filling her mouth. Dee dropped to her knees beside her and reached round behind her head for the straps that held the gag in place. She undid them and pulled it out of Kathy's mouth.

'Thank God for that,' gasped Kathy. 'I thought nobody would ever come.'

'What's going on, Kathy?' demanded Dee. 'What the hell are you doing here?'

'Well, I'm not exactly waiting for a bus.'

'I used to have a guy that liked to tie me up like that,' mused Trixie. 'It was quite exciting, really. First of all he'd strip all my clothes off. Then he'd get this big leather—'

'Never mind that now,' interrupted Dee. 'Kathy, what have you done with Lisa and Jenny?'

'What have *I* done?'

'Yeah. We know you're the jewel thief, because the policemen, Les and Akran told us so.'

'What? You thought those two were police?'

'Of course they are. That's why we put them onto you.

We know you stole those diamonds and planted them in Trixie's case.'

'Oh hell,' gasped Kathy. 'No wonder you all turned against me. You've got it all wrong.'

'What do you mean?'

'Look in the top drawer of my dresser. You'll find a leather card-case in there.'

Trixie opened the drawer and reached inside. She pulled out the case and opened it. Then her mouth fell open.

'What is it?' asked Dee.

'It's an identity card. Belonging to Detective Inspector Kathy Prender.'

'You don't mean—?'

'Yes. She's the bloody copper.'

'Oh shit.'

'So Les and Akran—'

'Are the thieves,' said Kathy. 'And we've got to stop them before they get those gems ashore.'

'Too late, I'm afraid,' said Dee. 'They've got them.'

'And Lisa and Jenny?'

'They've disappeared.'

'In that case, they're in serious trouble. We've got to get after them.'

'Should I call the Captain?' asked Dee.

'Not just yet. And certainly not whilst I'm in this state. Do you guys think you could release me now?'

'I guess so,' said Trixie. 'Although I must say you look very tempting lying there.'

She reached out and cupped Kathy's full breast in her hand, kneading the soft flesh.

'Look, Trixie,' said Kathy. 'You can have all the fun

you like with me after this thing is over. Meanwhile we've got to find your friends.'

'I might just take you up on that,' said Trixie.

'Come on then,' said Dee. 'Let's get her out of this. Then we've got some serious thinking to do.'

Chapter 29

Jenny stood in the centre of the brightly-lit room, her body trembling slightly, partly through fear and partly because she was naked, so that the slightest breeze chilled her bare skin. She shifted her position to try to relieve the ache in her arms, which were pulled up above her head by the chains that held her wrists. What on earth was happening to her? And where was Lisa? This was the most extraordinary predicament she had ever encountered, and she wished she at least had the comfort of her friend's presence. They had been separated since their arrival at this place and she had not encountered a friendly face since.

The journey in the van had not been a long one, the vehicle speeding along what were obviously metalled roads for most of the time before turning off onto a much rougher surface. Shortly afterwards they had stopped and she had heard the sound of gates being opened. Then the van had been reversed against the entrance to a building and the rear doors opened.

They had taken Lisa first, binding her hands behind her as before and leading her out of the vehicle. She had found time to throw a single glance of reassurance over her shoulder as she was led away, leaving Jenny alone with her guard. It was ten minutes before they came back for her. Then she too had her arms and legs released and her wrists cuffed behind her before she was led inside the building.

Whoever owned the house was clearly very rich indeed. Jenny was taken down a long, wide corridor, thickly carpeted and hung with exotic silken drapes. At the end a pair of double doors were flung open and she was led into a large room furnished with low divans, cushions scattered all over the floor and bowls of fruit and flowers set out on tables. It was the sort of setting in which a film maker might stage a Roman orgy, and she reflected nervously how well equipped she was to play a part in such revelries. At the moment, however, there were only a few people in the room, both men and women, all dressed as servants. They stopped working and stared with interest as the naked and blushing young girl was led past them.

Jenny was led on into a smaller room that smelled of eastern perfumes and incense. In the centre was a large bath, at the side of which sat two young maidservants, each no more than sixteen years old and dressed in simple silken gowns that hung down to the floor. The whole scene suddenly reminded Jenny less of the Romans than of something out of the Arabian Nights.

The maids rose as she came in and walked towards her. At the same time her guard removed the cuffs from her wrists and took a seat beside the door.

The two youngsters eyed her up and down, giggling to one another and exchanging words that Jenny did not understand. The guard barked an order and they were silent once more. Then they each took one of Jenny's arms and led her to the bath.

She stepped in, lowering herself into the water. It was deliciously warm, the water soft and perfumed, and as she lay back she felt the tensions in her muscles begin to relax after the discomfort of the van.

The maids began to wash her, their small hands travelling lovingly over her smooth skin, relaxing her still further as they massaged the soap into her pores. They left no part unwashed, being careful to sluice out from her vagina all traces of her seduction on the beach, the intimacy of their touch causing Jenny to gasp and writhe with pleasure, making the pair giggle at her obvious arousal.

When at last she was clean, they towelled her down, then sat her on a stool and brushed out her long hair. Once she was dry all over they anointed her with fragrant oils, dabbing them onto her flesh. Finally they stood her before a mirror, putting the final touches to her hair and even trimming her pubic bush until it was a neat triangle. Then they beckoned to the guard.

Jenny had been hoping that at this point they would dress her. She felt very embarrassed and vulnerable, naked as she was, and she longed to be able to hide herself. But modesty was not to be allowed her, and she was still totally naked when led from the bath chamber, her wrists cuffed behind her once more.

Her guard had taken her directly to the room she was now in. At the centre was a pulley set into the ceiling from which hung silvery chains. He had undone her wrists only to attach new manacles fastened to these chains. Then he had pulled them tight, dragging her arms above her. He had paused then, standing back and admiring her naked body before turning to leave, closing the door behind him.

That had been nearly an hour ago, and Jenny's arms now ached from the awkward position in which she was forced to hold them. Her legs too were becoming sore, and she shuffled from foot to foot in order to ease the pain. And all the time her mind was filled with thoughts of what was to happen to her.

It was clear that she was now a prisoner, denied even the comfort of clothes, and she could make a fair guess at what would be required of her by her captors. In fact the images that filled her mind were having a quite unexpected effect on her, and try as she might, she found herself unable to suppress the stirrings of arousal deep inside her as she imagined what was in store.

Just when she was beginning to think she'd been forgotten, she heard the sound of footsteps outside. She looked up as the door opened and two men walked in. They were both dressed in colourful uniforms which owed more to a bygone age than to modern military garb, with bejewelled turbans, and long curved swords hanging from their waists. They took up positions on either side of a small dais at the end of the room on which stood a row of soft chairs. Less than a minute later, a second group of men entered. These were led by a portly man who was very grandly dressed indeed, with long crimson robes in shining silk. He was about sixty years old, his hair grey and receding, his face clean shaven. With him were two younger men, equally well robed, and behind them Akran and Les.

Jenny felt her face redden as the eyes of the men fell on her nakedness. She dropped her gaze from theirs, staring down at the floor as they took their places on the dais. Only when the leader seated himself did the others sit down too.

There was a muttered discussion between the three men in robes, then the older man turned to Akran.

'So this is your new contribution to my collection?' he asked.

'This is one of them, my lord. The other is outside. We thought you might like to explain their positions to them.'

'A capital idea. Send the second one in.'

Jenny turned toward the door as it opened again, and her eyes widened as Lisa was brought into the room. Her friend wore a pair of baggy silk pantaloons and a small waistcoat that fastened with a single cord at the front, barely covering her full breasts. She had her hands cuffed behind her and was further hampered by shackles on her ankles attached together by a chain about fifteen inches long that obliged her to walk with a shuffling gait. She stopped short in surprise when she saw her friend's predicament.

'You okay, Jenny?' she asked.

'Silence!' roared the guard who had followed her in. All the same Jenny was able to give her friend a swift nod of affirmation.

Lisa was led round to the front of the dais and made to stand before the portly man Akran had spoken to earlier. At the same time Akran rose to his feet.

'My lord. This one is called Lisa. She will be the more headstrong of the pair. Girl, this is your master, the Hazrir. I suggest you bow down before him.'

'Get lost, Akran,' spat Lisa.

'I advise you to do as you are bidden,' said Akran. 'The Hazrir is a very important man.'

'I don't care if he's the Queen of Sheba. This has gone

far enough, Akran. You've got your precious diamonds. Now let us go.'

'I think you may regret those words,' said Akran darkly.

'Do what the hell you want to me. I don't care.'

Akran smiled. 'You know, I really don't think you do care. However, we have our methods. Now kneel before the Hazrir before I make you regret it.'

'Piss off.'

'Right,' said Akran. 'Give the girl in the middle six strokes with the horse whip.'

'No!' Lisa spun round, her eyes flaming. 'Leave her alone. She hasn't done anything.'

'Six strokes.'

Jenny watched in horror as one of the guards stepped forward. From his belt he withdrew a long leather horse-whip. It was thick at the handle, rapidly tapering to no more than a few millimetres at the end. The man wielded it a couple of times, the swish as it cut through the air bringing a chill to Jenny's stomach.

'No!' cried out Lisa once more. She made a lunge at the man but was brought up short by her escort, who held her by the arms facing the naked captive at the centre of the room.

Jenny stood silently, her face pale as the burly guard moved towards her. She stared across at her friend, whose face was a mask of rage as she watched the scenario unfold. She managed to smile weakly at Lisa, winking an eye. She wanted to say something reassuring, but her throat was too dry.

The man moved behind her, and she felt the cold of

the leather tap against her backside. Then he drew back his arm and she closed her eyes.

Swish! Whack!

The whip came down hard on Jenny's naked behind, sending a bolt of stinging pain through her as it fell and leaving a thin white stripe across her flesh that rapidly darkened to a vivid crimson.

Swish! Whack!

The second blow fell with equal force, shaking Jenny's small body as it cut into her backside. She gritted her teeth, determined not to cry out despite the excruciating pain.

Swish! Whack!

'All right,' shouted Lisa suddenly. 'I'll do what you ask. I'll kneel before the hasbeen, or whatever he's called.'

'Hazrir,' corrected Akran. 'And you'll do well to show him some respect. Still, I'm glad to know you're seeing some sense at last. Continue with the punishment.'

'Wait a minute,' cried Lisa indignantly. 'I've said I'll agree.'

'And I've said six strokes,' said Akran. 'The punishment must be carried out.'

'You sadistic bastard.'

'On the other hand, I could double it to twelve strokes.'

Lisa opened her mouth to reply, then obviously thought the better of it and closed it again. Instead she glared at Akran.

Swish! Whack!

Once again Jenny's backside stung abominably as the whip descended, leaving another bright stripe across the creamy flesh of her behind. Her whole rear seemed to be on fire now and it was all she could do to stand still as the man drew back his arm once more.

Swish! Whack!

The force of the blows was undiminished, each one rocking her forward in her chains and sending a shooting pain through her as she struggled to remain silent under the onslaught. Only one blow to go now and she closed her eyes as she heard the swish of the cane once more.

Swish! Whack!

The final stroke landed, cutting yet another stripe across her burning behind. Then it was over, and she hung panting from her manacles, her body shiny with sweat, her breasts rising and falling as she fought to remain in control. She opened her eyes to find herself staring into Lisa's. The girl had stopped struggling now and simply stood, staring in dismay at her friend. Once again Jenny managed a wink to reassure her friend.

'Now,' broke in Akran. 'I think you were about to kneel before our leader?'

'Not until you let her down.'

Akran's eyes narrowed. 'We had an agreement,' he said.

'And I'm quite prepared to keep my side of it. I'll do whatever you ask, Akran. Just undo her chains, that's all.'

Akran hesitated for a moment, then nodded to the guard who had carried out the beating. The man placed his whip in his belt and reached for Jenny's manacles. In no time she was free, staggering slightly as her legs took her full weight once more. The guard led her over to stand beside Lisa.

'You okay?'

Jenny nodded. 'I've had worse.'

'Now kneel before the Hazrir,' ordered Akran impatiently.

Obediently the two girls dropped to their knees. Jenny wondered at the sight they must both make, Lisa in her strangely sexy outfit, she naked, her backside striped with the evidence of the caning. There was something strangely erotic about the whole scene. Something that seemed to appeal to her basest desires. Even the pain in her stinging behind was, in a way, arousing and she felt an odd thrill as she bowed before the men.

Suddenly the older man began to speak. His voice was deep and authoritative, and Jenny found herself unexpectedly attracted by its sonorous tones.

'You are now part of my household,' he boomed. 'As such it will be your duty to please me or any of my guests in whatever way you are told. In time you will receive training in the more subtle arts of pleasing men and will be taught to suffer punishments far more severe than what you have just witnessed. Your duty will be to bring pleasure to men with your bodies. Do you understand?'

The two girls looked at one another, then Lisa shrugged.

'We don't seem to have much choice,' she said.

'A wise outlook,' said the Hazrir. 'If you behave yourselves you could find life here quite comfortable. My house is renowned for the beauty and obedience of its women, and men come a long way to sample their delights. I am certain you will be no exception. Tomorrow night you will be presented for the first time.' He turned to Akran. 'Had you anything in mind for their debut?'

Akran smiled. 'Naturally. You see these two have a

penchant for one another's pleasures. Something I thought we could exploit.'

'An excellent idea. The sight of two women giving pleasure to one another is something guaranteed to put my guests in the right mood.' He addressed the girls once more. 'Now you will be taken to your rooms. At tomorrow's party you will sample some of the duties of your new position. Take them away.'

The guards pulled the two girls to their feet, and Jenny felt the cold hardness of the cuffs as they closed about her wrists again behind her back. Akran was saying something to the Hazrir and Lisa was quick to take advantage, leaning close to her friend.

'Think you'll be all right?' she asked.

Jenny nodded. 'After all, we're only going to get fucked. I think I can stand that.'

Lisa smiled. 'Lie back and think of England and all that?'

'Lie back nothing. To be honest, the idea makes me horny as hell.'

'Shit, I thought that was just me. Still, we've got to find a way out of here.'

'Do you think Dee and Trixie will come looking for us?'

'I'm sure of it. Meanwhile, try to keep out of trouble. Your backside's red as a beetroot.'

At that moment the girls' respective guards pulled them apart, and Akran began to speak again.

'These two men are the Hazrir's sons,' he said, indicating the men in the bright robes who sat on either side of their leader. 'They have expressed a wish to sample your charms. Step up here.'

Lisa and Jenny received a shove from behind and each stepped up onto the dais in front of the men, who had risen to their feet. Jenny gazed into the face of the one in front of her. He was in his middle forties, with deep-set eyes and a thick moustache. He reached out a hand and ran it over her breast, his fingers caressing the nipple to hardness. Jenny felt a wetness seep into her sex as he stroked her, and all of a sudden she realised how turned on she was. The enforced nudity, the bondage, even the beating had all kindled a fire within her that yearned for satisfaction. When he slid a finger into her slit her cry could be heard all round the room.

The man smiled. 'It is good,' he said. 'I think you are ready for my cock.'

Jenny made no reply, but when he indicated the door she did not hesitate, allowing him to lead her from the room, her sex already throbbing in anticipation of what was to come.

There were some aspects of being a sex slave that she thought she was going to like.

Chapter 30

Dee and Trixie rose to their feet as Kathy entered the café and approached them.

'Any luck?'

'Have you found them?'

'Come on, Kathy, tell us!'

Kathy waved a hand. 'Sit down a minute,' she said. 'I'll tell you what I know.'

The two girls sat down once more at their table and gazed expectantly at the young policewoman.

It had been Kathy's idea to come into town to visit the local police station. The other two had been nervous about the idea, afraid to implicate themselves in the jewellery smuggling plot in such a foreign country. They knew that the law in Panavia was not exactly sacrosanct, and that those in positions of importance held great sway over the police. However Kathy had assured them that she would be as discreet as possible and that no mention of the diamonds would be made. She would simply flash her Interpol card and try to find out as much as she could about Akran.

'After all,' she argued, 'if they were waiting to search him when he left the ship they must know something about him.'

So she had come down to police headquarters with the other two in tow, and had deposited them in the café whilst she went into the imposing building. After some persuasion, she had been granted an interview with the Chief of Police that had lasted nearly half an hour. Now, the interview over, she sat before Dee and Trixie as they stared expectantly at her.

'Well, I spun him a yarn about Akran being under investigation for procuring women in Italy, and that seemed to satisfy him,' she began.

'And did they know who he was?' asked Dee.

'Oh, they knew all right. Apparently he's got something of a reputation around here.'

'And?'

'Apparently he works for one of the local bigwigs. A sort of local Mafia boss called the Hazrir.'

'The what?'

'It's an inherited title. According to the Chief, his ancestors were warlords who've ruled parts of this region for years. He's a pretty important guy.'

'Meaning he's not exactly restrained by the powers of law and order?'

'I'm afraid so. It's just what we feared. If Lisa and Jenny are in his power, the police aren't going to be much good in getting them back.'

'Then we'll have to do it ourselves,' said Trixie decisively. 'Where does this guy hang out?'

'His headquarters are on the edge of town. Apparently it's something of a fortress. Rumour has it that he keeps about thirty girls in there with him, as well as an entourage of thugs to maintain order. It's going to be quite a job to break into.'

'Sounds like a tall order,' said Dee. 'Any ideas?'

'Well, I got one snippet of information. Apparently there's a big party up there tomorrow night. All the local dignitaries invited. They're even busing in extra girls from local brothels and harems to make up the numbers.'

'Tomorrow night? That's cutting it a bit fine, isn't it?' said Dee. 'After all, the ship's due to sail at one in the morning.'

'I think it's the only chance we'll get,' said Kathy. 'Go in daylight and we'll be spotted immediately. Tomorrow night, though, with the place swarming with strangers, we might just stand a chance.'

'That's our time to move, then,' said Dee decisively. 'When we're less conspicuous.'

'Hold on, Dee,' said Kathy. 'Remember all the women there will be there for one purpose.'

'Meaning?'

'Meaning that if we're going to be mingling with them, we'll have to put on a fairly convincing act.'

'You mean we might get ourselves fucked?' said Trixie. 'Precisely.'

Dee turned to Trixie. 'You got a problem with that?'

Trixie shook her head. 'Just making sure I understood the way things are,' she said. 'We've got to get Lisa and Jenny out of there, no matter what it takes.'

'Right,' said Dee. 'The next problem is, how do we get in?'

'I've got a few ideas on that score,' said Kathy. 'Apparently the place has very extensive grounds surrounded by a high fence. It shouldn't be too difficult to cut a hole in it as far from the house as possible. Then, once we're inside, we find the girls and let them out by the same route.'

'You make it sound simple,' said Dee.

'That's one thing it won't be. Now let's get in the car and go out and reconnoitre the place. It's not far from here. Then we'll have to think about getting something suitable to wear.'

'I didn't think you had to dress for an orgy,' giggled Trixie.

'Well, you may not have to keep it on for long,' replied Kathy. 'Come on now, girls, there's work to be done.'

Kathy jumped to her feet and headed for the door, followed closely by her two companions.

Chapter 31

Jenny stood at the side of the small stage, her wrists pinned to the wall above her head. She was naked, as she had been since arriving at the Hazrir's house, and once again she was forced to contemplate her helplessness and vulnerability before the members of the household.

She wondered what time it was. She guessed it must be evening, though she had no way of telling since there were no windows visible from where she stood. Beyond the curtain that covered the front of the stage she could hear preparations in progress for the party, with much chatter and the rattle of crockery. Hanging where she was she felt extremely lonely. If only she could find out what had become of Lisa.

She hadn't seen her friend since the previous day, when they had been introduced to the Hazrir. After that she had spent the entire night with his son, who had fucked her with an enthusiasm she had been able to reciprocate, taking her in every way possible so that by morning the pair of them were exhausted. A guard had collected her soon after dawn and had taken her to be bathed once more, then locked her in a small cell where she had slept for hours. She had been wakened by the same guard, who had once again placed her in the charge of the two young handmaidens to be groomed for the evening. Then they had brought her here and left her chained to the wall.

She looked about her. Like many of the rooms in the Hazrir's house, the stage walls were hung with fine silks. In the centre stood a low divan, apart from which the area was bare. She wondered what role she would be called upon to play. What she couldn't understand was how, despite her natural fear as to what her fate would be, there was an undeniable excitement that coursed through her body as she waited there, shackled and helpless. She knew that her body would be used as an instrument of pleasure that evening, and that she should be outraged by the idea. The trouble was that the thought of it was more arousing than she had thought possible.

Pictures filled her mind. Erotic fantasies in which she was ravished by dark, handsome young men with enormous rampant cocks that they plunged into her mouth, backside and vagina. And the more she thought about it, the more it made her juices flow. She tried to suppress these wanton thoughts, but in vain. Suddenly she had an overwhelming desire to masturbate, and she groaned with frustration at her inability to do so. How much longer would they keep her chained like this? It was more than a randy young girl like her could bear.

Then Jenny tensed. She could hear a murmur of voices on the other side of the curtain, accompanied by a clinking of glasses, and she realised with a shock that the room beyond was beginning to fill with people. There were just one or two at first, but they were quickly joined by others. Over the next fifteen minutes or so the sound of the voices became louder as more and more people arrived. With the increase in volume came a heightening of apprehension in the young captive as she contemplated her proximity to this roomful of people.

All of a sudden, the door at the back of the stage opened and a figure emerged. It was Akran, dressed in a long silk robe, tied at the waist. On his head was a scarlet turban with an impressive plume rising from the front. Jenny caught her breath. He looked magnificent, and the contrast to her own nakedness made her face glow with embarrassment.

'So, I see they have prepared you for this evening's entertainment,' he said.

Jenny remained silent, simply glaring at him.

Akran turned and clapped his hands and a second person stepped onto the stage. It was Lisa, clad and chained as she had been the day before. She stopped short when she saw Jenny, a look of concern on her face, but the girl gave her a smile, determined not to show apprehension in front of their captor.

'Two such beautiful ladies,' mused Akran. 'I am sure you will both be extremely popular this evening. But first there is your little performance to discuss.'

'Performance?' said Lisa.

'Exactly. I am well aware that the pair of you have a certain penchant for your own sex. This is true, is it not?'

The girls said nothing.

'Well,' he went on. 'The coupling of two females is something I and my companions find most entertaining. For that reason, the two of you are going to perform for us, up here on the stage.'

'And what if we don't feel like performing?' asked Lisa.

'I am sure you can be persuaded,' he said. 'As you can see, yesterday's beating left a fine pattern of marks on your friend's backside. A new set can easily be applied. And the crowd would enjoy that too. How many strokes do you think? Ten? Twenty?'

'All right,' sighed Lisa. 'You win. What do you want us to do?'

'Simply to act out a little scenario for the audience. You shouldn't find it too difficult.'

'What scenario?'

'You play the mistress. The haughty one who is used to getting her own way. Your little friend there will act as your slave. She will wear a collar and follow you like a dog. Once the audience has seen enough of that, then you will get her to pleasure you with her hands and mouth. By the time you have finished, the watchers should be in the right mood for the rest of the party.'

'And I guess our roles will be just beginning.'

He smiled. 'Naturally. Now come with me to get changed. And you, little one, turn your face to the wall and make sure those watching get a good view of those stripes across your backside.'

Silently Jenny obeyed. Behind her she heard the other two cross the stage and exit once more. The sound from the other side of the curtain was getting even louder now, and she sensed the audience's impatience for the entertainment to begin.

She had to wait a further fifteen minutes, however, before she heard the footsteps return to the stage once more. She did not turn, but sensed the closeness of Akran as he walked up behind her. She gave a start as a hand closed over her breast, but still she didn't turn her head.

'Such smooth skin,' he mused. 'So perfect for the cut of the whip . . .'

Then he left her and she heard him walk across to centre stage. When she finally chanced a look, he had disappeared through the curtain, and as he did so a hush descended in the room beyond.

Akran began to speak, his words incomprehensible to the little captive. His audience clearly understood him, though, and his words were punctuated by outbreaks of laughter and applause.

Suddenly the hubbub ceased altogether and silence fell over the crowd. Jenny felt herself go tense as she waited for the curtain to open. At the same time, though, a thrill ran through her at the thought of the men who would soon see her naked body.

A murmur went up as the curtain swung aside, followed by applause and whistles as Jenny came into view. She remained still, staring at the wall, only too aware of the sight her punished backside made to those watching.

For a few seconds nothing happened. Then Jenny heard the door at the back of the stage open and another cheer went up, almost as loud as that which had greeted herself. Still she dared not turn to look, simply standing still, her face pressed against the wall.

Footsteps came across the stage. Footsteps that sounded unnaturally loud to the captive. It sounded as if Lisa was wearing a high heel. The footsteps came to a halt immediately behind her, as had Akran's. Then she felt something touch her flesh. It felt cool and hard as it traced the curve of her spine down to the crack of her buttocks. With a shiver she realised that it was the tip of a whip, of the kind she had experienced so memorably the previous day. It probed her behind, pressing against her anus, making her gasp as it seemed about to penetrate her there. Then it slid further down between her legs and Jenny bit her lip as it was pushed up against her sex lips whilst at the same time beginning a sawing motion, the rough surface gliding over her already wet clitoris.

The whip ran back and forth a number of times, until it was all Jenny could do to keep her backside still, such was her desire to press downwards against the roughness of its surface. She moaned softly at the sensation, only too aware of the lustful eyes that were on her body as she stood, chained and naked for all to see.

'Turn round!'

Lisa's command made her start, so close was it to her ear. Slowly, her face glowing red, she turned to face her friend, now become her mistress. Her eyes widened as they fell on Lisa. The girl wore a leotard in shiny red PVC that clung closely to her body, accentuating the smooth curve of her hips and the bulge of her full breasts. On her legs she wore red fishnet hold-up stockings with bright red boots that came up almost to her knees, the heels nearly four inches high. Over her eyes she wore a mask that partially obscured her face, giving her an air both of authority and mystery. Jenny felt very exposed indeed as she gave the audience their first view of her bare breasts and sex.

Lisa held the horse whip in one hand, and in the other was a leather collar to which a shiny chain was attached.

She slipped the whip into her belt and approached the helpless captive, reaching up to her throat. She buckled the collar in place about Jenny's slender neck, fastening it so that it made a snug fit. At the same time her mouth came close to Jenny's ear.

'Play it up for all you're worth,' she whispered. 'We might even enjoy it,'

She dropped a hand onto her friend's breast, caressing it gently, much to the approval of those watching.

For the first time, Jenny could see the audience. The room was in semi-darkness, but still the rows of seats were clearly visible, and the sight of the sea of upturned faces gave her yet another unexpected thrill as she contemplated her nudity.

Lisa reached up and released Jenny's wrists, freeing her at last. She rubbed the sore flesh where the manacles had been, then felt a sharp tug on her leash.

'Down on all fours, little puppy dog,' ordered Lisa.

Jenny obeyed at once, dropping to her hands and knees.

'Get those legs apart. Show us what you've got.'

Jenny spread her legs wide, pressing her backside back so that the pink gash of her sex and dark star of her anus were perfectly presented to those watching. Lisa had the whip in her hand again now, and once more Jenny felt its rough surface rub against her slit, leaving a gleaming trail of wetness along its length.

Smack!

Lisa brought the whip down on her buttocks with a loud crack that echoed about the room. After the whipping she had received the day before, it felt to Jenny no more than a tap, but still the slap of leather against bare flesh brought a murmur of approval from those watching.

'Move, puppy dog,' said Lisa.

Jenny began to shuffle forward on all fours, still being careful to keep her legs wide. She wondered at the sight she must make, her breasts dangling down and shaking deliciously with every movement, the nipples hard with arousal. There was something very erotic about her position, subservient before the red-clad dominatrix who wielded the whip so expertly.

Smack!

Another blow fell across her rear cheeks, which were already reddening from the first. Still she moved on, walking close to her mistress's heel like the small dog she was supposed to be imitating.

Lisa led her about the stage a number of times, occasionally making her sit up and beg before the approving audience, continuing to reward her with an occasional rub from the whip, the moans of pleasure this elicited being clearly audible to those watching. Every now and again she would administer a swift stroke across Jenny's bare buttocks, leaving a mark that shone with her own wetness, the accumulation of blows leaving her backside glowing bright red.

At last she brought Jenny to a halt in the centre of the stage and took up a position in front of her, facing the audience. She stood with her legs apart, her crotch close to Jenny's face, She traced the curve of Jenny's flank with the end of the whip before delivering another blow to her behind.

'Right, little puppy dog,' she said. 'It's time to give some pleasure to your mistress. Understand?'

Jenny nodded.

Lisa dropped her gaze to a shiny metal ring between her breasts. The ring was attached to a zipper that ran all the way from the top of the garment to her crotch.

'Undo me.'

The crowd was completely silent as Jenny raised herself to her knees so that her head was level with the bulge of Lisa's breasts. Still maintaining her canine role, she opened her mouth and took the ring between her teeth. Then she began slowly to drag it down, unzipping the shiny plastic garment as she did so. As the garment came undone, the scent of the other girl reached her nostrils, a pungent mixture of sweat, perfume and feminine arousal that sent a new burst of wetness through her.

The zipper came undone easily, the material parting to reveal soft pink flesh beneath. Jenny continued to pull it down until she felt the hard wiriness of Lisa's pubic thatch against her face. Then she sat back and allowed the garment to simply drop to the floor.

Lisa looked magnificent, her firm breasts without a hint of droop, her bare sex shaven about the lips. Her nakedness was somehow enhanced by the boots and stockings she still wore, and the mask, which gave her an air of mystery. Jenny knelt before her, gazing upwards, her eyes filled with lust for the girl.

Lisa took a step backwards, then lowered herself onto the couch, reclining on her back and stretching her legs apart so that the audience were presented with a perfect view of her open crotch.

'Suck my tits, little slave,' she ordered.

Jenny shuffled forward on her knees until she was beside her friend. She stared down at the lovely young body stretched out before her, and a new spasm of lust shook her frame. She stretched out a hand and grasped Lisa's right breast. Then she bent forward and closed her lips over the nipple.

The flesh swelled to hardness at once as she sucked at it, and Jenny was rewarded with a grunt of pleasure from the prostrate Lisa as she began to suck at the protruding teat. She allowed her own breasts to brush against Lisa's flank, shivering with pleasure at the contact. She began working Lisa's other nipple to erection with her fingers as she sucked, transferring her mouth to it as soon as it was fully hard. Lisa writhed and moaned beneath her, clearly genuinely turned on by her ministrations, her hips beginning to gyrate as her lust increased.

'My cunt,' she murmured almost inaudibly. 'Lick my cunt now.'

Jenny responded at once, straightening up and leaving Lisa's breasts wet and gleaming with saliva. She made her way down to the bottom of the couch where Lisa's legs were still open, her hips jabbing upwards rhythmically, almost as if she was actually being fucked. Jenny studied the pink furrow of her friend's slit, noting that the lips were already coated with a sheen of lubricant, the clitoris protruding stiff and hard. She ran her fingers lightly up the inside of Lisa's thigh, watching as the girl's sex lips contracted involuntarily, forcing a dribble of liquid onto her inside leg. Her fingers found Lisa's sex, stretching the lips apart slightly. She glanced over her shoulder at the men who craned forward for a better look.

'Oh shit, Jenny,' gasped Lisa, momentarily forgetting their little play-act. 'Lick me, for God's sake! Suck my clit! Now!'

Jenny placed a hand on each of Lisa's legs, pressing them apart. Then she let her face drop down onto the honeypot below.

The scent of arousal was almost overpowering as Lisa positively shoved her crotch up into Jenny's face. Jenny protruded her tongue and ran it up the shiny channel of her friend's slit, seeking out the hard little love bud and sucking hard at it, her tongue running back and forth over the little nodule of flesh.

'Aahhh!'

Lisa's cry rang about the room as she abandoned herself to the pleasure of Jenny's mouth, her backside pumping back and forth so hard that Jenny had to wrap her arms about her friend's thighs in order to keep her mouth locked against her love hole. Her tongue had found Lisa's vagina now and was probing deep inside, eliciting little squeaks of pleasure from the ecstatic girl.

Jenny licked and sucked for all she was worth, her saliva mingling with the copious juices that ran from Lisa's sex, the two forming a shining stream that ran down her neck and formed a silvery rivulet between her breasts, as they bounced up and down with every jab of Lisa's hips. The prostrate girl's squeaks had turned to moans now, which grew in volume by the minute. Jenny sensed that her friend was close to her climax, and she set about with renewed vigour, her tongue reaching deep into Lisa's pulsating vagina.

Lisa's orgasm was long and violent, her body thrashing about on the couch whilst Jenny kept her face locked to her sex. So strong was her climax that her screams of passion echoed about the auditorium, her backside slamming down hard against the upholstery. Jenny raised her eyes to watch as her friend's head shook from side to side, her breasts bouncing up and down as she lost herself in her pleasure.

It was fully five minutes before she was finally still once more, her chest heaving as she regained her breath. Only then did Jenny remove her mouth from the exhausted girl's sex, raising her head and staring round in triumph at her audience. For a moment there was silence, then they broke into rapturous applause.

Akran leapt up onto the stage again and taking each girl by the arm he pulled them to their feet and dragged them to the front of the stage.

'A truly memorable performance,' he said. 'Worthy of your host's house.'

The crowd roared their agreement.

He turned to the girls. 'Now,' he said. 'I think it's time you had some healthy cocks inside you. Woman to woman is all very well, but there's nothing like the real thing.'

Jenny felt a tremor of pure lust pass through her as she heard the words. The performance had left her more aroused than she could remember, and the thought of being fucked sent a new wetness to her hot sex.

'Right,' shouted Akran. 'Who would like to sample the charms of these naked lovelies?'

At once a cheer went up, along with a sea of hands.

Jenny took a deep breath. It was going to be quite a party!

Chapter 32

'What the hell's taking her so long?'

Jon Howland sat at the wheel of the hired car, strumming his fingers on the steering wheel impatiently. Outside the windows it was dark, and there was no moon. He turned to Dee, who sat beside him in the passenger seat.

'Do you think she's okay?' he asked.

'Kathy knows what she's doing. After all, she is a professional. Besides, that's some fence out there. It'll take her a while to cut a big enough hole. Just relax, Jon.'

Howland shuffled in his seat. 'It's all right saying relax,' he muttered. 'This whole thing is crazy. If we're not careful you'll all end up in there.'

'You got a better plan?'

'Well, couldn't we just try the police?'

'You might just as well knock on the door and announce you're breaking in,' said Dee. 'This isn't the UK, Jon. They do things differently here.'

'Even so, I'm worried.'

Dee put a reassuring hand on his knee. 'Don't be,' she said. 'After all, it's us that's going in there, not you. Your job is just to wait here and be ready to drive us back to the ship when we come out. Besides, we know what we're doing, don't we, Trixie?'

'Certainly,' came Trixie's voice from the back seat. 'Don't worry about us, Jon, we can look after ourselves.'

At that moment there was a knock at the window and Dee pressed the button that sent it whirring down. Outside she could just discern the features of Kathy.

'All right,' said the policewoman in a low voice. 'The coast seems to be clear.'

'Did you see any guards?'

'There's a couple strolling round the perimeter, but they shouldn't be a problem. From what I can see they're far more interested in what's going on up at the house. It's pretty noisy up there.'

'Good. The more people, the easier it'll be to mingle with them. What about the fence, Kathy?'

'I've managed to cut a sizeable hole near the bottom, in a spot where it's pretty bushy. Nobody will notice it in this light.'

'Great. Time to get going, then.'

'I think so. By my estimation those guards won't be by for another five minutes yet. That should give us ample time.'

'Okay. Come on then, Trixie.'

Howland laid a hand on Dee's arm. 'Just you be careful,' he said.

She smiled and kissed him on the cheek. 'Don't worry. We'll be back before you know it.'

Trixie and Dee climbed from the vehicle, closing the doors quietly behind them. Even in the dim starlight it would have been clear to anyone seeing them that their dress was unusual. Trixie wore a very short minidress, the neck cut low so that her succulent breasts almost spilled over the top. Dee had on a pair of baggy silk trousers and a very short top. In her belly button she wore a bright jewel. Kathy too wore jewellery, a heavy-looking necklace studded with gleaming gems that looked almost real. She was clothed in a long, elegant dress with buttons all the way down the front, the buttons unfastened below her crotch, so that as she walked, the full length of her thighs was visible with every step.

'All set?' she asked.

'As ready as we'll ever be.'

Kathy led the way from the quiet grove in which the car was parked towards the high, imposing fence that was visible through the trees. She took them down a dip in the land, at the foot of which was a clump of bushes. Here she paused.

'Hang on a sec while I check on the guards,' she whispered.

She moved close to the fence, taking hold of the mesh and pulling, and at once the other girls saw the hole she had cut, about three feet square and still attached on one side, so that it formed a sort of hinge. Beyond it was a wide expanse of lawn, dotted about with trees, that sloped up to a house about two hundred yards away. The house was brightly lit, with coloured lights strung across the front. Loud music was blasting from inside and several figures could be seen moving about the lawn.

'There're the guards.'

Kathy pointed across the garden to where two figures could just be discerned. They were facing away from the three girls, obviously fascinated by the goings-on at the house.

'Right,' said Kathy. 'Come on, ladies. Time we were moving.'

One by one the three crawled through the hole and crouched down in the shadows on the other side. Kathy came through last, then pushed the mesh back over the hole.

'Better split up,' she whispered. 'It won't do for all of us to arrive together. Dee and I will go left. You go right, Trixie, and try and distract those two guards.'

'How should I distract them?'

Kathy grinned. 'With a body like that, you have to ask? Now get going. And stay close to the fence until you get near the house. We'll meet up again inside.'

'Right,' whispered Trixie. 'Good luck.'

She turned her back on her two companions and began to move as quickly as she was able along the fence. Behind her Kathy and Dee set off in the opposite direction. Trixie's route took her directly towards the guards. After all, she mused, if anyone could distract them, she could.

She moved swiftly, all the time getting closer and closer to the two men, who stood with their backs to her watching the house. As she approached it she could make out the partygoers outside the building more clearly. There was quite a crowd on the lawn beside the house, with more people on a large patio that adjoined it. Some had drinks in their hands and were simply chatting. Others were locked in embraces. In the centre of the lawn two men were undressing a young woman whilst others looked on. At the edge a naked couple were screwing, his backside plunging up and down whilst she moaned noisily beneath him.

The two guards were only yards away now, and as she came closer one of them turned.

'Who is that?' he said, causing his companion to turn round too.

'Just little old me,' said Trixie gaily.

'What are you doing down there?'

'Just getting some fresh air. I guess I had a little too much to drink. I feel better now.'

The two men relaxed, and began eyeing Trixie up with interest.

'You not enjoying the party?' asked one.

'It's boring. There's no decent men at all.'

'You are looking for a man?'

'That's what parties are for, isn't it?'

'You are very beautiful.'

'Yeah, that's what they all say. I can't seem to get laid tonight, though. What do you think, boys? Reckon I'm overdressed?'

'Overdressed?'

'Yeah. Do you think maybe I should take the dress off?'

'I—'

But before he could answer, Trixie had reached for the zipper that ran up under her arm and pulled it down. The dress fell away and her breasts spilled out, plump and white in the low light. She stepped out of it and tossed it aside. Beneath she wore only a small black g-string that barely covered her pubic hair.

'Whaddaya think, boys?' she asked. 'Reckon that's better?'

The pair nodded dumbly their eyes fixed on her chest. She walked up close to the first one and felt for his crotch. His cock was hard beneath his trousers, fairly straining to get out.

'My, but you're excited,' she said, pressing her soft mammaries against his chest. 'Did I do that to you?'

He nodded.

'Better try and relieve some of that pressure,' she said.

She dropped to her knees in front of him and reached for his fly, sliding the zipper down quickly and delving within. In no time she had extricated his cock from his underpants and it was projecting stiffly before her eyes.

'My, what a beauty,' she marvelled. 'And so hard. I bet you please lots of girls with that, don't you?'

She wrapped her fingers about his shaft, feeling it twitch as she did so. She looked up at him, a mischievous grin in her face.

'Bet it tastes good too,' she said. 'Mind if I try it?'

The man shook his head wordlessly, his face a picture of surprise mingled with desire.

Trixie opened her mouth and took him inside, savouring the salty taste of his organ. She began to suck him, whilst at the same time working his foreskin back and forth with her fingers. He gave a groan of pleasure as she did so, his weapon seeming to swell to even greater dimensions between her lips.

Trixie glanced slyly out of the corner of her eye, and was just in time to see Kathy stepping into the house, the jewels about her neck catching the light as she did so. She searched for Dee, and spotted her on the patio. A man had her trapped up against a pillar, and for a second

Trixie feared that her friend had been discovered, but then noticed his hand was up Dee's top, fondling her breasts. Clearly his intentions toward her, far from being hostile, were of a much more amorous nature. It seemed that her diversion was working fine.

She returned her attention to the cock between her lips, sucking all the harder and wanking it vigorously. Then, unexpectedly, she felt a hand on her backside. She didn't need to look back to guess that the hand belonged to the other guard. Clearly he had gone down on his knees behind her, and her suspicions were confirmed when she felt him pulling her bottom toward him.

She complied, pressing her behind backwards and upwards. He reached for her panties and had them down in a second, with Trixie assisting him by raising her knees and then her feet, allowing him to slip them off her. Once she was nude he wasted no time, feeling for her sex, his index finger finding her vagina and penetrating it. She let out a gasp, the sound muffled by her mouthful of hard cock.

Seconds later something else was nuzzling up against the cool flesh of her behind. Something stiff and hot that probed the crack of her bottom, then worked its way lower towards the most intimate part of her.

'Oh!'

He slid his cock into her with a single thrust, momentarily putting her off her rhythm as a spasm of lust rocked her naked body. His cock was large and long, and it filled her deliciously as he pressed it all the way in, gripping her hips for purchase, dragging her back until she felt the mat of his pubic hair pressed hard against her backside.

He began to fuck her hard, his fingers digging into her hips as he pulled her onto his shaft. She let him rock her body back and forth, allowing the first man's erection to slip in and out of her mouth as she did so. Trixie was ecstatic, her two favourite pastimes occupying her at the same time. She loved to suck cock, and she loved to be fucked, and here she was getting a full helping of both.

As the man pounded against her, her heavy breasts swung back and forth beneath her, quivering with each thrust. The man in front of her bent forward and reached for them, taking one in each hand and squeezing them, to the delight of the excited girl. At the same time his friend removed one of his hands from her hip and sought out her love bud, sending her into a near-frenzy of passion as he rubbed the sensitive little nodule with his coarse fingers.

Suddenly the cock in her mouth gave its most violent twitch yet, and she braced herself for what was to follow. Seconds later the man was coming, pumping thick spunk down her throat. Trixie didn't miss a beat, swallowing hard as spurt after spurt splashed against her tongue. She kept her lips locked about his glans, determined to take every drop into her as his hips jabbed at her face with renewed vigour, almost knocking her off balance.

She had almost drained him to the last dregs when the second man let go, grunting aloud as he discharged himself into her pulsating vagina. Only then did she let herself come, her hips thrusting back as her orgasm shook her.

The climax was wonderful, her body rocked back and forth between her two lovers, her mouth still filled with the one whilst the other shot his load into her. Trixie allowed the two men to take full charge, the thrusts of one transmitting themselves to the other as she felt herself filled with spunk at both ends.

When they had both shot their loads they withdrew, and Trixie flopped to the ground, rolling onto her back and staring up at them, a silly grin playing about her lips. The men grinned too as they tucked themselves back into their pants, clearly satisfied with their conquest. For a moment they lingered, gazing down at her. Then the two of them blew a kiss at the sprawling girl and turned away to resume their sentry duty, blissfully unaware of the trick that had been played on them.

Trixie watched them disappear into the gloom, then pulled herself to her feet. She glanced down at her dress and panties, lying where they had been discarded on the grass. Then she gave a little shrug and turned her back on them, heading towards the bright lights and people, her naked behind swaggering as she scanned the partygoers in search of her next lover.

Chapter 33

Kathy Prender pushed her way through the crowds that thronged the ballroom, deftly avoiding the hands that reached for her as she passed. Fingers groped for her breasts or slid up the slit in her dress, trying to restrain her, but each time she was too quick for them, twisting her body away and moving on, determined not to be deflected from her quest. On the far side of the room she had espied a door, and it was towards this she was single-mindedly headed.

She knew she had only a few minutes to herself. Dee was being seduced on the patio and she had seen Trixie taking on the two guards. It meant that she could at least try to do what she wanted to do before having to concentrate on rescuing Jenny and Lisa.

Kathy Prender was a single-minded woman, and a true professional. It hurt her badly to think that she had lost the diamonds she had come so close to retrieving. Worst of all she knew it was partly her own fault. She had had numerous opportunities to regain the jewels, but had chosen not to, and had finally given the thieves the opportunity to take them ashore. True, her motives had been good. Like any detective worth her salt, she had wanted to positively identify the villain. But it was in playing that cat-and-mouse game that she had allowed the jewels to be snatched from under her nose. Now, though, she was pretty certain that she was under the same roof as them once more, and she had to make the effort to get them back.

She burst through the door and found herself in a large reception hall. On one side was a wide entrance through which guests were still arriving. Opposite was an ornate marble staircase that swept upwards. It was towards this that she turned her steps.

She began to climb the stairs. As she did so, she noted that during her struggle through the ballroom she had lost two buttons from her dress. It now fell open almost to her navel as she climbed. She wore no knickers, so that her crotch was displayed with every step. Ordinarily she would have considered such a loss to be a crisis, but somehow tonight it didn't seem to matter.

She reached the top of the staircase and found herself on a wide landing. Corridors ran off on either side, each one lined with closed doors. She chose the one to her left, and set off along it, trying each door as she passed. The first three or four were offices, all deserted. Then there was a laundry room and a small kitchen. At the end of the corridor was a door facing her. She opened it and stepped through, then froze as she realised she was not alone.

In the centre of the room was a kind of wooden frame to which a man had been tied, his arms and legs chained at the four corners so that his body was spreadeagled. He was totally naked. Behind him a woman dressed in black leather was wielding a whip, bringing it down hard across his buttocks with a steady rhythm. In front crouched another leatherclad beauty, her lips wrapped around his stiff cock, her hands caressing his balls.

Behind this tableau, her arms chained above her, was a girl. She stood facing the wall whilst yet another of the young Amazons buggered her with a strap-on dildo. There were others in the room too, tied to chairs, hung from the ceiling or simply bound with ropes, each one naked, and each receiving both torture and stimulation from one or more of the young women. Kathy paused long enough to check that none of them was Lisa or Jenny, then retreated, for fear she would be asked to join in.

She made her way back to the stairs and then tried the other corridor. This time most of the rooms were bedrooms, many of them occupied by copulating couples or threesomes. On more than one occasion she was invited to join in, but she shook her head and withdrew.

She came to the final door and pushed it open. The room was in darkness and she fumbled for a light switch. She found it and pressed, filling the room with light.

She was in an office. But this was no ordinary office. For a start it was huge, with a leather suite on one side and a vast mahogany desk beside the far wall. The carpet was thick and expensive and the walls were hung with erotic art. She stared about her in awe. This was clearly the office of someone very important indeed.

Kathy hesitated for a moment, then stepped inside, closing the door behind her. She padded across the carpet to the desk. It was the biggest one she had ever seen, with a green leather surface that looked wide enough to accommodate a tennis court. On it was a jotter and a diary, as well as a box containing a set of gold pens. She tried the desk drawers, but they were locked. Then, on the far side, set low in the wall, she spotted precisely what she was seeking: a safe. Her heart beating fast, she made her way round to it. She was about to crouch down for a closer look when she heard the handle on the door turn. She spun round just in time to see the door swing open and a man enter. He was in his sixties, his hair grey, his stature portly. He was extremely well-dressed, and his fingers flashed with expensive rings.

'What are you doing here?' he asked.

'I'm sorry. I was looking for someone.'

'In my private office?'

'Your office?'

'Yes. I am the Hazrir. Surely you knew that?'

'I'm sorry, sir. I didn't.'

His eyes narrowed. 'Who are you?'

Kathy thought fast. 'My boyfriend works for the Chief of Police,' she said. 'He got us the invitation.'

'I see. And where is this boyfriend?'

'I don't know. That's who I was looking for. He wandered off about an hour ago and I haven't seen him since.'

The man moved closer. 'He must be very stupid to abandon one as beautiful as you,' he said.

Kathy smiled. 'Thank you.'

'Would you care for a drink?'

'I really couldn't impose. After all, this is your office.'

'It is no imposition. I insist you join me. After all, I am your host.'

'Well, if you put it that way . . . You're very kind. A whisky, please.'

'Make yourself comfortable.'

The man opened a cabinet in the wall and took out a bottle and two glasses. Kathy meanwhile perched herself on the edge of his desk. As she did so her dress fell apart, revealing her bare crotch. The man's eyes dropped to it immediately.

Kathy blushed, trying to pull the material together.

'Sorry,' she said.

'There's no need to apologise. Leave it. I like a woman who is not afraid to show off her body.'

He handed her her drink, then sat down in the large chair that stood behind the desk. 'Tell me,' he went on. 'Does your boyfriend fuck you very often?'

'That's a rather personal question.'

'Nevertheless, does he satisfy your needs?'

'Sometimes.'

'Not all the time?'

'Well, I—'

'For instance, where do you suppose he is now?'

'He's here somewhere.'

'Fucking some slut? This house is full of sluts tonight.'

'Present company excepted, I hope.'

'Naturally. But doesn't it anger you that, even as we speak, he probably has his cock in another woman's cunt?'

'A bit.'

'Would you like to get back at him?'

'What do you mean?'

'Would it anger him to discover you naked with another man?'

'Yes.'

'Why not remove your dress, then?'

'Now?'

'Yes.'

Kathy stared at him for a moment. He was not a handsome man, though he clearly had been in his youth. There was a certain air about him, though. He positively radiated power, and whilst this scared her slightly, it also excited her. Besides, as long as she remained in the room, there was a chance she might get to see in the safe. If stripping for him kept his interest alive, then she was more than happy to comply.

Slowly she placed her drink down on the desk top. Then her hands went to her breasts and she began undoing the buttons on her dress. She undid it all the way down, then climbing from the desk she shrugged it off, discarding it on the carpet. She turned to face him, her legs planted apart, her hands on her hips, allowing him to take in the full length of her body, her breasts jutting proudly forward, her slit in plain view.

He nodded his satisfaction.

'You truly are very beautiful,' he said. 'Come here.'

She moved closer to where he sat, coming to a halt inches from him, her body tingling with excitement at her brazenness.

'Your face is red,' he observed. 'Does this embarrass you?'

'A little.'

'Yet you stand with your legs apart.'

'Does that offend you?'

'Not at all. A woman's cunt is a beautiful thing. The object of many men's desires. Will you make your nipples hard for me?'

Kathy hesitated for a moment, staring hard at him. Then she raised her hands to her breasts and began to caress them, taking her brown teats between finger and thumb and teasing them to hardness. She toyed with them until they were fully erect, standing out long and prominent from her firm breasts. Then she dropped her hands to her hips again.

'Your presence is very arousing,' he murmured. 'Tell me, what do you think your boyfriend would say if he found you sucking another man's cock?'

'He'd be pretty mad.'

'Would that bother you?'

'No.'

He glanced down at his lap. Beneath his robe Kathy could clearly see a bulge. She raised her eyes to his once more. Then, without a word, she sank down into a kneeling position.

She pulled his robes apart to reveal a pair of briefs against which his erection was straining. She slid them down to his knees and it sprang free. It was thick and stiff as a pole, a pulsing vein running up the centre. Clearly he had not lost any of his virility with age.

She went down on him enthusiastically, closing her lips about his manhood and sucking hard at it, a thrill running through her as she felt its stiffness. She reached between his legs and took his balls in her hand. They were large and heavy and she rolled them about in her fingers as she fellated him.

'Mmmm, that's good,' he murmured. 'Your boyfriend is a very lucky man.'

He reached for her breasts, taking one in each hand and

rubbing his palm against the nipples. She raised her eyes to his as he did so, and he winked at her.

'Do you see that desk?' he asked.

'Mmm.' Kathy's mouth was too full of cock to allow her to answer properly.

'That desk cost fifteen thousand pounds. It's made of the finest mahogany. The handles are gold-plated and the top is covered with calf leather. I had it made especially by the best furniture maker in England. Don't you think it's a lovely object?'

'Mmm.'

'I've transacted many extremely valuable deals at that desk,' he went on. 'I've signed cheques worth millions on it. But do you know what I've never done?'

'Mmm?'

'I've never fucked a woman over it. Would you care to be the first?'

She raised her head. 'What about my boyfriend?'

'I presume it would make him angry?'

'Yes.'

'Well, then . . .'

Kathy hesitated for a moment, then she rose to her feet. She moved to the edge of the desk, standing close against it so that the edge of the wood felt hard and cold against her erect clitoris. Then she bent forward, reclining onto her front, gasping slightly as her nipples met the cool softness of the leather. Slowly she spread her legs as wide as she was able. Then she turned her head round and stared back at him, her eyebrows raised.

He stood up and moved close. A shiver ran through her as she felt his thick weapon pressed against the soft flesh of her behind. He ran a finger down her crack and found her cunt, delving his fingers into it, the juices within making a faint squelching sound.

'I see you are ready for me,' he said.

Kathy did not answer, simply pressing her lovely behind back at him in an unambiguous invitation to him to enter her.

'Oh!'

A small cry escaped her lips as she felt the tip of his tool press against her sex. He pushed harder, and her vagina resisted for a moment longer. Then he was inside, sliding the length of his cock all the way into the moist wetness of her sex until his body was pressed against hers. He slid his hands round her flanks, squeezing them in under her breasts. Then he began to fuck her.

He fucked her with long, smooth strokes, his tool sliding evenly in and out of her pulsating sex. He played her expertly, his experience showing as he found a perfect rhythm, thrusting against her buttocks, each thrust rocking her body and eliciting a grunt from deep within her. The lip of the desk was hard against her love bud, and the stimulation was delicious, each stroke sending a new spasm of pleasure through her.

Kathy revelled in the treatment she was receiving, even forgetting the jewels for a moment, such was the pleasure he was giving her. The sensation of the Hazrir's cock deep within her was wonderful, and the feel of his hands squeezing and caressing her breasts doubled the pleasure.

As they copulated, the man's rhythm began gradually to increase, and she could sense that he too was becoming intensely stimulated by their coupling. What had begun as smooth thrusts were rapidly becoming urgent jabs, and the urgency was transmitting itself to her. As his motions became more violent, his hands left her breasts and rested on her shoulders, permitting him to lever himself forward against her body and penetrate her even more deeply. She reciprocated by flinging back her head, her breasts slapping down on the green leather, her mouth open in a soundless scream.

He came suddenly, his spunk pumping deep into her vagina and triggering an immediate orgasm in her. Both cried out with pleasure as their juices mingled inside her love hole, Kathy gripping the far edge of the desk until her knuckles turned white whilst he continued to pump his hips back and forth.

They seemed to come and come, their bodies still in motion long after the last of the semen had leaked from the end of his member. At last, though, his energy was spent, and Kathy gave a little sigh as she felt his cock slip from within her.

Slowly she raised herself from the desk. The sweat from her body had left an imprint across the surface, with two circular marks where her breasts had been and another showing the outline of her belly. On the edge was a smear of wetness and a white blob of semen. She bent forward and licked this from the wood, then turned to face him, running her tongue over her lips as she did so.

'You are a very sensuous woman,' he said as he adjusted his clothing. 'What is your name?'

'Kathy.' She felt a mild shock at the idea that she had just been fucked by a man who hadn't even known her name. It amazed her how her life and attitudes had changed since leaving England.

He stood before her, his eyes still drinking in her nakedness, fingered the necklace about her neck.

'Why do you wear this cheap bauble when you could have the real thing?' he asked. He gave it a tug, snapping the chain that held it and tossed it into the bin.

'Hey!' said Kathy.

He held up a hand. 'Let me show you what could be yours,' he said.

Kathy could scarcely believe her luck when she saw him crouch down at the safe and fiddle with the dial. And she wasn't disappointed. When the door swung open he pulled out a small bag. One which Kathy knew well.

'Look at these,' he said, spilling the contents onto the desk.

Kathy gazed down at the glittering diamonds.

'Are they real?'

'Of course. I only have the best things about me. You could have the best things too, Kathy.'

'What do you mean?'

'Come and live at my house. Forget this stupid boyfriend of yours.'

'And become one of your sex slaves?'

'No. You know I could not do that. Even I cannot enslave a friend of the Chief of Police. It wouldn't be discreet.'

'What would you want of me then? One of the attendants in that torture chamber at the end of the corridor?'

'If you wish. Or one of its victims. All I would ask is that you were at my side when necessary.'

'And in your bed?'

He inclined his head. 'Naturally.'

He began to gather the diamonds up again, placing them in their bag and pulling the drawstring closed. Kathy watched, her heart beating fast. This was her last chance, she had to think of something!

'I'll consider your offer,' she said suddenly. 'Only right now I've got to go down and find my boyfriend. Is the coast clear outside? I wouldn't want to be seen leaving this office.'

He smiled. 'Don't worry,' he said. I'll check for you.'

He went to the door and stepped out. He was gone no more than thirty seconds. When he returned he found her slipping on her dress again.

'It's all clear,' he said, picking up the bag of gems from the desk. 'I must put these away. I have a valuer visiting me this evening to assess their worth.'

Kathy buttoned down her dress as far as she was able, then kissed him on the cheek.

'It has been a valuable experience meeting you,' she said. 'One I shall remember.'

'Think on my offer.'

'I certainly shall. Goodnight.'

And with that she set off across the carpet and down the corridor.

Chapter 34

The first person Kathy saw on entering the ballroom was Dee. The girl had lost her clothes and was dancing naked with a young man, her body pressed against him. All around the other guests were in various stages of undress. Some were fully and formally clothed, with evening dresses and suits, as if attending some kind of high society affair. Others, like Dee, were totally nude. Here and there, on the floor, on couches or against the walls couples were copulating or stimulating one another's bodies. Some smoked pipes of strange-smelling substances or dragged at small screwed-up cigarettes before passing them on to others in their group. Some simply sat around sipping drinks and chatting. It was the most bizarre gathering Kathy had ever seen.

'The Vice Squad would have a field day here,' she murmured.

She made her way across to Dee and cut in on her partner. The man protested, but was clearly too drunk to do much about it, and soon wandered off. Kathy put her arms round Dee and the two of them swayed to the music.

'Where the hell have you been?' asked Dee.

'Just checking the place out. Any success?'

'Yeah. Lisa's in that room over there. There's a kind of stage rigged up and they've got her dancing on it, wearing a pair of boots and nothing else. The crowd seem to like her.'

'And Jenny?'

'That's a little more awkward. She's in another room off the one with the stage. They've got her chained to a bench and the guys are taking it in turns to go in and fuck her.'

'Is she okay?'

'Judging from the noises she's making, I don't think she's complaining. But we've got to get in there and free her as soon as we can. Time's getting a bit short. It's nearly midnight.'

'Right,' said Kathy. 'That's our priority then. Once she's free we pick up Lisa on the way out and head back for the car. Where's Trixie?'

'Over there, mingling with the guests.'

Kathy followed Dee's look and soon caught sight of the third member of their group. The girl was stretched naked across a table on her back. Between her legs stood a naked man, fucking her for all he was worth so that her magnificent breasts shook like jellies with every stroke. Her head was hanging back over the far edge of the table, her mouth filled by another man's thick erection.

'She certainly knows how to entertain,' said Kathy admiringly.

The shouts and gasps from that direction told the two friends that it was a good moment to intervene. As the two men withdrew their cocks from the spunk-soaked girl,

Kathy brushed aside another who was about to take his turn and pulled Trixie to her feet.

'Time we were moving, Trixie,' she said.

'What already? I was just starting to enjoy myself.'

Kathy grinned. 'So we saw. Come on, now, we're going to get Jenny.'

The three pushed their way through the crowds, receiving their fair share of gropes as they did so. By the time Kathy reached the room with the stage in it, two more buttons had gone from the bottom of her dress and one from the top.

'That's the room over there,' said Dee, indicating a door on the far side.

They crossed the room. Kathy glanced up at the stage as they did so. Lisa was gyrating sexily up there, still wearing the boots, and still proving extremely popular with the cheering audience. So absorbed was she with her performance that Kathy was certain she had not noticed the three of them, though a number of her audience had.

Dee pushed open the door of the room and they slipped inside. The lights were low, and it took a few seconds before their eyes adjusted to the gloom. Finding Jenny, however, was simple. Even despite the loud music that was coming from the speakers on the wall, they could clearly hear the gasps and groans that were emanating from the bed in the corner.

They moved closer to the source of the noise. Jenny was stretched out naked on the bed. Her arms were above her head, held there by a pair of cuffs that were threaded through the bars in the bedhead. Her ankles were manacled at each corner, leaving her legs splayed wide apart. The man on top of her was screwing her for all he was worth, his backside pumping up and down, each stroke wringing a cry of pleasure from the tethered girl. There was no doubt that she was enjoying the man's attentions.

There were two others in the room. One stood at the foot of the bed, his cock standing from his trousers. He was wanking as he watched the tableau, clearly awaiting his turn with the young captive. The other wore the uniform of a servant, a bunch of keys hanging from his belt. It was obvious to the girls that he was Jenny's jailer. Both men were intent on what was happening in front of them, and neither gave any sign of having noticed the girls' arrival.

At the side of the room was a table, laden with drinks. Kathy nudged Dee and indicated it, banging her fist against her open palm at the same time. Dee gave a nod of understanding and made a similar gesture to Trixie. The three moved over to the table and each picked up a bottle.

To have taken on all three men at the same time would have been impossible, since it would have necessitated giving away their presence. Better to deal with the watchers first, then concentrate on the man who was screwing Jenny. For this reason Kathy hung back whilst Dee and Trixie crept up behind the two men standing beside the bed.

The bottles descended together, each one landing with a dull thud on the back of the men's necks. Both froze for a second, then slumped back into the arms of their attackers, who lowered them to the ground. So swift and silent had been the attacks that the man having his way with Jenny never noticed.

Jenny did, though. Her eyes opened wide as she stared over her ravisher's shoulder at her three friends. They opened wider still as she saw Kathy raise her bottle over the man's head.

'No!'

The man paused a second, then shook his head.

'Too late to stop now,' he said, and began pumping his hips back and forth with renewed vigour.

'It is,' muttered Jenny, and Kathy understood. She remained where she was, the bottle poised as Jenny came, her body thrashing about as best as it was able, given the restraints on her. The three girls smiled at one another as their red-faced friend rode out her passion with cries of delight. It was a full minute before she finally relaxed and stared into Kathy's eyes.

'Now,' she said.

Kathy's blow was hard and accurate, catching the man just behind the ear. His eyes glazed over almost immediately, and he fell with a thump to the floor. Jenny, her face still flushed with embarrassment, looked up at her friends.

'Sorry,' she said. 'But I couldn't stop then. I was too close.'

'That's okay,' smiled Kathy. 'Dee, grab those keys and get her undone. How long have you been here, Jenny?'

'I'm not sure. I guess I lost count.'

'Where're your clothes?'

'I haven't any. I've been naked since they captured me.'

Dee worked quickly at the locks and soon Jenny was on her feet, her hair dishevelled, her body spattered with semen, a thin trickle running down both thighs.

'Boy, do *you* look as if you've been fucked,' said Trixie.

'No time to worry about that now,' said Kathy. 'We've got to get out of here. Is there a back way out of that stage that Lisa's on?'

'If you mean the one next door, yes there is,' said Jenny. 'They brought me in that way.'

'All right,' said Kathy. 'Let's get out there. We'll pretend to join her up on the stage, then make a break for it.'

The four of them filed from the room, leaving the three men slumped where they had fallen. Next door Lisa was still dancing languidly about the stage, with all eyes upon her. The friends made their way around the side of the room, then on a nod from Kathy, they stepped up to join her.

The room rang with catcalls at the sight of the four girls, three naked and one semi-naked, as they began to drop into the rhythm with Lisa. For her part, Lisa simply stared, taken completely by surprise by their sudden arrival.

'Keep dancing,' hissed Dee. 'We're going to get you out of here.'

It was at that moment that Jenny spotted Akran. He had not been in the room earlier, but suddenly there he was. He was talking to another man. She grabbed Kathy's arm.

'We're in trouble,' she murmured. 'Look over there.'

Dee followed her gaze, and her face fell.

'Oh shit,' she said. 'Do you think he's spotted us?'

'Not yet. But he's bound to any second.'

Even as she spoke, Akran broke off his conversation and glanced idly across the room. Then he froze, his mouth dropping open as he recognised the five. For a second he didn't move.

'We're in trouble,' said Jenny. 'He's seen us.'

'Damn,' said Kathy. 'We're going to have to move fast.'

Whether the five of them would have made a clean escape with Akran in pursuit was somewhat doubtful. However, something unexpected happened then that was to make the escape a great deal easier. It took the form of a sudden roar of anger that rang through the house. A roar that Kathy, Jenny and Lisa all recognised at once as coming from the mouth of the Hazrir. Everybody in the room fell silent at that moment. Even the girls were rooted to the spot.

There came a sudden tirade in equally loud tones. It was in a language none of the girls understood. There were, however, two words all five recognised. The names Akran and Les.

'The jewel valuer,' breathed Kathy to herself. 'He must have arrived. Thank God.'

In a second there was pandemonium as three servants moved in on Akran, grabbing him from all sides. He shouted in protest, trying in vain to indicate the girls on the stage, but the men paid him no heed. They pinned his arms behind him and dragged him from the room amid considerable noise and confusion.

Kathy surveyed their audience. All eyes had now turned away from the stage and were fixed on what was happening behind.

This was their chance!

'Right, girls,' she said. 'Let's go.'

She pulled open the door at the back of the stage and ushered the other four through it. There was a bolt on the other side and she slid it across. As she did so she heard someone shout from beyond the stage. Their departure had been noticed.

'Which way?' she said to Jenny.

'Well, that way leads to the cells,' said the girl, pointing right.

'We'll go left then. Come on.'

The five girls set off as fast as they were able as a loud banging began on the stage door. They ran down the corridor and round a bend, to be confronted by another door. Kathy pulled it open and they followed her through. It was an empty office with no other doors.

Behind them came a crash that announced that the bolt had finally given way.

'The windows,' said Kathy, closing the office door.

Dee tried the first window, but it was stuck fast. Trixie and Lisa hauled at the second. For a moment, this too refused to move. Then with a creak it slid upwards. Trixie glanced out.

'It's okay,' she said. 'It leads onto the lawn.'

One by one the five lowered themselves from the sill onto the grass below. Outside the door they could hear footsteps and voices, and it was obvious that time was short. Kathy was last through, and Dee slammed the window shut as she cleared it. Then they were off across the grass.

They found themselves in a part of the garden to the right of the house. Across to their left was the patio, where many guests were still gathered. Because of a high wall to their right, their escape route took them across in front of the patio, and Kathy hesitated for a moment.

'We're going to have to make a dash for it,' said Kathy. 'Time's too short for anything else. The ship sails in half an hour. You all game?'

All four nodded.

'Right. Let's go.'

They set off at a sprint, their route taking them closer and closer to the people on the patio. By the time they were twenty yards away they were spotted, a group of men pointing and laughing at the naked lovelies as they streaked across the grass, their breasts bouncing up and down with each step. Then somebody behind shouted something and the expressions on the men's faces changed.

The shout had come just too late, however. The girls had rounded the wall and were heading off toward the bottom of the lawn and the hole in the fence, well clear of their pursuers. Kathy reached it first, pulling aside the wire as each of the girls jumped through. The men were coming closer now, but in the nick of time Kathy followed Trixie through the gap and let the wire spring closed behind her. Then she sprinted up to the copse where they had left Jon.

By the time she reached the car the engine was running. She threw herself onto the back seat. Immediately there was a crunch of gears and the car lurched forward, accelerating rapidly away and leaving their pursuers staring at the rear lights as they disappeared into the night.

Chapter 35

Jon drove hard through the deserted streets, aware that there was now less than half an hour until the ship was due to sail. The girls were all silent, too exhausted to talk, huddled together as they stared out at the empty streets.

They reached the ship with twenty minutes to spare, finding the gangplanks still in place. The sailor guarding the rear gangway gaped as the five climbed from the car, followed closely by Jon. Fortunately for the four band members the ship's decks were deserted. To anyone watching they would have made quite a sight as they trooped on board, naked and dishevelled. It wasn't until all five girls were safely on the after-deck that they collapsed in a giggling heap onto a bench, oblivious to the spectacle they made, hugging one another in triumph.

'That was incredible,' gasped Lisa. 'You guys were wonderful. How the hell did you find us?'

'Thank Kathy for that,' said Dee. 'I reckon we all owe her an apology. She was fantastic.'

'Just part of the job,' said Kathy, blushing. 'Anyhow, I couldn't have done it without all of you.'

'It's a shame about the diamonds, though,' said Jenny. 'I'm really sorry about that, Kathy. If only we'd realised.'

'Don't worry,' said Kathy. 'Look at this.'

She reached into the pocket of the tattered remains of her dress and pulled something out. Something that glittered in the light of the bulb above them.

'The diamonds,' gasped Trixie. 'But how did you manage that?'

'More luck than good judgement,' smiled Kathy. 'You remember the necklace I wore this evening?'

'They glittery one?'

'That's it. You see, I had some fake diamonds sent out from London to Naples with the intention of switching them with the ones in the cassette machine.'

'Is that what you were trying to do when we caught you lurking outside Lisa's room?' asked Jenny.

'Exactly. But you soon put paid to that idea. So when we hatched our little plan for tonight, I bought a jewellery-making kit from the ship's shop. You know, a kid's toy.'

'And the jewels in the necklace were the fakes,' said Jenny.

'Right again. When we got to the party I found the Hazrir's office, and lo and behold, the idiot showed me the real gems.'

'Why?'

'Trying to lure me into his harem. Anyhow, I got him out of the office for a few seconds and managed to rip the jewels out of the necklace and substitute them.'

'And I suppose all that kerfuffle with Akran was because the Hazrir had found out.'

'Precisely. Bit of a stroke of luck, that.'

'Wow,' said Jenny. 'You really are a great cop, Kathy.'

Kathy shook her head. 'Trouble is, the crooks got away,' she said.

But she spoke too soon. At that very moment, the sound of a car's engine reached their ears. The five girls rose to their feet and looked out over the ship's rail. The last of the gangplanks was just being inched away from the ship's side when the car roared into view, hotly pursued by another. It screeched to a halt at the foot of the gangplank in a puff of blue smoke, and the girls stared in surprise as two men got out.

It was Les and Akran. Both were naked and both looked somewhat the worse for wear. As they raced up the gangplank, which had already been pulled away from the ship, the second car ground to a halt and a gang of dark-skinned heavies leapt out. They ran after the two escapees, waving sticks and shouting. By now a four-foot wide gap had opened between the top of the gangplank and the ship, but neither Les nor Akran faltered, leaping across and coming to rest in a heap at the girls' feet. As the others tried to follow, the crane holding the gangway dropped it suddenly, precipitating them on the dockside, and leaving them to stand and shake their fists as the ship eased away from its mooring.

The girls helped the men to their feet. Both had bruised and bloody faces, and their skin was striped all over with whip marks. They gazed about themselves, as if barely aware of where they were, then stared at the naked girls.

'Well, guys,' said Dee. 'It looks like your friends didn't take too kindly to being charged a small fortune for a few pieces of glass.'

'You bloody bitches,' snapped Les. 'I'll make you sorry for this.'

'I think you may find that rather difficult,' said Kathy. 'Seeing as you'll be spending the rest of the voyage in the ship's cell.' She turned to the others. 'What do you think of this pair now, then?'

Trixie moved in front of them, taking their cocks in her hands. They were limp and lifeless.

'They're certainly no good to me in this condition,' she said.

Lisa put her arm round Jenny, cupping her breast and kissing her on the mouth.

'Jenny and I aren't going to need any cocks tonight,' she said. 'We're going to take up where we left off on that beach.'

Dee reached for Jon's hand. 'You free tonight, Jon?'

He eyed her lovely young body up and down. 'Can't think of anything I'd like better,' he said.

'Well, I've got to get these two under lock and key,' said Kathy. 'Come on.'

'Wait a minute,' said Jenny. 'What about poor Trixie?'

'Don't worry about me,' said Trixie. 'I've just seen that guy who was manning the gangplank go into the cabin over there, and judging from the bulge in his trousers he could use some company.'

And with that she swaggered off in pursuit of the man, whilst behind her the others collapsed with mirth.

Headline Delta Erotic Survey

In order to provide the kind of books you like to read – and to
qualify for a free erotic novel of the Editor's choice – we
would appreciate it if you would complete the following
survey and send your answers, together with any further
comments, to:

> Headline Book Publishing
> FREEPOST (WD 4984)
> London
> NW1 0YR

1.   Are you male or female?
2.   Age? Under 20 / 20 to 30 / 30 to 40 / 40 to 50 /
      50 to 60 / 60 to 70 / over
3.   At what age did you leave full-time education?
4.   Where do you live? (Main geographical area)
5.   Are you a regular erotic book buyer / a regular book
      buyer in general / both?
6.   How much approximately do you spend a year on erotic
      books / on books in general?
7.   How did you come by this book?
7a.   If you bought it, did you purchase from:
      a national bookchain / a high street store / a newsagent /
      a motorway station / an airport / a railway station /
      other . . .
8.   Do you find erotic books easy / hard to come by?
8a.   Do you find Headline Delta erotic books easy / hard
      to come by?
9.   Which are the best / worst erotic books you have ever
      read?
9a.   Which are the best / worst Headline Delta erotic books
      you have ever read?
10.   Within the erotic genre there are many periods,
      subjects and literary styles. Which of the following
      do you prefer:
10a. (period) historical / Victorian / C20th /contemporary /
      future?
10b. (subject) nuns / whores & whorehouses /
      Continental frolics / s&m / vampires / modern realism /
      escapist fantasy / science fiction?

10c. (styles) hardboiled / humorous / hardcore / ironic / romantic / realistic?

10d. Are there any other ingredients that particularly appeal to you?

11. We try to create a cover appearance that is suitable for each title. Do you consider them to be successful?

12. Would you prefer them to be less explicit / more explicit?

13. We would be interested to hear of your other reading habits. What other types of books do you read?

14. Who are your favourite authors?

15. Which newspapers do you read?

16. Which magazines?

17 Do you have any other comments or suggestions to make?

If you would like to receive a free erotic novel of the Editor's choice (available only to UK residents), together with an up-to-date listing of Headline Delta titles, please supply your name and address. Please allow 28 days for delivery.

Name ....

Address ....

....

....

A selection of Erotica from Headline